25 Greatest Stories
for Young Readers

Ruskin Bond is known for his signature simplistic and witty writing style. He is the author of several bestselling short stories, novellas, collections, essays and children's books; and has contributed a number of poems and articles to various magazines and anthologies. At the age of twenty-three, he won the prestigious John Llewellyn Rhys Prize for his first novel, *The Room on the Roof*. He was also the recipient of the Padma Shri in 1999, Lifetime Achievement Award by the Delhi Government in 2012 and the Padma Bhushan in 2014.

Born in 1934, Ruskin Bond grew up in Jamnagar, Shimla, New Delhi and Dehradun. Apart from three years in the UK, he has spent all his life in India, and now lives in Landour, Mussoorie, with his adopted family.

RUSKIN BOND

25 Greatest Stories for Young Readers

Published by
Rupa Publications India Pvt. Ltd 2022
7/16, Ansari Road, Daryaganj
New Delhi 110002

Sales centres:
Bengaluru Chennai
Hyderabad Jaipur Kathmandu
Kolkata Mumbai Prayagraj

Copyright © Ruskin Bond 2022

Illustration courtesy: Roopkatha Ray Krishnan

This is a work of fiction. Names, characters, places and incidents are either the product of the author's imagination or are used fictitiously and any resemblance to any actual person, living or dead, events or locales is entirely coincidental.

All rights reserved.
No part of this publication may be reproduced, transmitted, or stored in a retrieval system, in any form or by any means, electronic, mechanical, photocopying, recording or otherwise, without the prior permission of the publisher.

P-ISBN: 978-93-5520-900-9
E-ISBN: 978-93-5520-901-6

Second impression 2024

10 9 8 7 6 5 4 3 2

Moral right of the author has been asserted.

Printed in India

This book is sold subject to the condition that it shall not, by way of trade or otherwise, be lent, resold, hired out, or otherwise circulated, without the publisher's prior consent, in any form of binding or cover other than that in which it is published.

CONTENTS

Introduction   vii

1. Cricket for the Crocodile   1
2. The School among the Pines   14
3. When the Guavas Are Ripe   37
4. Home   45
5. Mukesh Starts a Zoo   51
6. The King and the Tree-Goddess   57
7. The Window   62
8. The Visitor   68
9. Angry River   74
10. Koki Plays the Game   101
11. The Lost Ruby   107
12. Seven Brides for Seven Princes   112
13. The Ugly Prince and the Heartless Princess   119
14. The Tunnel   128
15. The Elephant and the Cassowary Bird   136
16. The Parrot Who Wouldn't Talk   139
17. A Rupee Goes a Long Way   143
18. The Flute Player   149
19. The Kitemaker   159
20. The Last Tiger   165
21. The Last Truck Ride   194

22. The Boy Who Broke the Bank	202
23. Romi and the Wildfire	209
24. Panther's Moon	218
25. Dust on the Mountain	249

INTRODUCTION

The best part of a story is the characters we meet on the pages of books and the tales we hear growing up—princes and princesses, parents and children, lovers and enemies, the mighty and the weak, talking animals and plants, and many more. Some we fall in love with, while others we adore or look up to, and some we just can't stand. We live with them, laugh with them, cry with them, we root for them, such are their qualities—they stay with us.

Over the years, of all the characters I have written about, some of them hold a special place in my heart. Some were inspired by the people I met or what I observed roaming around the streets and mountain villages, and remembered with fondness as I sat down to write. While others made an appearance in my imagination when I went looking for them.

All these characters have stories to tell—of journeys into the world or the inner self; of discoveries and disappointments; of successes and failures; of joys and sorrows. They have been my companions all these years.

I hope they will hold your hand, too, as they usher you into their worlds for a while and leave a mark or a lesson in living.

Ruskin Bond

CRICKET FOR THE CROCODILE

Ranji was up at dawn.

It was Sunday, a school holiday. Although he was supposed to be preparing for his exams, only a fortnight away, he couldn't resist one or two more games before getting down to history and algebra and other unexciting things.

'I'm going to be a Test cricketer when I grow up,' he told his mother. 'Of what use will maths be to me?'

'You never know,' said his mother, who happened to be more of a cricket fan than his father. 'You might need maths to work out your batting average. And as for history, wouldn't you like to be a part of history? Famous cricketers make history!'

'Making history is all right,' said Ranji. 'As long as I don't have to remember the date on which I make it!'

∞

Ranji met his friends and teammates in the park. The grass was still wet with dew, the sun only just rising behind the distant hills. The park was full of flower beds, and swings and slides for smaller children. The boys would have to play on the riverbank against their rivals, the village boys. Ranji did not have a full team that morning, but he was looking for a 'friendly' match. The really important game would be held the following Sunday.

The village team was quite good because the boys lived near each other and practised a lot together, whereas Ranji's team was drawn from all parts of the town. There was the baker's boy, Nathu; the tailor's son, Sunder; the postmaster's son, Prem; and the bank manager's son, Anil. These were some of the better players. Sometimes their fathers also turned up for a game. The fathers weren't very good, but you couldn't tell them that. After all, they helped to provide bats and balls and pocket money.

A regular spectator at these matches was Nakoo, the crocodile, who lived in the river. Nakoo means Nosey, but the village boys were very respectful and called him Nakoo-ji or Nakoo sir. He had a long snout, rows of ugly-looking teeth (some of them badly in need of fillings), and a powerful, scaly tail.

He was nearly fifteen feet long, but you did not see much of him; he swam low in the water and glided smoothly through the tall grasses near the river. Sometimes he came out on the riverbank to bask in the sun. He did not care for people, especially cricketers. He disliked the noise they made, frightening away the waterbirds and other creatures required for an interesting menu, and it was also alarming to have cricket balls plopping around in the shallows where he liked to rest.

Once Nakoo crept quite close to the bank manager, who was resting against one of the trees near the riverbank. The bank manager was a portly gentleman, and Nakoo seemed to think he would make a good meal. Just then a party of villagers had come along, beating drums for a marriage party. Nakoo retired to the muddy waters of the river. He was a little tired of swallowing frogs, eels, and herons. That juicy bank manager would make a nice change—he'd grab him one day!

∞

The village boys were a little bigger than Ranji and his friends, but they did not bring their fathers along. The game made very little sense to the older villagers. And when balls came flying across fields to land in milk pails or cooking pots, they were as annoyed as the crocodile.

CRICKET FOR THE CROCODILE

Today, the men were busy in the fields, and Nakoo was wallowing in the mud behind a screen of reeds and water lilies. How beautiful and innocent those lilies looked! Only sharp eyes would have noticed Nakoo's long snout thrusting above the broad, flat leaves of the lilies. His eyes were slits. He was watching.

Ranji struck the ball hard and high. Splash! It fell into the river about thirty feet from where Nakoo lay. Village boys and town boys dashed into the shallow water to look for the ball. Too many of them! Crowds made Nakoo nervous. He slid away, crossed the river to the opposite bank, and sulked.

As it was a warm day, nobody seemed to want to get out of the water. Several boys threw off their clothes, deciding that it was a better day for swimming than for cricket. Nakoo's mouth watered as he watched those bare limbs splashing about.

'We're supposed to be practising,' said Ranji, who took his cricket seriously. 'We won't win next week.'

'Oh, we'll win easily,' said Anil, joining him on the riverbank. 'My father says he's going to play.'

'The last time he played, we lost,' said Ranji. 'He made two runs and forgot to field.'

'He was out of form,' said Anil, ever loyal to his father, the bank manager.

Sheroo, the captain of the village team, joined them. 'My cousin from Delhi is going to play for us. He made a hundred in one of the matches there.'

'He won't make a hundred on this wicket,' said Ranji. 'It's slow at one end and fast at the other.'

'Can I bring my father?' asked Nathu, the baker's son.

'Can he play?'

'Not too well, but he'll bring along a basket of biscuits, buns, and pakoras.'

'Then he can play,' said Ranji, always quick to make up his mind. No wonder he was the team's captain! 'If there are too many of us, we'll make him twelfth man.'

The ball could not be found, and as they did not want to risk their spare ball, the practice session was declared over.

'My grandfather's promised me a new ball,' said little Mani, from the village team, who bowled tricky leg breaks which bounced off to the side.

'Does he want to play too?' asked Ranji.

'No, of course not. He's nearly eighty.'

'That's settled, then,' said Ranji. 'We'll all meet here at nine o'clock next Sunday. Fifty overs a side.'

They broke up, Sheroo and his team wandering back to the village, while Ranji and his friends got onto their bicycles (two or three to a bicycle, since not everyone had one), and cycled back to town.

Nakoo, left in peace at last, returned to his favourite side of the river and crawled some way up the riverbank, as if to inspect the wicket. It had been worn smooth by the players, and looked like a good place to relax. Nakoo moved across it. He felt pleasantly drowsy in the warm sun, so he closed his eyes for a little nap. It was good to be out of the water for a while.

The following Sunday morning, a cycle bell tinkled at the gate. It was Nathu, waiting for Ranji to join him. Ranji hurried out of the house, carrying his bat and a thermos of lime juice thoughtfully provided by his mother.

'Have you got the stumps?' he asked.

'Sunder has them.'

'And the ball?'

CRICKET FOR THE CROCODILE

'Yes. And Anil's father is bringing one too, provided he opens the batting!'

Nathu rode, while Ranji sat on the cross bar with bat and thermos. Anil was waiting for them outside his house.

'My father's gone ahead on his scooter. He's picking up Nathu's father. I'll follow with Prem and Sunder.'

Most of the boys got to the riverbank before the bank manager and the baker. They left their bicycles under a shady banyan tree and ran down the gentle slope to the river. And then, one by one, they stopped, astonished by what they saw.

They gaped in awe at their cricket pitch. Across it, basking in the soft warm sunshine, was Nakoo the crocodile.

'Where did it come from?' asked Ranji.

'Usually he stays in the river,' said Sheroo, who had joined them. 'But all this week he's been coming out to lie on our wicket. I don't think he wants us to play.'

'We'll have to get him off,' said Ranji.

'You'd better keep out of reach of his tail and jaws!'

'We'll wait until he goes away,' said Prem.

But Nakoo showed no signs of wanting to leave. He rather liked the smooth, flat stretch of ground which he had discovered. And here were all the boys again, doing their best to disturb him.

After some time the boys began throwing pebbles at Nakoo. These had no effect, simply bouncing off the crocodile's tough hide. They tried mud balls and an orange. Nakoo twitched his tail and opened one eye, but refused to move on.

Then Prem took a ball, and bowled a fast one at the crocodile. It bounced just short of Nakoo and caught him on the snout. Startled and stung, he wriggled off the pitch and moved rapidly down the riverbank and into the water. There was a mighty splash as he dived for cover.

'Well bowled, Prem!' said Ranji. 'That was a good ball.' 'Nakoo-ji will be in a bad mood after that,' warned Sheroo. 'Don't get too close to the river.'

The bank manager and the baker were the last to arrive. The scooter had given them some trouble. No one mentioned the crocodile, just in case the adults decided to call the match off.

After inspecting the wicket, which Nakoo had left in fair condition, Sheroo and Ranji tossed a coin. Ranji called 'Heads!' but it came up tails. Sheroo chose to bat first.

∞

The tall Delhi player came out to open the innings with little Mani.

CRICKET FOR THE CROCODILE

Mani was a steady bat, who could stay at the wicket for a long time; but in a one-day match, quick scoring was needed. This the Delhi player provided. He struck a four, then took a single off the last ball of the over.

In the third over, Mani tried to hit out and was bowled for a duck. So the village team's score was 13 for 1.

'Well done!' said Ranji to fast bowler Prem. 'But we'll have to get that tall fellow out soon. He seems quite good.'

The tall fellow showed no sign of getting out. He hit two more boundaries and then swung one hard and high towards the river.

Nakoo, who had been sulking in the shallows, saw the ball coming towards him. He opened his jaws wide, and with a satisfying 'clunk!' the ball lodged between his back teeth.

Nakoo got his teeth deep into the cricket ball and chewed. Revenge was sweet. And the ball tasted good too! The combination of leather and cork was just right. Nakoo decided that he would snap up any other balls that came his way.

'Harmless old reptile,' said the bank manager. He produced a new ball and insisted that he bowl with it.

It proved to be the most expensive over of the match. The bank manager's bowling was quite harmless and the Delhi player kept hitting the ball into the field for fours and sixes. The score soon mounted to 40 for 1. The bank manager modestly took himself off.

By the time the tenth over had been bowled, the score had mounted to 70. Then Ranji, bowling slow spin, lost his grip on the ball and sent the batsman a full toss. Having played the good balls perfectly, the Delhi player couldn't resist taking a mighty swipe at the bad ball. He mistimed his shot and was astonished to see the ball fall into the hands of a fielder near the boundary. 70 for 2. The game was far from being lost for Ranji's team.

A couple of wickets fell cheaply, and then Sheroo came in and started playing rather well. His drives were straight and clean. The ball cut down the buttercups and hummed over the grass. A big hit landed in a poultry yard. Feathers flew and so did curses. Nakoo raised his head to see what all the noise was about. No further cricket balls came his way, and he gazed balefully at a heron who was staying just out of his reach.

The score mounted steadily. The fielding grew slack, as it often does when batsmen gain the upper hand. A catch was dropped. And Nathu's father, keeping wicket, missed a stumping chance.

'No more grown-ups in our team,' grumbled Nathu.

The baker made amends by taking a good catch behind the wicket. The score was 115 for 5, with about half the overs remaining.

Sheroo kept his end up, but the remaining batsmen struggled for runs and the end came with about 5 overs still to go. A modest total of 145.

'Should be easy,' said Ranji.

'No problem,' said Prem.

'Lunch first,' said the bank manager, and they took a half-hour break.

The village boys went to their homes for rest and refreshment, while Ranji and his team spread themselves out under the banyan tree.

Nathu's father had brought patties and pakoras; the bank manager brought a basket of oranges and bananas; Prem had brought a jackfruit curry; Ranji had brought a halwa made from carrots, milk, and sugar; Sunder had brought a large container full of pulao rice cooked with peas and fried onions; and the others had brought various curries, pickles, and sauces. Everything was shared, and with the picnic in full swing no one noticed that Nakoo the crocodile had left the water. Using some tall reeds as cover, he had crept halfway up the riverbank. Those delicious food smells had reached him too, and he was unwilling to be left out of the picnic. Perhaps the boys would leave something for him. If not...

∽

'Time to start,' announced the bank manager, getting up. 'I'll open the batting. We need a good start if we are going to win!'

The bank manager strode out to the wicket in the company of young Nathu. Sheroo opened the bowling for the village team.

The bank manager took a run off the first ball. He puffed himself up and waved his bat in the air as though the match had already been won. Nathu played out the rest of the over without taking any chances.

The tall Delhi player took up the bowling from the other end. The bank manager tapped his bat impatiently, then raised it above his shoulders, ready to hit out. The bowler took a long, fast run up to the bowling crease. He gave a little leap, his arm swung over, and the ball came at the bank manager in a swift, curving flight.

The bank manager still had his bat raised when the ball flew past him and uprooted his middle stump.

A shout of joy went up from the fielders. The bank manager was on his way back to the shade of the banyan tree.

'A fly got in my eye,' he muttered. 'I wasn't ready. Flies everywhere!' And he swatted angrily at flies that no one else could see.

The villagers, hearing that someone as important as a bank manager was in their midst, decided that it would be wrong for him to sit on the ground like everyone else. So they brought him a cot from the village. It was one of those light wooden beds, taped with strands of thin rope. The bank manager lowered himself into it rather gingerly. It creaked but took his weight.

The score was 1 for 1.

Anil took his father's place at the wicket and scored 10 runs in two overs. The bank manager pretended not to notice but he was really quite pleased. 'Takes after me,' he said, and made himself comfortable on the cot.

Nathu kept his end up while Anil scored the runs. Then Anil was out, skying a catch to midwicket.

25 for 2 in six overs. It could have been worse.

'Well played!' called the bank manager to his son, and then lost interest in the proceedings. He was soon fast asleep on the cot. The flies did not seem to bother him any more.

Nathu kept going, and there were a couple of good partnerships for the fourth and fifth wickets. When the Delhi player finished his share of overs, the batsmen became more free in their stroke play. Then little Mani got a ball to spin sharply, and Nathu was caught by the wicketkeeper.

It was 75 for 4 when Ranji came in to bat.

Before he could score a run, his partner at the other end was bowled. And then Nathu's father strode up to the wicket, determined to do better than the bank manager. In this he succeeded by 1 run.

The baker scored 2, and then in trying to run another 2 when there was only one to be had, found himself stranded halfway up the wicket. The wicketkeeper knocked his stumps down.

The boys were too polite to say anything. And as for the bank manager he was now fast asleep under the banyan tree.

So intent was everyone on watching the cricket that no one noticed that Nakoo, the crocodile, had crept further up the riverbank to slide beneath the cot on which the bank manager was sleeping.

CRICKET FOR THE CROCODILE

There was just room enough for Nakoo to get between the legs of the cot. He thought it was a good place to lie concealed, and he seemed not to notice the large man sleeping peacefully just above him.

Soon the bank manager was snoring gently, and it was not long before Nakoo dozed off, too. Only, instead of snoring, Nakoo appeared to be whistling through his crooked teeth.

∞

75 for 5 and it looked as though Ranji's team would soon be crashing to defeat.

Sunder joined Ranji and, to everyone's delight, played two lovely drives to the boundary. Then Ranji got into his stride and cut and drove the ball for successive fours. The score began to mount steadily. 112 for 5. Once again, there were visions of victory.

After Sunder was out, stumped, Ranji was joined by Prem, a big hitter. Runs came quickly. The score reached 140. Only 6 runs were needed for victory.

Ranji decided to do it in style. Receiving a half-volley, he drove the ball hard and high towards the banyan tree.

Thump! It struck Nakoo on the jaw and loosened one of his teeth.

It was the second time that day he'd been caught napping. He'd had enough of it.

Nakoo lunged forward, tail thrashing and jaws snapping. The cot, with the manager still on it, rose with him. Crocodile and cot were now jammed together, and when Nakoo rushed forward, he took the cot with him.

The bank manager, dreaming that he was at sea in a rowing boat, woke up to find the cot pitching violently from side to side.

'Help!' he shouted. 'Help!'

The boys scattered in all directions, for the crocodile was now advancing down the wicket, knocking over stumps and digging up the pitch. He found an abandoned sun hat and swallowed it. A wicketkeeper's glove went the same way. A batsman's pad was caught up on his tail.

All this time the bank manager hung on to the cot for safety, but would he be able to get out of reach of Nakoo's jaw and tail? He decided to hang on to the cot until it was dislodged.

'Come on, boys, help!' he shouted. 'Get me off!'

But the cot remained firmly attached to the crocodile, and so did the bank manager.

The problem was solved when Nakoo made for the river and plunged into its familiar waters. Then the bank manager tumbled into the water and scrambled up the bank, while Nakoo made for the opposite shore.

The bank manager's ordeal was over, and so was the cricket match.

'Did you see how I dealt with that crocodile?' he said, still dripping, but in better humour now that he was safe again. 'By the way, who won the match?'

'We don't know,' said Ranji, as they trudged back to their bicycles. 'That would have been a 6 if you hadn't been in the way.'

Sheroo, who had accompanied them as far as the main road, offered a return match the following week.

'I'm busy next week,' said the baker.

'I have another game,' said the bank manager.

'What game is that, sir?' asked Ranji.

'Chess,' said the bank manager.

Ranji and his friends began making plans for the next match. 'You won't win without us,' said the bank manager.

'Not a chance,' said the baker.

CRICKET FOR THE CROCODILE

But Ranji's team did, in fact, win the next match.

Nakoo the crocodile did not trouble them because the cot was still attached to his back, and it took him several weeks to get it off.

A number of people came to the riverbank to look at the crocodile who carried his own bed around.

Some even stayed to watch the cricket.

THE SCHOOL AMONG THE PINES

I

A leopard, lithe and sinewy, drank at the mountain stream, and then lay down on the grass to bask in the late February sunshine. Its tail twitched occasionally and the animal appeared to be sleeping. At the sound of distant voices it raised its head to listen, then stood up and leapt lightly over the boulders in the stream, disappearing among the trees on the opposite bank.

A minute or two later, three children came walking down the forest path. They were a girl and two boys, and they were singing in their local dialect an old song they had learnt from their grandparents.

'Five more miles to go!
We climb through rain and snow.
A *river to cross...*
A *mountain to pass...*
Now *we've four more miles to go!*'

Their school satchels looked new, their clothes had been washed and pressed. Their loud and cheerful singing startled a spotted forktail. The bird left its favourite rock in the stream and flew down the dark ravine.

'Well, we have only three more miles to go,' said the bigger boy, Prakash, who had been this way hundreds of times. 'But first we have to cross the stream.'

THE SCHOOL AMONG THE PINES

He was a sturdy twelve-year-old with eyes like raspberries and a mop of bushy hair that refused to settle down on his head. The girl and her small brother were taking this path for the first time.

'I'm feeling tired, Bina,' said the little boy.

Bina smiled at him, and Prakash said, 'Don't worry, Sonu, you'll get used to the walk. There's plenty of time.' He glanced at the old watch he'd been given by his grandfather. It needed constant winding. 'We can rest here for five or six minutes.'

They sat down on a smooth boulder and watched the clear water of the shallow stream tumbling downhill. Bina examined the old watch on Prakash's wrist. The glass was badly scratched and she could barely make out the figures on the dial. 'Are you sure it still gives the right time?' she asked.

'Well, it loses five minutes every day, so I put it ten minutes forward at night. That means by morning it's quite accurate! Even our teacher, Mr Mani, asks me for the time. If he doesn't ask, I tell him! The clock in our classroom keeps stopping.'

They removed their shoes and let the cold mountain water run over their feet. Bina was the same age as Prakash. She had pink cheeks, soft brown eyes, and hair that was just beginning to lose its natural curls. Hers was a gentle face, but a determined little chin showed that she could be a strong person. Sonu, her younger brother, was ten. He was a thin boy who had been sickly as a child but was now beginning to fill out. Although he did not look very athletic, he could run like the wind.

Bina had been going to school in her own village of Koli, on the other side of the mountain. But it had been a primary school, finishing at Class Five. Now, in order to study in the Sixth, she would have to walk several miles every day to Nauti, where there was a high school going up to the Eighth. It had been decided that Sonu would also shift to the new school, to give Bina company.

Prakash, their neighbour in Koli, was already a pupil at the Nauti school. His mischievous nature, which sometimes got him into trouble, had resulted in his having to repeat a year.

But this didn't seem to bother him. 'What's the hurry?' he had told his indignant parents. 'You're not sending me to a foreign land when I finish school. And our cows aren't running away, are they?'

'You would prefer to look after the cows, wouldn't you?' asked Bina, as they got up to continue their walk.

'Oh, school's all right. Wait till you see old Mr Mani. He always gets our names mixed up, as well as the subjects he's supposed to be teaching. At out last lesson, instead of maths, he gave us a geography lesson!'

'More fun than maths,' said Bina.

'Yes, but there's a new teacher this year. She's very young, they say, just out of college. I wonder what she'll be like.'

Bina walked faster and Sonu had some trouble keeping up with them. She was excited about the new school and the prospect of different surroundings. She had seldom been outside her own village, with its small school and single ration shop. The day's routine never varied—helping her mother in the fields or with household tasks like fetching water from the spring or cutting grass and fodder for the cattle. Her father, who was a soldier, was away for nine months in the year and Sonu was still too small for the heavier tasks.

As they neared Nauti village, they were joined by other children coming from different directions. Even where there were no major roads, the mountains were full of little lanes and shortcuts. Like a game of snakes and ladders, these narrow paths zigzagged around the hills and villages, cutting through fields and crossing narrow ravines until they came together to form a fairly busy road along which mules, cattle and goats joined the throng.

THE SCHOOL AMONG THE PINES

Nauti was a fairly large village, and from here a broader but dustier road started for Tehri. There was a small bus, several trucks and (for part of the way) a road roller. The road hadn't been completed because the heavy diesel roller couldn't take the steep climb to Nauti. It stood on the roadside half way up the road from Tehri.

Prakash knew almost everyone in the area, and exchanged greetings and gossip with other children as well as with muleteers, bus drivers, milkmen and labourers working on the road. He loved telling everyone the time, even if they weren't interested.

'It's nine o'clock,' he would announce, glancing at his wrist. 'Isn't your bus leaving today?'

'Off with you!' the bus driver would respond, 'I'll leave when I'm ready.'

As the children approached Nauti, the small flat school buildings came into view on the outskirts of the village, fringed with a line of long-leaved pines. A small crowd had assembled on the playing field. Something unusual seemed to have happened. Prakash ran forward to see what it was all about. Bina and Sonu stood aside, waiting in a patch of sunlight near the boundary wall.

Prakash soon came running back to them. He was bubbling over with excitement.

'It's Mr Mani!' he gasped. 'He's disappeared! People are saying a leopard must have carried him off!'

II

Mr Mani wasn't really old. He was about fifty-five and was expected to retire soon. But for the children, adults over forty seemed ancient! And Mr Mani had always been a bit absent-minded, even as a young man.

He had gone out for his early morning walk, saying he'd be

back by eight o'clock, in time to have his breakfast and be ready for class. He wasn't married, but his sister and her husband stayed with him. When it was past nine o'clock his sister presumed he'd stopped at a neighbour's house for breakfast (he loved tucking into other people's breakfast) and that he had gone on to school from there. But when the school bell rang at ten o'clock, and everyone but Mr Mani was present, questions were asked and guesses were made.

No one had seen him return from his walk and enquiries made in the village showed that he had not stopped at anyone's house. For Mr Mani to disappear was puzzling; for him to disappear without his breakfast was extraordinary.

Then a milkman returning from the next village said he had seen a leopard sitting on a rock on the outskirts of the pine forest. There had been talk of a cattle-killer in the valley, of leopards and other animals being displaced by the construction of a dam. But as yet, no one had heard of a leopard attacking a man. Could Mr Mani have been its first victim? Someone found a strip of red cloth entangled in a blackberry bush and went running through the village showing it to everyone. Mr Mani had been known to wear red pyjamas. Surely, he had been seized and eaten! But where were his remains? And why had he been in his pyjamas?

Meanwhile, Bina and Sonu and the rest of the children had followed their teachers into the school playground. Feeling a little lost, Bina looked around for Prakash. She found herself facing a dark, slender young woman wearing spectacles, who must have been in her early twenties—just a little too old to be another student. She had a kind expressive face and she seemed a little concerned by all that had been happening.

Bina noticed that she had lovely hands—it was obvious that the new teacher hadn't milked cows or worked in the fields!

THE SCHOOL AMONG THE PINES

'You must be new here,' said the teacher, smiling at Bina. 'And is this your little brother?'

'Yes, we've come from Koli village. We were at school there.'

'It's a long walk from Koli. You didn't see any leopards, did you? Well, I'm new too. Are you in the Sixth class?'

'Sonu is in the Third. I'm in the Sixth.'

'Then I'm your new teacher. My name is Tania Ramola. Come along, let's see if we can settle down in our classroom.'

Mr Mani turned up at twelve o'clock, wondering what all the fuss was about. No, he snapped, he had not been attacked by a leopard; and yes, he had lost his pyjamas and would someone kindly return them to him?

'How did you lose your pyjamas, sir?' asked Prakash.

'They were blown off the washing line!' snapped Mr Mani.

After much questioning, Mr Mani admitted that he had gone further than he had intended, and that he had lost his way coming back. He had been a bit upset because the new teacher, a slip of a girl, had been given charge of the Sixth, while he was still with the Fifth, along with that troublesome boy Prakash, who kept on reminding him of the time! The headmaster had explained that as Mr Mani was due to retire at the end of the year, the school did not wish to burden him with a senior class. But Mr Mani looked upon the whole thing as a plot to get rid of him. He glowered at Miss Ramola whenever he passed her. And when she smiled back at him, he looked the other way!

Mr Mani had been getting even more absent-minded of late—putting on his shoes without his socks, wearing his homespun waistcoat inside out, mixing up people's names and, of course, eating other people's lunches and dinners. His sister had made a special mutton broth (*pai*) for the postmaster, who was down with flu and had asked Mr Mani to take it over in a thermos. When the postmaster opened the thermos, he found only a few drops of broth at the bottom—Mr Mani had drunk the rest somewhere along the way.

When sometimes Mr Mani spoke of his coming retirement, it was to describe his plans for the small field he owned just behind the house. Right now, it was full of potatoes, which did not require much looking after; but he had plans for growing dahlias, roses, French beans, and other fruits and flowers.

The next time he visited Tehri, he promised himself, he would buy some dahlia bulbs and rose cuttings. The monsoon season would be a good time to put them down. And meanwhile, his potatoes were still flourishing.

III

Bina enjoyed her first day at the new school. She felt at ease with Miss Ramola, as did most of the boys and girls in her class. Tania Ramola had been to distant towns such as Delhi and Lucknow—places they had only read about—and it was said that she had a brother who was a pilot and flew planes all over the world. Perhaps he'd fly over Nauti some day!

Most of the children had, of course, seen planes flying overhead, but none of them had seen a ship, and only a few had been on a train. Tehri mountain was far from the railways and hundreds of miles from the sea. But they all knew about the big dam that was being built at Tehri, just forty miles away.

Bina, Sonu and Prakash had company for part of the way home, but gradually the other children went off in different directions. Once they had crossed the stream, they were on their own again.

It was a steep climb all the way back to their village. Prakash had a supply of peanuts which he shared with Bina and Sonu, and at a small spring they quenched their thirst.

When they were less than a mile from home, they met a postman who had finished his round of the villages in the area and was now returning to Nauti.

'Don't waste time along the way,' he told them. 'Try to get home before dark.'

'What's the hurry?' asked Prakash, glancing at his watch. 'It's only five o'clock.'

'There's a leopard around. I saw it this morning, not far from the stream. No one is sure how it got here. So don't take any chances. Get home early.'

'So there really is a leopard,' said Sonu.

They took his advice and walked faster, and Sonu forgot to complain about his aching feet.

They were home well before sunset.

There was a smell of cooking in the air and they were hungry.

'Cabbage and roti,' said Prakash gloomily. 'But I could eat anything today.' He stopped outside his small slate-roofed house, and Bina and Sonu waved him goodbye, then carried on across a couple of ploughed fields until they reached their small stone house.

'Stuffed tomatoes,' said Sonu, sniffing just outside the front door.

'And lemon pickle,' said Bina, who had helped cut, sun and salt the lemons a month previously.

Their mother was lighting the kitchen stove. They greeted her with great hugs and demands for an immediate dinner. She was a good cook who could make even the simplest of dishes taste delicious. Her favourite saying was, 'Homemade pai is better than chicken soup in Delhi,' and Bina and Sonu had to agree.

Electricity had yet to reach their village, and they took their meal by the light of a kerosene lamp. After the meal, Sonu settled down to do a little homework, while Bina stepped outside to look at the stars.

Across the fields, someone was playing a flute. It *must be Prakash*, thought Bina. *He always breaks off on the high notes.* But the flute music was simple and appealing, and she began singing softly to herself in the dark.

IV

Mr Mani was having trouble with the porcupines. They had been getting into his garden at night and digging up and eating his potatoes. From his bedroom window—left open, now that the mild-April weather had arrived—he could listen to them enjoying the vegetables he had worked hard to grow. Scrunch, scrunch! *Katar, katar,* as their sharp teeth sliced through the largest and juiciest of potatoes. For Mr Mani, it was as though they were biting through his own flesh. And the sound of them digging industriously as they rooted up those healthy, leafy plants, made him tremble with rage and indignation. The unfairness of it all!

Yes, Mr Mani hated porcupines. He prayed for their destruction, their removal from the face of the earth. But, as his friends were quick to point out, 'Bhagwan protected porcupines too,' and in any case you could never see the creatures or catch them, they were completely nocturnal.

Mr Mani got out of bed every night, torch in one hand, a stout stick in the other, but as soon as he stepped into the garden the crunching and digging stopped and he was greeted by the most infuriating of silences. He would grope around in the dark, swinging wildly with the stick, but not a single porcupine was to be seen or heard. As soon as he was back in bed—the sounds would start all over again. Scrunch, scrunch, *katar, katar*...

Mr Mani came to his class tired and dishevelled, with rings

beneath his eyes and a permanent frown on his face. It took some time for his pupils to discover the reason for his misery, but when they did, they felt sorry for their teacher and took to discussing ways and means of saving his potatoes from the porcupines.

It was Prakash who came up with the idea of a moat or waterditch. 'Porcupines don't like water,' he said knowledgeably.

'How do you know?' asked one of his friends.

'Throw water on one and see how it runs! They don't like getting their quills wet.'

There was no one who could disprove Prakash's theory, and the class fell in with the idea of building a moat, especially as it meant getting most of the day off.

'Anything to make Mr Mani happy,' said the headmaster, and the rest of the school watched with envy as the pupils of Class Five, armed with spades and shovels collected from all parts of the village, took up their positions around Mr Mani's potato field and began digging a ditch.

By evening the moat was ready, but it was still dry and the porcupines got in again that night and had a great feast.

'At this rate,' said Mr Mani gloomily 'there won't be any potatoes left to save.'

But next day Prakash and the other boys and girls managed to divert the water from a stream that flowed past the village. They had the satisfaction of watching it flow gently into the ditch. Everyone went home in a good mood. By nightfall, the ditch had overflowed, the potato field was flooded, and Mr Mani found himself trapped inside his house. But Prakash and his friends had won the day. The porcupines stayed away that night!

A month had passed, and wild violets, daisies and buttercups now sprinkled the hill slopes, and on her way to school Bina gathered enough to make a little posy. The bunch of flowers fitted easily into an old inkwell. Miss Ramola was delighted to find this little display in the middle of her desk.

'Who put these here?' she asked in surprise.

Bina kept quiet, and the rest of the class smiled secretively. After that, they took turns bringing flowers for the classroom.

On her long walks to school and home again, Bina became aware that April was the month of new leaves. The oak leaves were bright green above and silver beneath, and when they rippled in the breeze they were like clouds of silvery green. The path was strewn with old leaves, dry and crackly. Sonu loved kicking them around.

Clouds of white butterflies floated across the stream. Sonu was chasing a butterfly when he stumbled over something dark and repulsive. He went sprawling on the grass. When he got to his feet, he looked down at the remains of a small animal.

'Bina! Prakash! Come quickly!' he shouted.

It was part of a sheep, killed some days earlier by a much larger animal.

'Only a leopard could have done this,' said Prakash.

'Let's get away, then,' said Sonu. 'It might still be around!'

'No, there's nothing left to eat. The leopard will be hunting elsewhere by now. Perhaps it's moved on to the next valley.'

'Still, I'm frightened,' said Sonu. 'There may be more leopards!'

Bina took him by the hand. 'Leopards don't attack humans!' she said.

'They will, if they get a taste for people!' insisted Prakash.

'Well, this one hasn't attacked any people as yet,' said Bina, although she couldn't be sure. Hadn't there been rumours of a leopard attacking some workers near the dam? But she did not want Sonu to feel afraid, so she did not mention the story. All she said was, 'It has probably come here because of all the activity near the dam.'

THE SCHOOL AMONG THE PINES

All the same, they hurried home. And for a few days, whenever they reached the stream, they crossed over very quickly, unwilling to linger too long at that lovely spot.

V

A few days later, a school party was on its way to Tehri to see the new dam that was being built.

Miss Ramola had arranged to take her class, and Mr Mani, not wishing to be left out, insisted on taking his class as well. That meant there were about fifty boys and girls taking part in the outing. The little bus could only take thirty. A friendly truck driver agreed to take some children if they were prepared to sit on sacks of potatoes. And Prakash persuaded the owner of the diesel roller to turn it round and head it back to Tehri—with him and a couple of friends up on the driving seat.

Prakash's small group set off at sunrise, as they had to walk some distance in order to reach the stranded road roller. The bus left at 9.00 a.m. with Miss Ramola and her class, and Mr Mani and some of his pupils. The truck was to follow later.

It was Bina's first visit to a large town and her first bus ride.

The sharp curves along the winding, downhill road made several children feel sick. The bus driver seemed to be in a tearing hurry. He took them along at rolling, rollicking speed, which made Bina feel quite giddy. She rested her head on her arms and refused to look out of the window. Hairpin bends and cliff edges, pine forests and snowcapped peaks, all swept past her, but she felt too ill to want to look at anything. It was just as well—those sudden drops, hundreds of feet to the valley below, were quite frightening. Bina began to wish that she hadn't come—or that she had joined Prakash on the road roller instead!

Miss Ramola and Mr Mani didn't seem to notice the lurching

and groaning of the old bus. They had made this journey many times. They were busy arguing about the advantages and disadvantages of large dams—an argument that was to continue on and off for much of the day; sometimes in Hindi, sometimes in English, sometimes in the local dialect!

Meanwhile, Prakash and his friends had reached the roller. The driver hadn't turned up, but they managed to reverse it and get it going in the direction of Tehri. They were soon overtaken by both the bus and the truck but kept moving along at a steady chug. Prakash spotted Bina at the window of the bus and waved cheerfully. She responded feebly.

Bina felt better when the road levelled out near Tehri. As they crossed an old bridge over the wide river, they were startled by a loud bang which made the bus shudder. A cloud of dust rose above the town.

'They're blasting the mountain,' said Miss Ramola.

'End of a mountain,' said Mr Mani mournfully.

While they were drinking cups of tea at the bus stop, waiting for the potato truck and the road roller, Miss Ramola and Mr Mani continued their argument about the dam. Miss Ramola maintained that it would bring electric power and water for irrigation to large areas of the country, including the surrounding area. Mr Mani declared that it was a menace, as it was situated in an earthquake zone. There would be a terrible disaster if the dam burst! Bina found it all very confusing. *And what about the animals in the area*, she wondered. *What would happen to them?*

The argument was becoming quite heated when the potato truck arrived. There was no sign of the road roller, so it was decided that Mr Mani should wait for Prakash and his friends while Miss Ramola's group went ahead.

Some eight or nine miles before Tehri the road roller had broken down, and Prakash and his friends were forced to walk. They had not gone far, however, when a mule train came along—five or six mules that had been delivering sacks of grain in Nauti. A boy rode on the first mule, but the others had no loads.

'Can you give us a ride to Tehri?' called Prakash.

'Make yourselves comfortable,' said the boy.

There were no saddles, only gunny sacks strapped on to the mules with rope. They had a rough but jolly ride down to the Tehri bus stop. None of them had ever ridden mules; but they had saved at least an hour on the road.

Looking around the bus stop for the rest of the party, they could find no one from their school. And Mr Mani, who should have been waiting for them, had vanished.

VI

Tania Ramola and her group had taken the steep road to the hill above Tehri. Half an hour's climbing brought them to a little plateau which overlooked the town, the river and the dam site.

The earthworks for the dam were only just coming up, but a wide tunnel had been bored through the mountain to divert the river into another channel. Down below, the old town was still spread out across the valley and from a distance it looked quite charming and picturesque.

'Will the whole town be swallowed up by the waters of the dam?' asked Bina.

'Yes, all of it,' said Miss Ramola. 'The clock tower and the old palace. The long bazaar, and the temples, the schools and the jail, and hundreds of houses, for many miles up the valley. All those people will have to go—thousands of them! Of course, they'll be resettled elsewhere.'

'But the town's been here for hundreds of years,' said Bina. 'They were quite happy without the dam, weren't they?'

'I suppose they were. But the dam isn't just for them—it's for the millions who live further downstream, across the plains.'

'And it doesn't matter what happens to this place?'

'The local people will be given new homes, somewhere else.' Miss Ramola found herself on the defensive and decided to change the subject. 'Everyone must be hungry. It's time we had our lunch.'

Bina kept quiet. She didn't think the local people would want to go away. And it was a good thing, she mused, that there was only a small stream and not a big river running past her village. To be uprooted like this—a town and hundreds of villages—and put down somewhere on the hot, dusty plains—seemed to her unbearable.

'Well, I'm glad I don't live in Tehri,' she said.

She did not know it, but all the animals and most of the birds had already left the area. The leopard had been among them.

They walked through the colourful, crowded bazaar, where fruit sellers did business beside silversmiths, and pavement vendors sold everything from umbrellas to glass bangles. Sparrows attacked sacks of grain, monkeys made off with bananas, and stray cows and dogs rummaged in refuse bins, but nobody took any notice. Music blared from radios. Buses blew their horns. Sonu bought a whistle to add to the general din, but Miss Ramola told him to put it away. Bina had kept ten rupees aside, and now, she used it to buy a cotton head scarf for her mother.

As they were about to enter a small restaurant for a meal, they were joined by Prakash and his companions; but of Mr Mani there was still no sign.

'He must have met one of his relatives,' said Prakash. 'He has relatives everywhere.'

After a simple meal of rice and lentils, they walked the length of the bazaar without seeing Mr Mani. At last, when they were about to give up the search, they saw him emerge from a bylane, a large sack slung over his shoulder.

'Sir, where have you been?' asked Prakash. 'We have been looking for you everywhere.'

On Mr Mani's face was a look of triumph.

'Help me with this bag,' he said breathlessly.

'You've bought more potatoes, sir,' said Prakash.

'Not potatoes, boy. Dahlia bulbs!'

VII

It was dark by the time they were all back in Nauti. Mr Mani had refused to be separated from his sack of dahlia bulbs, and had been forced to sit in the back of the truck with Prakash and most of the boys.

Bina did not feel so ill on the return journey. Going uphill was definitely better than going downhill! But by the time the bus reached Nauti it was too late for most of the children to walk back to the more distant villages. The boys were put up in different homes, while the girls were given beds in the school verandah.

The night was warm and still. Large moths fluttered around the single bulb that lit the verandah. Counting moths, Sonu soon fell asleep. But Bina stayed awake for some time, listening to the sounds of the night. A nightjar went *tonk tonk* in the bushes, and somewhere in the forest an owl hooted softly. The sharp call of a barking deer travelled up the valley, from the direction of the stream. Jackals kept howling. It seemed that there were more of them than ever before.

Bina was not the only one to hear the barking deer. The leopard, stretched full length on a rocky ledge, heard it too. The leopard raised its head and then got up slowly. The deer was its natural prey. But there weren't many left, and that was why the leopard, robbed of its forest by the dam, had taken to attacking dogs and cattle near the villages.

As the cry of the barking deer sounded nearer, the leopard left its lookout point and moved swiftly through the shadows towards the stream.

THE SCHOOL AMONG THE PINES

VIII

In early June, the hills were dry and dusty, and forest fires broke out, destroying shrubs and trees, killing birds and small animals. The resin in the pines made these trees burn more fiercely, and the wind would take sparks from the trees and carry them into the dry grass and leaves, so that new fires would spring up before the old ones had died out. Fortunately, Bina's village was not in the pine belt, the fires did not reach it. But Nauti was surrounded by a fire that raged for three days, and the children had to stay away from school.

And then, towards the end of June, the monsoon rains arrived and there was an end to forest fires. The monsoon lasts three months and the lower Himalayas would be drenched in rain, mist and cloud for the next three months.

The first rain arrived while Bina, Prakash and Sonu were returning home from school. Those first few drops on the dusty path made them cry out with excitement. Then the rain grew heavier and a wonderful aroma rose from the earth.

'The best smell in the world!' exclaimed Bina.

Everything suddenly came to life. The grass, the crops, the trees, the birds. Even the leaves of the trees glistened and looked new.

That first wet weekend, Bina and Sonu helped their mother plant beans, maize and cucumbers. Sometimes, when the rain was very heavy, they had to run indoors. Otherwise they worked in the rain, the soft mud clinging to their bare legs.

Prakash now owned a black dog with one ear up and one ear down. The dog ran around getting in everyone's way, barking at cows, goats, hens and humans, without frightening any of them. Prakash said it was a very clever dog, but no one else seemed to think so. Prakash also said it would protect the village from the leopard, but others said the dog would be the first to be taken—he'd run straight into the jaws of Mr Spots!

In Nauti, Tania Ramola was trying to find a dry spot in the quarters she'd been given. It was an old building and the roof was leaking in several places. Mugs and buckets were scattered about the floor in order to catch the drip.

Mr Mani had dug up all his potatoes and presented them to the friends and neighbours who had given him lunches and dinners. He was having the time of his life, planting dahlia bulbs all over his garden.

'I'll have a field of many-coloured dahlias!' he announced. 'Just wait till the end of August!'

'Watch out for those porcupines,' warned his sister. 'They eat dahlia bulbs too!'

Mr Mani made an inspection tour of his moat, no longer in flood, and found everything in good order. Prakash had done his job well.

Now, when the children crossed the stream, they found that the water level had risen by about a foot. Small cascades had turned into waterfalls. Ferns had sprung up on the banks. Frogs chanted.

Prakash and his dog dashed across the stream. Bina and Sonu followed more cautiously. The current was much stronger now and the water was almost up to their knees. Once they had crossed the stream, they hurried along the path, anxious not to be caught in a sudden downpour.

By the time they reached school, each of them had two or three leeches clinging to their legs. They had to use salt to remove them. The leeches were the most troublesome part of the rainy season. Even the leopard did not like them. It could not lie in the long grass without getting leeches on its paws and face.

THE SCHOOL AMONG THE PINES

One day, when Bina, Prakash and Sonu were about to cross the stream they heard a low rumble, which grew louder every second. Looking up at the opposite hill, they saw several trees shudder, tilt outwards and begin to fall. Earth and rocks bulged out from the mountain, then came crashing down into the ravine.

'Landslide!' shouted Sonu.

'It's carried away the path,' said Bina. 'Don't go any further.'

There was a tremendous roar as more rocks, trees and bushes fell away and crashed down the hillside.

Prakash's dog, who had gone ahead, came running back, tail between his legs.

They remained rooted to the spot until the rocks had stopped falling and the dust had settled. Birds circled the area, calling wildly. A frightened barking deer ran past them.

'We can't go to school now,' said Prakash. 'There's no way around.'

They turned and trudged home through the gathering mist.

In Koli, Prakash's parents had heard the roar of the landslide. They were setting out in search of the children when they saw them emerge from the mist, waving cheerfully.

IX

They had to miss school for another three days, and Bina was afraid they might not be able to take their final exams. Although Prakash was not really troubled at the thought of missing exams, he did not like feeling helpless just because their path had been swept away. So he explored the hillside until he found a goat track going around the mountain. It joined up with another path near Nauti. This made their walk longer by a mile, but Bina did not mind. It was much cooler now that the rains were in full swing.

The only trouble with the new route was that it passed close to the leopard's lair. The animal had made this area its own since being forced to leave the dam area.

One day Prakash's dog ran ahead of them, barking furiously. Then he ran back, whimpering.

'He's always running away from something,' observed Sonu. But a minute later he understood the reason for the dog's fear.

They rounded a bend and Sonu saw the leopard standing in their way. They were struck dumb—too terrified to run. It was a strong, sinewy creature. A low growl rose from its throat. It seemed ready to spring.

They stood perfectly still, afraid to move or say a word. And the leopard must have been equally surprised. It stared at them for a few seconds, then bounded across the path and into the oak forest.

Sonu was shaking. Bina could hear her heart hammering. Prakash could only stammer, 'Did you see the way he sprang? Wasn't he beautiful?'

He forgot to look at his watch for the rest of the day.

A few days later Sonu stopped and pointed to a large outcrop of rock on the next hill.

The leopard stood far above them, outlined against the sky. It looked strong, majestic. Standing beside it were two young cubs.

'Look at those little ones!' exclaimed Sonu.

'So it's a female, not a male,' said Prakash.

'That's why she was killing so often,' said Bina. 'She had to feed her cubs too.'

They remained still for several minutes, gazing up at the leopard and her cubs. The leopard family took no notice of them.

'She knows we are here,' said Prakash, 'but she doesn't care. She knows we won't harm them.'

'We are cubs too!' said Sonu.

'Yes,' said Bina. 'And there's still plenty of space for all of us.

Even when the dam is ready there will still be room for leopards and humans.'

X

The school exams were over. The rains were nearly over too. The landslide had been cleared, and Bina, Prakash and Sonu were once again crossing the stream.

There was a chill in the air, for it was the end of September.

Prakash had learnt to play the flute quite well, and he played on the way to school and then again on the way home. As a result he did not look at his watch so often.

One morning they found a small crowd in front of Mr Mani's house.

'What could have happened?' wondered Bina. 'I hope he hasn't got lost again.'

'Maybe he's sick,' said Sonu.

'Maybe it's the porcupines,' said Prakash.

But it was none of these things.

Mr Mani's first dahlia was in bloom, and half the village had turned out to look at it! It was a huge red double dahlia, so heavy that it had to be supported with sticks. No one had ever seen such a magnificent flower!

Mr Mani was a happy man. And his mood only improved over the coming week, as more and more dahlias flowered—crimson, yellow, purple, mauve, white—button dahlias, pompom dahlias, spotted dahlias, striped dahlias...Mr Mani had them all! A dahlia even turned up on Tania Romola's desk—he got on quite well with her now—and another brightened up the headmaster's study.

A week later, on their way home—it was almost the last day of the school term—Bina, Prakash and Sonu talked about what they might do when they grew up.

'I think I'll become a teacher,' said Bina. 'I'll teach children about animals and birds, and trees and flowers.'

'Better than maths!' said Prakash.

'I'll be a pilot,' said Sonu. 'I want to fly a plane like Miss Ramola's brother.'

'And what about you, Prakash?' asked Bina.

Prakash just smiled and said, 'Maybe I'll be a flute player,' and he put the flute to he lips and played a sweet melody.

'Well, the world needs flute players too,' said Bina, as they fell into step beside him.

The leopard had been stalking a barking deer. She paused when she heard the flute and the voices of the children. Her own young ones were growing quickly, but the girl and the two boys did not look much older.

They had started singing their favourite song again:

'*Five more miles to go!*
We climb through rain and snow.
A river to cross...
A mountain to pass...
Now we've four more miles to go!'

The leopard waited until they had passed, before returning to the trail of the barking deer.

WHEN THE GUAVAS ARE RIPE

Guava trees are easy to climb. And guavas are good to eat. So it's little wonder that an orchard of guava trees is a popular place with boys and girls.

Just across the road from Ranji's house, on the other side of a low wall, was a large guava orchard. The monsoon rains were almost over. It was a warm, humid day in September, and the guavas were ripening, turning from green to gold; no longer hard, but growing soft and sweet and juicy.

The schools were closed because of a religious festival. Ranji's father was at work in his office. Ranji's mother was enjoying an afternoon siesta on a cot in the backyard. His grandmother was busy teaching her pet parrot to recite a prayer.

'I feel like getting into those guava trees,' said Ranji to himself. 'It's been months since I climbed a tree.'

He was soon across the road and over the wall and among the trees. He chose a tree that grew in the middle of the orchard, where it was unlikely that he would be disturbed; then he climbed swiftly into its branches. A cluster of guavas swung just above him. He reached up for one of them, but to his surprise he found himself clutching a small, bare foot which had suddenly been thrust through the foliage.

Having caught the foot, Ranji did not let go. Instead he pulled hard on it. There was a squeal and someone came toppling down on him. Ranji found himself clutching at arms and legs. Together they crashed through a couple of branches and landed with a thud on the soft ground beneath the tree.

Ranji and the intruder struggled fiercely. They rolled about on the grass. Ranji tried a judo hold—without any success. Then he saw that his opponent was a girl. It was his friend and neighbour, Koki.

'It's you!' he gasped.

'It's me,' said Koki. 'And what are *you* doing here?'

'Get your knee out of my stomach and I'll tell you.'

When he had recovered his breath, he said, 'I just felt like climbing a tree.'

'So did I.'

He stared at her. There was guava juice at the corners of her mouth and on her chin.

'Are the guavas good?' he asked.

'Quite sweet, in this tree,' said Koki. 'You find another tree for yourself, Ranji. There must be thirty or forty trees to choose from.'

'And all going to waste,' said Ranji. 'Look, some of the guavas have been spoilt by the birds.'

'Nobody wants them, it seems.'

Koki climbed back onto her tree, and Ranji obligingly walked a little further and climbed another tree. After a few polite exchanges they fell silent, their attention given over entirely to the eating of guavas.

'I've eaten five,' said Koki after some time.

'You'd better stop.'

'You're only saying that because you've just started.'

'Well, three's enough for me.'

'I'm getting a tummy ache, I think.'

'I warned you. Come on, I'll take you home. We can come back tomorrow. There are still lots of guavas left.'

'I don't think I want to eat any more,' said Koki.

∞

WHEN THE GUAVAS ARE RIPE

She felt better the next day—so well, in fact, that Ranji found her leaning on the gate, waiting for him to join her. She was accompanied by her small brother, Teju, who was only six and very mischievous.

'How are you feeling today?' asked Ranji.

'Hungry,' said Koki.

'Why did you bring your brother?'

'He wants to start climbing trees.'

Soon they were in the orchard. Ranji and Koki helped Teju onto the branches of one of the smaller trees and then made for other trees, disturbing a party of parrots who flew in circles around the orchard, screaming their protests.

Two boys and a girl talking to each other from three different trees can make quite a lot of noise, and it wasn't only the birds who were disturbed. Though they did not know it, the orchard belonged to a wealthy property dealer and he employed a watchman, whose duty it was to keep away birds, children, monkeys, flying foxes, and other fruit-eating pests. But on a hot, sultry afternoon, Gopal, the watchman, could not resist taking a nap. He was stretched out under a shady jackfruit tree, snoring so loudly that the flies who had been buzzing around him felt that a storm was brewing and kept their distance.

He woke to the sound of voices raised high in glee. Sitting up, he brushed a ladybird from his long moustache, then seized his lathi, a long, stout stick usually carried by watchmen.

'Who's there?' he shouted, struggling to his feet.

There was a sudden silence on the trees.

'Who's there?' he called again.

No answer.

'I must have been dreaming,' he muttered, and was preparing to lie down and take another nap when Teju, who had been watching him, burst into laughter.

'Ho!' shouted the watchman, coming to life again. 'Thieves! I'll settle you!' And he began striding towards the centre of the orchard, boasting all the time of his physical prowess. 'I'm not afraid of thieves, bandits, or wild beasts! I'll have you know that I was once the wrestling champion of the entire district of Dehra. Come on out and fight me if you dare!'

'Run!' hissed Koki, scrambling down from her tree.

'Run!' shouted Ranji, as though it were a cricket match.

Teju was so startled by the sudden activity that he tumbled

out of his tree and began crying and Ranji and Koki had to go to his aid.

The sight of an enormous ex-wrestler bearing down on them was enough to make Teju stop crying and get to his feet. Then all three were fleeing across the grove, the watchman a little way behind them, waving his lathi and shouting at the top of his voice. Although he was an ex-wrestler (or perhaps because of it) he could not run very fast and was still huffing and puffing some twenty metres behind them when they climbed up and over the wall. He could not climb walls either. They ran off in different directions before returning home.

Next day, Ranji met Koki and Teju at the far end of the road.

'Is he there?' asked Koki.

'I haven't seen him. But he must be around somewhere.'

'Maybe he's gone for his lunch. We'll just walk past and take a quick look.'

The three of them strolled casually down the road. Koki said the gardens were looking very pretty. Teju gazed admiringly at a boy flying a kite from a rooftop. Ranji kept one eye on the road and one eye on the orchard wall. A squirrel ran along the top of the wall; the parrots were back in the guava trees.

They moved closer to the wall. Ranji leaned casually against it and Koki began to pick little daisies growing at the edge of the road. Teju, unable to hide his curiosity, pulled himself up on the wall and looked over. At the same time, Gopal, the watchman, who had been hiding behind the wall waiting for them, stood up slowly and glared fiercely at Teju.

Teju gulped, but he did not flinch. He was looking straight into the watchman's red angry eyes.

'And what can I do for you?' growled Gopal.

'I was just looking,' said Teju.

'At what?'

'At the view.'

Gopal was a little baffled. They looked just like the children he'd chased away yesterday, but he couldn't be sure. They didn't *look* guilty. But did children ever look guilty?

'There's a better view from the other side of the road,' he said gruffly. 'Now be off!'

'What lovely guavas,' said Koki, smiling sweetly. There weren't many people who could resist that smile!

'True,' said Ranji, with the air of one who was an expert on guavas and all things good to eat. 'They are just the right size and colour. I don't think I've seen better. But they'll be spoilt by the birds if you don't gather them soon.'

'It's none of your business,' said the watchman.

'Just look at his muscles,' said Teju, trying a different approach. 'He's really strong!'

Gopal looked pleased for once. He was proud of his former prowess, even though he was now rather flabby around the waist.

'You look like a wrestler,' said Ranji.

'I *am* a wrestler,' said Gopal.

'I told you so,' said Koki. 'What else could he be?'

'I'm a retired wrestler,' said Gopal.

'You don't look retired,' said Teju, fast learning that flattery can get you almost anywhere.

Gopal swelled with pride; such admiration hadn't come his way for a long time. To Koki he looked like a bullfrog swelling up, but she thought it better not to say so.

'Do you want to see my muscles?' he asked.

'Yes, yes!' they cried. 'Do show us!'

Gopal peeled off his shirt and thumped his chest. It sounded like a drum. They were really impressed. Then he bent his elbow and his biceps bulged like cricket balls.

'You can touch them,' he said generously.

Teju poked a finger into Gopal's biceps.

'Mister Universe!' he exclaimed.

Gopal glowed all over. He liked these children. How intelligent they were! Not everyone had the sense to appreciate his strength, his manliness, his magnificent physique!

'Climb over the wall and join me,' he said. 'Come sit on the grass and I'll tell you about the time when I was a wrestling champion.'

Over the wall they came and sat politely on the grass. Gopal told them about some of his exploits: how he had vanquished a world-famous wrestler in five seconds flat, and how he had saved a carload of travellers from drowning by single-handedly dragging their car out of a river. They listened patiently. Then Teju mentioned that he was feeling hungry.

'Hungry?' said Gopal. 'Why didn't you tell me before? I'll bring you some guavas, that's all there is to eat here. I know which tree has the best ones. And they're all going to rot if no one eats them—no one's buying the crop this year, the owner's price is too high!'

Gopal hurried off and soon returned with a basket full of guavas.

'Help yourselves,' he said. 'But don't eat too many, you'll get sick.'

So they munched guavas and listened to Gopal tell them about the time he was waylaid by three bandits and how he threw them all into the village pond.

'Will you come again tomorrow?' asked Gopal eagerly, when the guavas were finished and the children got up to leave. 'Come tomorrow and I'll tell you another story.'

'We'll come tomorrow,' said Teju, looking at all the guava trees still laden with fruit.

Somehow it seemed very important to Gopal that they should come again. It was lonely in the orchard. Koki sensed this and said, 'We like your stories.'

'They are good stories,' said Ranji, *even if they were not entirely true*, he thought...

They climbed over the wall and waved goodbye to Gopal.

They came again the next day.

And even when the guava season was over and Gopal had nothing to offer them but his stories, they went to see him, because by that time they had grown to like him.

HOME

'The boy's useless,' said Mr Kapoor, speaking to his wife but making sure his son could hear. 'I don't know what he'll do with himself when he grows up. He takes no interest in his studies.'

Suraj's father had returned from a business trip and was seeing his son's school report for the first time. 'Good at cricket,' said the report. 'Poor in studies. Does not pay attention in class.'

Suraj's mother, a quiet, dignified woman, said nothing. Suraj stood at the window, refusing to speak. He stared out at the light drizzle that whispered across the garden. He had angry black eyes and bushy eyebrows, and he was feeling rebellious.

His father was doing all the talking. 'What's the use of spending money on his education if he can't show anything for it? He comes home, eats as much as three boys, asks for money, and then goes out to loaf with his friends!'

Mr Kapoor paused, expecting Suraj to reply and give cause for further scolding; but Suraj knew that silence would irritate his father even more, and there were times when he enjoyed watching his father get irritated.

'Well, I won't stand for it,' said Mr Kapoor finally. 'If you don't make some effort, my boy, you can leave this house!' And having at last addressed Suraj directly, he stormed out of the room.

Suraj remained a few moments at the window. Then he went to the front door, opened it, stepped out into the rain, and banged the door behind him.

His mother made as if to call out after him, but she thought better of it, and turned and walked into the kitchen.

Suraj stood in the drizzle, looking back at the house.

'I'll never go back,' he said fiercely. 'I can manage without them. If they want me back, they can come and ask me to return!'

And he thrust his hands into his pockets and walked down the road with an independent air.

His fingers came into contact with a familiar crispness, a five rupee note. It was all the money he had in the world. He clutched it tight. He had meant to spend it at the cinema, but

HOME

now it would have to serve more urgent needs. He wasn't sure what these needs would be because just now he was angry and his mind wasn't running on practical lines. He walked blindly, unconscious of the rain, until he reached the maidaan.

When he reached the maidaan, the sun came out.

Though there was still a drizzle, the sun seemed to raise Suraj's spirits at once. He remembered his friend Ranji and decided he would stay with Ranji until he found some sort of work. He knew that if he didn't find work, he wouldn't be able to stay away from home for long. He wondered what kind of work a thirteen-year-old could get. He did not fancy delivering newspapers or serving tea in a small tea shop in the bazaar; it was much better being a customer.

The drizzle ceased altogether, and Suraj hurried across the maidaan and down a quiet road until he reached Ranji's house. When he went in at the gate, his spirits sank.

The house was shut. There was a lock on the front door. Suraj went round the house three times but he couldn't find an open door or window. Perhaps, he thought, *the family have gone out for the morning—a picnic or birthday treat; they were sure to be back for lunch.* With spirits mounting once again, he strolled leisurely down the road, in the direction of the bazaar.

Suraj had a weakness for the bazaar, for its crowded variety of goods, its smells and colours and the music playing over the loudspeakers. He lingered now at a tea-and-pakora shop, tempted by the appetizing smells that came from inside; but decided that he would eat at Ranji's house and spend his money on something other than food. He couldn't resist the big yellow yo-yo in the toy-seller's glass case; it was set with pieces of different shine, coloured glass which shone and twinkled in the sunshine.

'How much?' asked Suraj.

'Two rupees,' said the shop-keeper. 'But to a regular customer like you I give it for one rupee.'

'It must be an old one,' said Suraj, but he paid the rupee and took possession of the yo-yo. He immediately began working it, strolling through the bazaar with the yo-yo swinging up and down from his index finger.

Fingering the four remaining notes in his pocket, he decided that he was thirsty. Not tap water, nor a fizzy drink, but only a vanilla milkshake would meet his need. He sat at a table and sucked milkshake through a straw. One eye caught sight of the clock on the wall. It was nearly one o'clock. Ranji and his family should be home by now.

Suraj slipped off his chair, paid for the drink—that left him with two rupees—and went sauntering down the bazaar road, the yo-yo making soothing sounds beside him.

Ranji's house was still shut.

This was something Suraj hadn't anticipated. He walked quickly round the house, but it was locked as before. On his second round he met the gardener, an old man over sixty.

'Where is everybody?' asked Suraj.

'They have gone to Delhi for a week,' said the gardener, looking sharply at Suraj. 'Why, is anything the matter?'

Suraj had never seen the old man before, but he did not hesitate to confide in him. 'I've left home. I was going to stay with Ranji. Now there's nowhere to go.'

The old man thought this over for a minute. His face was wrinkled like a walnut, his hands and feet hard and cracked; but his eyes were bright and almost youthful.

He was a part-time gardener, who worked for several families along the road; there were no big gardens in this part of the town.

'Why don't you go home again?' he suggested.

'It's too soon,' said Suraj. 'I haven't really run away as yet. They must know I've run away. Then they'll feel sorry!'

HOME

The gardener smiled. 'You should have planned it better,' he said. 'Have you saved any money?' 'I had five rupees this morning. Now there are two rupees left.' He looked down at his yo-yo. 'Would you like to buy it?'

'I wouldn't know how to work it,' said the gardener. 'The best thing for you to do is to go home, wait till Ranji gets back, and then run away.'

Suraj considered this interesting advice, and decided that there was something in it. But he didn't make up his mind right away. A little suspense at home would be a good thing for his parents.

He returned to the maidaan and sat down on the grass. As soon as he sat down, he felt hungry.

He had never felt so hungry before. Visions of tandoori chickens and dripping spangled sweets danced before him. He wondered if the toy-seller would take back the yo-yo. He probably would, for half the price; but, as much as Suraj wanted food, he did not want to give up the yo-yo.

There was nothing to do but go home. His mother, he was sure, would be worried by now. His father (he hoped) would be pacing up and down the verandah, glancing at his watch every few seconds. It would be a lesson to them. He would walk back into the house as if doing them a favour.

He only hoped they had kept his lunch.

Suraj walked into the sitting room and threw his yo-yo on the sofa.

Mr Kapoor was sitting in his favourite armchair, reading a newspaper prior to going back to his office. He stood up for a moment as Suraj came into the room, said 'You're very late,' and returned to his newspaper.

Suraj found his mother and his food in the kitchen. She did not speak to him, but was smiling to herself.

'Feeling hungry?' she asked.

'No,' said Suraj, and seized the tray and tucked into his food.

When he returned to the sitting room he was surprised to see his father fumbling with the yo-yo.

'How do you work this stupid thing?' said Mr Kapoor.

Suraj didn't reply. He just stood there gloating over his father's clumsiness. At last he couldn't help bursting into laughter.

'It's easy,' he said. 'I'll show you.' And he took the yo-yo from his father and gave a demonstration.

When Mrs Kapoor came into the room she did not appear at all surprised to find her husband and son deeply absorbed in the working of a cheap bazaar toy. She was used to such absurdities. Men never really grew up.

Mr Kapoor had forgotten he was supposed to be returning to his office, and Suraj had forgotten about running away. They had both forgotten the morning's unpleasantness. That had been a long, long time ago.

MUKESH STARTS A ZOO

On a visit to Delhi with his parents, Mukesh spent two crowded hours at the zoo. He was dazzled by the many colourful birds, fascinated by the reptiles, charmed by the gibbons and chimps, and awestruck by the big cats—the lions, tigers and leopards. There was no zoo in the small town of Dehra where he lived, and the jungle was some way across the river bed. So, as soon as he got home, he decided that he would have a zoo of his own.

'I'm going to start a zoo,' he announced at breakfast, the day after his return.

'But you don't have any birds or animals,' said Dolly, his little sister.

'I'll soon find them,' said Mukesh. 'That's what a zoo is all about—collecting animals.'

He was gazing at the whitewashed walls of the verandah, where a gecko, a small wall lizard, was in pursuit of a fly. A little later Mukesh was trying to catch the lizard. But it was more alert than it looked, and always managed to keep a few inches ahead of his grasp.

'That's not the way to catch a lizard,' said Teju, appearing on the verandah steps. Teju and his sister Koki lived next door.

'You catch it, then,' said Mukesh.

Teju fetched a stick from the garden, where it had been used to prop up sweet peas. He used the stick to tip the lizard off the wall and into a shoebox.

'You'll be my Head Keeper,' said Mukesh, and soon he and Teju were at work in the back garden setting up enclosures with a roll of wire netting they had found in the poultry shed.

'What else can we have in the zoo?' asked Teju. 'We need more than a lizard.'

'There's your grandmother's parrot,' said Mukesh.

'That's a good idea. But we won't tell her about it—not yet. I don't think she'd lend it to us. You see, it's a *religious* parrot. She's taught it lots of prayers and chants.'

'Then people are sure to come and listen to it. They'll pay, too.'

'We must have the parrot, then. What else?'

'Well, there's my dog,' said Mukesh. 'He's very fierce.'

'But a dog isn't a zoo animal.'

'Mine is—he's a wild dog. Look, he's black all over and he's got yellow eyes. There's no other dog like him.'

Mukesh's dog, who spent most of his time sleeping on the verandah, raised his head and obligingly revealed his yellow eyes.

'He's got jaundice,' said Teju. 'They've always been yellow.'

'All right, then, we've got a lizard, a parrot and a black dog with yellow eyes.'

'Koki has a white rabbit. Will she lend it to us?'

'I don't know. She thinks a lot of her rabbit. Maybe we can rent it from her.'

'And there's Sitaram's donkey.'

Sitaram, the dhobi-boy, usually used a donkey to deliver and collect the laundry from the houses along this particular street.

'Do you really want a donkey?' asked Teju doubtfully.

'Why not? It's a wild donkey. Haven't you heard of them?'

'I've heard of a wild ass, but not a wild donkey.'

'Well, they're all related to each other—asses, donkeys and mules.'

'Why don't you paint black stripes on it and call it a zebra?'

'No, that's cheating. It's got to be a proper zoo. No tricks—it's not a circus!'

MUKESH STARTS A ZOO

On Saturday afternoon, a large placard with corrected spelling announced the opening of the zoo. It hung from the branches of the jackfruit tree. Children were allowed in free but grown-ups had to buy tickets at fifty paise each, and Koki and Dolly were selling home-made tickets to the occasional passerby or parent who happened to look in. Mukesh and his friends had worked hard at making notices for the various enclosures and each resident of the zoo was appropriately named.

The first attraction was a large packing case filled with an assortment of house lizards. They looked rather sluggish, having been generously fed with a supply of beetles and other insects.

Then came an enclosure in which Koki's white rabbit was on display. Freshly washed and brushed, it looked very cuddly and was praised by all.

Staring at it with evil intent from behind wire netting was Mukesh's dog—RARE BLACK DOG WITH YELLOW EYES—read the notice. Those yellow eyes were now trying hard to hypnotize the pink eyes of Koki's nervous rabbit. The dog pawed at the ground, trying to dig its way out from under the fence to get at the rabbit.

Tethered to a mango tree was Sitaram's small donkey. And tacked to the tree was a placard saying—WILD ASS FROM KUTCH. A distant relative it may have been, but everyone recognized it as the local washerman's beast of burden. Every now and then it tried to break loose, for it was long past its feeding time.

There was also a duck that did not seem to belong to anyone, and a small cow that had strayed in on its own; but the star attraction was the parrot. As it could recite three different prayers, over and over again, it was soon surrounded by a group of admiring parents, all of whom wished they had a parrot who could pray, or rather, do their praying for them. Oddly enough, Koki's grandmother had chosen that day for visiting the temple, so she was unaware of the fuss that was being made of her pet, or even that it had been made an honorary member of the zoo. Teju had convinced himself she wouldn't mind.

While Mukesh and Teju were escorting visitors around the zoo, lecturing them on wild dogs and wild asses, Koki and Dolly were doing a brisk trade at the ticket counter. They had collected about ten rupees and were hoping for yet more, when there was a disturbance in the enclosures.

The black dog with yellow eyes had finally managed to dig his way out of his cage, and was now busy trying to dig his way into the rabbit's compartment. The rabbit was running round and round in panic-stricken circles. Meanwhile, the donkey had finally snapped the rope that held it and, braying loudly, scattered the spectators and made for home.

MUKESH STARTS A ZOO

Koki went to the rescue of her rabbit and soon had it cradled in her arms. The dog now turned his attention to the duck. The duck flew over the packing case, while the dog landed in it, scattering lizards in all directions.

In all this confusion, no one noticed that the door of the parrot's cage had slipped open. With a squawk and a whirr of wings, the bird shot out of the cage and flew off into a nearby orchard.

'The parrot's gone!' shouted Dolly, and almost immediately a silence fell upon the assembled visitors and children. Even the dog stopped barking. Granny's praying parrot had escaped! How could they possibly face her? Teju wondered if she would believe him if he told her it had flown off to heaven.

'Can anyone see it?' he asked tearfully.

'It's in a mango tree,' said Dolly. 'It won't come back.'

The crowd fell away, unwilling to share any of the blame when Koki's grandmother came home and discovered what had happened.

'What are we going to do now?' asked Teju, looking to Koki for help; but Koki was too upset to suggest anything. Mukesh had an idea.

'I know!' he said. 'We'll get another one!'

'How?'

'Well, there's the ten rupees we've collected. We can buy a new parrot for ten rupees!'

'But won't Granny know the difference?' asked Teju.

'All these hill parrots look alike,' said Mukesh.

So, taking the cage with them, they hurried off to the bazaar, where they soon found a bird-seller who was happy to sell them a parrot not unlike Granny's. He assured them it would talk.

'It looks like your grandmother's parrot,' said Mukesh on the way home. 'But can it pray?'

'Of course not,' said Koki. 'But we can teach it.'

Koki's grandmother, who was short-sighted, did not notice the substitution; but she complained bitterly that the bird had stopped repeating its prayers and was instead making rude noises and even swearing occasionally.

Teju soon remedied this sad state of affairs.

Every morning he stood in front of the parrot's cage and repeated Granny's prayers. Within a few weeks the bird had learnt to repeat one of them. Granny was happy again—not only because her parrot had started praying once more, but because Teju had started praying too!

THE KING AND
THE TREE-GODDESS

This is one of the stories Koki's grandmother told the children on a wet monsoon evening, when it was impossible to play outside. Grandmother loved trees, and this was one of her favourite tree stories.

There was once a king living in the Himalayan foothills, who longed to build himself a palace more beautiful than any he had seen in that part of the world. He could not make it richer, taller or stronger than any other without going to a great deal of expense and trouble. So he decided to build something different; the entire palace was to be supported by one column only, and that column was to be made from the tallest tree in the kingdom.

In the Himalayas there are many tall trees—spruce and pine, oak and deodar. And the tallest and the strongest are the deodars, whose very name, *Deo-Dar*, means Tree of God.

The King sent for his Prime Minister and said, 'Send men to my forests far and near, and tell them to cut down and bring to this city, without delay, the largest deodar they can find.'

'But the deodar is a sacred tree,' protested his daughter. 'It is used only for building temples.'

'All the more reason for me to have one,' said the King. 'My palace shall be as magnificent as any temple!'

The Prime Minister sent out thirty men but they soon returned, saying that though there were many great deodars in the kingdom, they could never carry or drag them over so much difficult country as lay between the forests and the city.

When the King heard this, he called his son and said, 'Take your horsemen, and with the help of your horses, bring me one of these trees.'

The prince rode out with his horsemen but returned after a few days, saying, 'No horses could move such a tree an inch. We have tried oxen too, but without any success.'

'Well, then, try elephants,' said the King.

Elephants were brought from the plains, but the hills were too steep for them, and the paths too narrow; they had to return to the valley.

'Very well,' said the King angrily. 'In one of my own parks you must find me a tree just as big as any in the forests. Bring it to me within seven days.'

After much searching, the King's men found a splendid deodar tree growing not far from the city. It was worshipped by the people of many villages round about, because within it lived a Goddess, and it was she who gave to the tree its great strength, size and beauty.

When the Prime Minister and his men had decided that the column for the King's palace must be made from this lofty deodar tree, they came with garlands, lamps and music to pay their respects to the Goddess inside, and to warn her that she must leave her abode. Within seven days it had to be cut to the ground.

They lit their lamps and placed them in a circle round the tree. They hung their garlands upon the branches and tied nosegays among the leaves. Then, joining hands, some danced, and others sang:

THE KING AND THE TREE-GODDESS

'With cruel axe we've come
To fell your age-long home;
Forgive us, great Tree-Gdddess–
We dance before your throne!
To please the King must we
Cut down your loveliest tree.'

The Tree-Goddess heard, and understood what was about to happen. She remained quiet as a resting breeze for a few moments, and then all her leaves began to whisper and her topmost branches bowed. The men went away satisfied that she had heard and understood.

That night, when the King was asleep, a glorious figure draped in shining green foliage appeared to him, and spoke in a voice that was like the rustle of autumn leaves:

'I am the Goddess of the Deodar tree, great King. Your men have told me that you intend to cut me down. I have come to beg you to change your mind.'

'No, my mind is made up,' answered the King in his dream. 'Yours is the only tree in all my parks strong enough to support by itself a palace, and therefore I must have it.'

'But consider, oh King! For hundreds of years I have been worshipped by the people of all the villages in your kingdom, and nothing but good has gone out from me to them. The birds nest in me. I send a most lovely shade upon the grass. Men rest against my trunk and wild creatures rub themselves against me. The earth blesses me, and sends up new plants and herbs under my protective arms. I bind the earth with my strong roots. Children play at my feet, and women returning from the fields seek refuge in my coolness.'

'All true enough, good Tree-Goddess,' said the King, 'but all the same I cannot spare you. My mind is made up, my will cannot be shaken.'

The Tree-Goddess sank her head upon her breast and spoke in tones of great sorrow.

'Then, mighty King, grant me one last request. Let me be felled in three parts. First my head, with its crown of waving greenery. Next my middle, with its hundred strong arms and hands. And last my base, which bears the heaviest and knottiest of my limbs upon it.'

'This is a strange request,' said the King. 'I have never before heard of someone who wished to suffer the death stroke *thrice*! Why not suffer it once, and have done with it?'

'The reason is plain,' said the Tree-Goddess. 'Dozens of young deodar trees have sprung from me, and have grown up around me. Should you fell me with one mighty stroke, my weight would certainly crush all my children to death. But if I suffer the stroke

THE KING AND THE TREE-GODDESS

three times, and fall in three pieces, some of the young ones may escape. Is my prayer granted?'

'Indeed, it is,' said the astonished King, as the Tree-Goddess faded from his vision.

The next morning the King called his children and his ministers and his foresters to him, and told them that he had changed his mind, and that the column for the new palace should be built of stone, not wood.

'For,' said he, 'within the deodar tree lives a spirit nobler than my own.' And he told them of his vision, and they all marvelled.

And the King built his palace upon a great column of stone, and around its base he created a beautiful park, and the children of the city and the surrounding villages flocked to the gardens to sit on the grass and enjoy the many beautiful flowers and trees that had been planted on all sides.

Taking the example of the King, no one built their houses of wood any more. The houses were made of stone, and the great deodars were able to spread freely through the forests.

'And if you go up into the mountains,' said Grandmother, 'you can still see those forests, all the way up the sacred river Ganga, to its source near the eternal snows.'

THE WINDOW

I came in the spring, and took the room on the roof. It was a long low building which housed several families; the roof was flat, except for my room and a chimney. I don't know whose room owned the chimney, but my room owned the roof. And from the window of my room I owned the world.

But only from the window.

The banyan tree, just opposite, was mine, and its inhabitants my subjects. They were two squirrels, a few mynah, a crow, and at night, a pair of flying foxes. The squirrels were busy in the afternoons, the birds in the mornings and evenings, the foxes at night. I wasn't very busy that year; not as busy as the inhabitants of the banyan tree.

There was also a mango tree but that came later, in the summer, when I met Koki, and the mangoes were ripe.

At first, I was lonely in my room. But then I discovered the power of my window. I looked out on the banyan tree, on the garden, on the broad path that ran beside the building, and out over the roofs of other houses, over roads and fields, as far as the horizon. The path was not a very busy one but it held variety: an ayah, with a baby in a pram; the postman, an event in himself; the fruit seller, the toy seller, calling their wares in high-pitched familiar cries; the rent collector; a posse of cyclists; a long chain of schoolgirls; a lame beggar...all passed my way, the way of my window.

In the early summer, a tonga came rattling and jingling down the path and stopped in front of the house. A girl and an elderly lady climbed down, and a servant unloaded their baggage. They

THE WINDOW

went into the house and the tonga moved off, the horse snorting a little.

The next morning the girl looked up from the garden and saw me at my window.

She had long black hair that fell to her waist, tied with a single red ribbon. Her eyes were black like her hair and just as shiny. She must have been about ten or eleven years old.

'Hallo,' I said with a friendly smile.

She looked suspiciously at me. 'Who are you?' she asked.

'I'm a ghost.'

She laughed, and her laugh had a gay, mocking quality. 'You look like one!'

I didn't think her remark particularly flattering, but I had asked for it. I stopped smiling anyway. Most children don't like adults smiling at them all the time.

'What have you got up there?' she asked.

'Magic,' I said.

She laughed again but this time without mockery. 'I don't believe you,' she said.

'Why don't you come up and see for yourself?'

She hesitated a little but came round to the steps and began climbing them, slowly, cautiously. And when she entered the room, she brought a magic of her own.

'Where's your magic?' she asked, looking me in the eye.

'Come here,' I said, and I took her to the window, and showed her the world.

She said nothing but stared out of the window uncomprehendingly at first, and then with increasing interest. And after some time she turned round and smiled at me, and we were friends.

I only knew that her name was Koki, and that she had come with her aunt for the summer months; I didn't need to know

any more about her, and she didn't need to know anything about me except that I wasn't really a ghost—not the frightening sort anyway…

She came up my steps nearly every day, and joined me at the window. There was a lot of excitement to be had in our world, especially when the rains broke.

At the first rumblings, women would rush outside to retrieve the washing on the clothes line and if there was a breeze, to chase a few garments across the compound. When the rain came, it came with a vengeance, making a bog of the garden and a river of the path. A cyclist would come riding furiously down the path, an elderly gentleman would be having difficulty with an umbrella, naked children would be frisking about in the rain. Sometimes Koki would run out on the roof, and shout and dance in the rain. And the rain would come through the open door and window of the room, flooding the floor and making an island of the bed.

But the window was more fun than anything else. It gave us the power of detachment: we were deeply interested in the life around us, but we were not involved in it.

'It is like a cinema,' said Koki. 'The window is the screen, the world is the picture.'

Soon the mangoes were ripe, and Koki was in the branches of the mango tree as often as she was in my room. From the window I had a good view of the tree, and we spoke to each other from the same height. We ate far too many mangoes, at least five a day.

'Let's make a garden on the roof,' suggested Koki. She was full of ideas like this.

'And how do you propose to do that?' I asked.

'It's easy. We bring up mud and bricks and make the flowerbeds. Then we plant the seeds. We'll grow all sorts of flowers.'

'The roof will fall in,' I predicted.

But it didn't. We spent two days carrying buckets of mud up the steps to the roof and laying out the flowerbeds. It was very hard work, but Koki did most of it. When the beds were ready, we had the opening ceremony. Apart from a few small plants collected from the garden below we had only one species of seeds—pumpkin...

We planted the pumpkin seeds in the mud, and felt proud of ourselves.

But it rained heavily that night, and in the morning I discovered that everything—except the bricks—had been washed away.

So we returned to the window.

A mynah had been in a fight—with a crow perhaps—and the feathers had been knocked off its head. A bougainvillaea that had been climbing the wall had sent a long green shoot in through the window.

Koki said, 'Now we can't shut the window without spoiling the creeper.'

'Then we will never close the window,' I said.

And we let the creeper into the room.

The rains passed, and an autumn wind came whispering through the branches of the banyan tree. There were red leaves on the ground, and the wind picked them up and blew them about, so that they looked like butterflies. I would watch the sun rise in the morning, the sky all red, until its first rays splashed the windowsill and crept up the walls of the room. And in the evening Koki and I watched the sun go down in a sea of fluffy clouds; sometimes the clouds were pink, and sometimes orange; they were always coloured clouds, framed in the window.

'I'm going tomorrow,' said Koki one evening.

I was too surprised to say anything.

'You stay here forever, don't you?' she said.

I remained silent.

'When I come again next year you will still be here, won't you?'

'I don't know,' I said. 'But the window will still be here.'

'Oh, do be here next year,' she said, 'or someone will close the window!'

In the morning the tonga was at the door, and the servant, the aunt and Koki were in it. Koki waved to me at my window. Then the driver flicked the reins, the wheels of the carriage

THE WINDOW

creaked and rattled, the bell jingled. Down the path went the tonga, down the path and through the gate, and all the time Koki waved; and from the gate I must have looked like a ghost, standing alone at the high window, amongst the bougainvillaea.

When the tonga was out of sight I took the spray of bougainvillaea in my hand and pushed it out of the room. Then I closed the window. It would be opened only when the spring and Koki came again.

THE VISITOR

Amir was sitting on his bed, staring out of the door that opened out onto the roof. The bald mynah bird stared back at him. Then he heard someone calling from downstairs.

'Does anyone live up there?'

'No,' shouted Amir. 'Nobody lives up here.'

'Then can I come up?' asked the person below.

Amir didn't answer. Presently he heard footsteps coming up. The mynah bird flew off the roof and settled in a mango tree.

A boy stood in the doorway, smiling at Amir. He was a little taller than Amir, and much thinner. He wore a white shirt outside striped pyjamas. On his feet were open slippers. A tray hung from his shoulders, filled with an assortment of goods.

'Would you like to buy something?' he asked.

In his tray were combs, buttons, reels of thread, shoelaces, little vials of cheap perfume.

'I have everything you need,' he said.

'I don't need anything,' said Amir.

'You need buttons.'

'I don't.'

'Your top button is missing.'

Amir felt for the top button of his shirt and was surprised to find it missing.

'I don't like buttoning my shirt,' he said.

'That's different,' said his visitor, and looked him up and down for further signs of wear and tear. 'You'd better buy a new pair of shoelaces.'

Amir looked down at his shoes and said, 'I've got laces.'

THE VISITOR

'Very poor quality,' said the boy, and taking hold of one of the laces, he tugged at it and snapped it in two.

'See how easily it breaks? Now you need laces.'

'Well, I'm not buying any,' said Amir.

The boy sighed, shrugged, and moved towards the door. As he walked slowly down the steps, Amir stood in the doorway, watching him go. On an impulse, he called out, 'What's your name?'

'Mohan,' replied the boy.

'Well, come again in a week,' said Amir. 'I may need something then.'

Amir went downstairs for his lunch. He returned to his room to study, but dozed off instead. Towards evening he felt hungry and restless. He could not remain in his room when everyone else was pouring into the streets to shop and talk and eat, and visit the cinema.

From the roof he could see the bazaar lights coming on, and hear the jingle of tonga bells and the blare of bus horns. It was a cool evening and he put on his coat before going downstairs.

It was not easy to walk fast on the road to the bazaar. Apart from the great number of pedestrians, there were cyclists and scooter-rickshaws, handcarts, and cows, all making movement difficult. A little tea shop played film music over a loudspeaker, adding noise to the general confusion.

The balloon-man was having a trying time. He was surrounded by a swarm of children who were more intent on bursting his balloons than on buying any. One or two got loose and went sailing over the heads of the crowd to burst over the fire in the chaat shop.

Amir stood outside the chaat shop and ate a variety of spicy snacks. Then he wiped his fingers on the banana leaves on which he had been served, and moved on down the bazaar road.

Towards the clock tower the road grew wider and less crowded. There was a street lamp at the corner of the road. A boy was sitting on the pavement beneath the lamp, bent over a book, absorbed in what he was reading. He seemed not to notice the noise of the bazaar or the chill in the air. As Amir came nearer, he saw that the boy was Mohan.

He did not know whether to stop and talk to him, or carry on down the road. After walking some distance, he felt ashamed at not having stopped to greet the boy, so he turned and retraced his steps. But when he came to the lamp post, Mohan had gone.

When Mohan came again he did not call out from below but came straight up to the room. He looked at Amir's shirt and shoes and saw that one of the shoes was still done up with half a lace. With an air of triumph he dropped a pair of shoelaces on the desk.

'I can't pay for them now,' said Amir.

'You can pay me later.'

Amir sat on the edge of his table while Mohan leaned against the wall.

'Do you go to school?' asked Amir.

'Sometimes I go to evening classes,' Mohan said. 'I am sitting privately for my high school exams next month. If I pass...'

He stopped to think about the things he could do if he passed. The way to a career would be open to him, he could study further, become an engineer, or a scientist or an administrator. No more selling combs and buttons at street corners...

'Where are your parents?' asked Amir.

'My father is dead. My mother is in our village in the hills. I have brothers and sisters at home, but I am the only one old

THE VISITOR

enough to work.'

'Then where do you stay?'

'Anywhere. On somebody's verandah, or on the maidan; it doesn't matter much in the summer. These days I sleep on the station platform. It's quite warm there.'

'You can sleep here,' said Amir.

One morning, when he opened the door of his room, Amir found Mohan asleep at the top of the steps. He had wrapped himself up in a thin blanket. His tray of merchandise lay a short distance away.

Amir shook him gently and he woke up immediately, blinking in the bright sunlight.

'Why didn't you come in?' asked Amir. 'Why didn't you let me know you were here?'

'It was late,' said Mohan. 'I did not want to wake you. Besides, it was a fine night, not too cold.'

'Someone could have stolen your things. '

Amir made Mohan promise to sleep in the room that night. He came quite early. Amir lent him another blanket, and he lay down on the floor-mat and slept soundly, while Amir stayed awake worrying if his guest was comfortable enough.

Mohan came quite often, leaving early in the morning before Amir could offer him a meal. He ate at little places in the bazaar.

The high school exams were nearing, and Mohan sat up late with his books. Apart from his occasional evening classes, he received no teaching.

The exams lasted for ten days, and during this time Mohan put aside his tray of odds and ends. He did his papers with confidence. He thought he had done rather well. And when it

THE VISITOR

was over, he took up his tray again and walked all over the town, trying to make up for lost sales.

※

On the day the exam results were due, Amir rose early. He got to the news agency at five o'clock, just as the morning papers arrived. Bhartu gave him a paper to look at and he found the page on which the results were listed. He looked down the 'passes' column for the town, but couldn't find Mohan's number on the list. He looked twice to make sure, and then returned the paper to Bhartu with a glum look.

'Failed?' said Bhartu.

Amir nodded and turned away. When he returned to the room, he found Mohan sitting at the top of the steps. He didn't have to tell him anything. Mohan knew by the look on the other's face.

Amir sat down beside him, and they said nothing for a while.

'Never mind,' said Mohan. 'I'll pass next year.' It seemed that Amir was more in need of comforting than himself.

'If only you'd had more time,' said Amir.

'I have plenty of time now. Another year... Can I still stay in your room?'

'For as long as it's my room. That means I shall have to work too, otherwise my grandfather will drag me downstairs again.'

Mohan laughed and went into the room. When he came out, the tray was hanging from his shoulders.

'What would you like to buy?' he asked. 'I have everything you need.'

ANGRY RIVER

In the middle of the big river—the river that began in the mountains and ended in the sea—was a small island. The river swept round the island, sometimes clawing at its banks, but never going right over it. It was over twenty years since the river had flooded the island, and at that time no one had lived there. But for the last ten years a small hut had stood there, a mud-walled hut with a sloping thatched roof. The hut had been built into a huge rock, so only three of the walls were mud, and the fourth was rock.

Goats grazed on the short grass which grew on the island, and on the prickly leaves of thorn bushes. A few hens followed them about. There was a melon patch and a vegetable patch. In the middle of the island stood a peepul tree. It was the only tree there. Even during the Great Flood, when the island had been under water, the tree had stood firm.

It was an old tree. A seed had been carried to the island by a strong wind some fifty years back, had found shelter between two rocks, had taken root there, and had sprung up to give shade and shelter to a small family. Indians love peepul trees, especially during the hot summer months when the heart-shaped leaves catch the least breath of air and flutter eagerly, fanning those who sit beneath.

A sacred tree, the peepul: the abode of spirits, good and bad.

'Don't yawn when you are sitting beneath the tree,' Grandmother used to warn Sita.

'And if you must yawn, always snap your fingers in front of

your mouth. If you forget to do that, a spirit might jump down your throat!'

'And then what will happen?' asked Sita.

'It will probably ruin your digestion,' said Grandfather, who wasn't much of a believer in spirits.

The peepul had a beautiful leaf, and Grandmother likened it to the body of the mighty god Krishna—broad at the shoulders, then tapering down to a very slim waist.

It was an old tree, and an old man sat beneath it. He was mending a fishing net. He had fished in the river for ten years, and he was a good fisherman. He knew where to find the slim silver chilwa fish and the big, beautiful mahseer and the long-moustached singhara; he knew where the river was deep and where it was shallow; he knew which baits to use—which fish liked worms and which liked gram. He had taught his son to fish, but his son had gone to work in a factory in a city, nearly a hundred miles away. He had no grandson; but he had a granddaughter, Sita, and she could do all the things a boy could do, and sometimes she could do them better. She had lost her mother when she was very small. Grandmother had taught her all the things a girl should know, and she could do these as well as most girls. But neither of her grandparents could read or write, and as a result Sita couldn't read or write either.

There was a school in one of the villages across the river, but Sita had never seen it. There was too much to do on the island.

While Grandfather mended his net, Sita was inside the hut, pressing her grandmother's forehead, which was hot with fever. Grandmother had been ill for three days and could not eat. She had been ill before, but she had never been so bad. Grandfather had brought her some sweet oranges from the market in the nearest town, and she could suck the juice from the oranges, but she couldn't eat anything else.

She was younger than Grandfather, but because she was sick, she looked much older. She had never been very strong.

When Sita noticed that Grandmother had fallen asleep, she tiptoed out of the room on her bare feet and stood outside.

The sky was dark with monsoon clouds. It had rained all night, and in a few hours it would rain again. The monsoon rains had come early, at the end of June. Now it was the middle of July, and already the river was swollen. Its rushing sound seemed nearer and more menacing than usual.

Sita went to her grandfather and sat down beside him beneath the peepul tree.

'When you are hungry, tell me,' she said, 'and I will make the bread.'

'Is your grandmother asleep?'

'She sleeps. But she will wake soon, for she has a deep pain.'

The old man stared out across the river, at the dark green of the forest, at the grey sky, and said, 'Tomorrow, if she is not better, I will take her to the hospital at Shahganj. There they will know how to make her well. You may be on your own for a few days—but you have been on your own before...'

Sita nodded gravely; she had been alone before, even during the rainy season. Now she wanted Grandmother to get well, and she knew that only Grandfather had the skill to take the small dugout boat across the river when the current was so strong. Someone would have to stay behind to look after their few possessions.

Sita was not afraid of being alone, but she did not like the look of the river. That morning, when she had gone down to fetch water, she had noticed that the level had risen. Those rocks which were normally spattered with the droppings of snipe and curlew and other water birds had suddenly disappeared.

They disappeared every year—but not so soon, surely?

'Grandfather, if the river rises, what will I do?'

'You will keep to the high ground.'
'And if the water reaches the high ground?'
'Then take the hens into the hut, and stay there.'
'And if the water comes into the hut?'
'Then climb into the peepul tree. It is a strong tree. It will not fall. And the water cannot rise higher than the tree!'
'And the goats, Grandfather?'
'I will be taking them with me, Sita. I may have to sell them to pay for good food and medicines for your grandmother. As for the hens, if it becomes necessary, put them on the roof. But do not worry too much'—and he patted Sita's head—'the water will not rise as high. I will be back soon, remember that.'
'And won't Grandmother come back?'
'Yes, of course, but they may keep her in the hospital for some time.'

Towards evening, it began to rain again—big pellets of rain, scarring the surface of the river. But it was warm rain, and Sita could move about in it. She was not afraid of getting wet, she rather liked it. In the previous month, when the first monsoon shower had arrived, washing the dusty leaves of the tree and bringing up the good smell of the earth, she had exulted in it, had run about shouting for joy. She was used to it now, and indeed a little tired of the rain, but she did not mind getting wet. It was steamy indoors, and her thin dress would soon dry in the heat from the kitchen fire.

She walked about barefooted, bare-legged. She was very sure on her feet; her toes had grown accustomed to gripping all kinds of rocks, slippery or sharp. And though thin, she was surprisingly strong.

Black hair streaming across her face. Black eyes. Slim brown arms. A scar on her thigh—when she was small, visiting her mother's village, a hyena had entered the house where she was sleeping, fastened on to her leg and tried to drag her away, but her screams had roused the villagers and the hyena had run off.

She moved about in the pouring rain, chasing the hens into a shelter behind the hut. A harmless brown snake, flooded out of its hole, was moving across the open ground. Sita picked up a stick, scooped the snake up, and dropped it between a cluster of rocks. She had no quarrel with snakes. They kept down the rats and the frogs. She wondered how the rats had first come to the island—probably in someone's boat, or in a sack of grain. Now it was a job to keep their numbers down.

When Sita finally went indoors, she was hungry. She ate some dried peas and warmed up some goat's milk. Grandmother woke once and asked for water, and Grandfather held the brass tumbler to her lips.

∞

It rained all night.

The roof was leaking, and a small puddle formed on the floor. They kept the kerosene lamp alight. They did not need the light, but somehow it made them feel safer.

The sound of the river had always been with them, although they were seldom aware of it; but that night they noticed a change in its sound. There was something like a moan—like a wind in the tops of tall trees—and a swift hiss as the water swept round the rocks and carried away pebbles. And sometimes there was a rumble, as loose earth fell into the water.

Sita could not sleep.

She had a rag doll, made with Grandmother's help, out of bits

ANGRY RIVER

of old clothing. She kept it by her side every night. The doll was someone to talk to, when the nights were long and sleep elusive. Her grandparents were often ready to talk—and Grandmother, when she was well, was a good storyteller—but sometimes Sita wanted to have secrets, and though there were no special secrets in her life, she made up a few, because it was fun to have them. And if you have secrets, you must have a friend to share them with, a companion of one's own age. Since there were no other children on the island, Sita shared her secrets with the rag doll whose name was Mumta.

Grandfather and Grandmother were asleep, though the sound of Grandmother's laboured breathing was almost as persistent as the sound of the river.

'Mumta,' whispered Sita in the dark, starting one of her private conversations.

'Do you think Grandmother will get well again?'

Mumta always answered Sita's questions, even though the answers could only be heard by Sita.

'She is very old,' said Mumta.

'Do you think the river will reach the hut?' asked Sita.

'If it keeps raining like this, and the river keeps rising, it will reach the hut.'

'I am a little afraid of the river, Mumta. Aren't you afraid?'

'Don't be afraid. The river has always been good to us.'

'What will we do if it comes into the hut?'

'We will climb on to the roof.'

'And if it reaches the roof?'

'We will climb the peepul tree. The river has never gone higher than the peepul tree.'

As soon as the first light showed through the little skylight, Sita got up and went outside. It wasn't raining hard, it was drizzling, but it was the sort of drizzle that could continue for days, and it probably meant that heavy rain was falling in the hills where the river originated.

Sita went down to the water's edge. She couldn't find her favourite rock, the one on which she often sat dangling her feet in the water, watching the little chilwa fish swim by. It was still there, no doubt, but the river had gone over it.

She stood on the sand, and she could feel the water oozing and bubbling beneath her feet.

The river was no longer green and blue and flecked with white, but a muddy colour.

She went back to the hut. Grandfather was up now. He was getting his boat ready.

Sita milked a goat. Perhaps it was the last time she would milk it.

The sun was just coming up when Grandfather pushed off in the boat. Grandmother lay in the prow. She was staring hard at Sita, trying to speak, but the words would not come. She raised her hand in a blessing.

Sita bent and touched her grandmother's feet, and then Grandfather pushed off. The little boat, with its two old people and three goats—riding swiftly on the river, moved slowly, very slowly, towards the opposite bank. The current was so swift now that Sita realized the boat would be carried about half a mile downstream before Grandfather could get it to dry land.

It bobbed about on the water, getting smaller and smaller, until it was just a speck on the broad river.

And suddenly Sita was alone.

There was a wind, whipping the raindrops against her face; and there was the water, rushing past the island; and there was the distant shore, blurred by rain; and there was the small hut; and there was the tree.

Sita got busy. The hens had to be fed. They weren't bothered about anything except food. Sita threw them handfuls of coarse grain and potato peelings and peanut shells.

Then she took the broom and swept out the hut, lit the charcoal burner, warmed some milk, and thought, 'Tomorrow there will be no milk...' She began peeling onions. Soon her eyes started smarting and, pausing for a few moments and glancing around the quiet room, she became aware again that she was alone. Grandfather's hookah stood by itself in one corner. It was a beautiful old hookah, which had belonged to Sita's great-grandfather. The bowl was made out of a coconut encased in silver. The long winding stem was at least four feet in length. It was their most valuable possession. Grandmother's sturdy shisham wood walking stick stood in another corner.

Sita looked around for Mumta, found the doll beneath the cot, and placed her within sight and hearing.

Thunder rolled down from the hills. BOOM–BOOM–BOOM...

'The gods of the mountains are angry,' said Sita. 'Do you think they are angry with me?'

'Why Should they be angry with you?' asked Mumta.

'They don't have to have a reason for being angry. They are angry with everything, and we are in the middle of everything. We are so small—do you think they know we are here?'

'Who knows what the gods think?'

'But I made you,' said Sita, 'and I know you are here.'

'And will you save me if the river rises?'

'Yes, of course. I won't go anywhere without you, Mumta.'

Sita couldn't stay indoors for long. She went out, taking Mumta with her, and stared out across the river, to the safe land on the other side. But was it safe there? The river looked much wider now. Yes, it had crept over its banks and spread far across the flat plain. Far away, people were driving their cattle through waterlogged, flooded fields, carrying their belongings in bundles on their heads or shoulders, leaving their homes, making for the high land. It wasn't safe anywhere.

She wondered what had happened to Grandfather and Grandmother. If they had reached the shore safely, Grandfather would have to engage a bullock cart, or a pony-drawn carriage, to get Grandmother to the district town, five or six miles away, where there was a market, a court, a jail, a cinema, and a hospital.

She wondered if she would ever see Grandmother again. She had done her best to look after the old lady, remembering the times when Grandmother had looked after her, had gently touched her fevered brow, and had told her stories—stories about the gods: about the young Krishna, friend of birds and animals, so full of mischief, always causing confusion among the other Gods; and Indra, who made the thunder and lightning; and Vishnu, the preserver of all good things, whose steed was a great white bird; and Ganesh, with the elephant's head; and Hanuman, the monkey god, who helped the young Prince Rama in his war with the King of Ceylon. Would Grandmother return to tell her more about them, or would she have to find out for herself?

The island looked much smaller now. In parts, the mud banks had dissolved quickly, sinking into the river. But in the middle of the island there was rocky ground, and the rocks would never crumble, they could only be submerged. In a space in the middle of the rocks, grew the tree.

Sita climbed up the tree to get a better view. She had climbed the tree many times and it took her only a few seconds to reach the higher branches. She put her hand to her eyes to shield them from the rain, and gazed upstream.

ANGRY RIVER

There was water everywhere. The world had become one vast river. Even the trees on the forested side of the river looked as though they had grown from the water, like mangroves. The sky was banked with massive, moisture-laden clouds. Thunder rolled down from the hills and the river seemed to take it up with a hollow, booming sound.

Something was floating down with the current, something big and bloated. It was closer now, and Sita could make out the bulky object—a drowned buffalo, being carried rapidly downstream.

So the water had already inundated the villages further upstream. Or perhaps the buffalo had been grazing too close to the rising river.

Sita's worst fears were confirmed when, a little later, she saw planks of wood, small trees and bushes, and then a wooden bedstead, floating past the island.

How long would it take for the river to reach her own small hut?

As she climbed down from the tree, it began to rain more heavily. She ran indoors, shooing the hens before her. They flew into the hut and huddled under Grandmother's cot. Sita thought it would be best to keep them together now. And having them with her took away some of the loneliness.

There were three hens and a cock bird. The river did not bother them. They were interested only in food, and Sita kept them happy by throwing them a handful of onion skins.

She would have liked to close the door and shut out the swish of the rain and the boom of the river, but then she would have no way of knowing how fast the water rose.

She took Mumta in her arms, and began praying for the rain to stop and the river to fall. She prayed to the god Indra, and, just in case he was busy elsewhere, she prayed to other Gods too. She prayed for the safety of her grandparents and for her own safety. She put herself last but only with great difficulty.

She would have to make herself a meal. So she chopped up some onions, fried them, then added turmeric and red chilli powder and stirred until she had everything sizzling; then she added a tumbler of water, some salt, and a cup of one of the cheaper lentils. She covered the pot and allowed the mixture to simmer. Doing this took Sita about ten minutes. It would take at least half an hour for the dish to be ready.

When she looked outside, she saw pools of water amongst the rocks and near the tree. She couldn't tell if it was rainwater or overflow from the river.

She had an idea.

A big tin trunk stood in a corner of the room. It had belonged to Sita's mother. There was nothing in it except a cotton-filled quilt, for use during the cold weather. She would stuff the trunk with everything useful or valuable, and weigh it down so that it wouldn't be carried away—just in case the river came over the island... Grandfather's hookah went into the trunk. Grandmother's walking stick went in too. So did a number of small tins containing the spices used in cooking—nutmeg, caraway seeds, cinnamon, coriander, and pepper—a bigger tin of flour and a tin of raw sugar. Even if Sita had to spend several hours in the tree, there would be something to eat when she came down again.

A clean white cotton shirt of Grandfather's, and Grandmother's only spare sari also went into the trunk. Never mind if they got stained with yellow curry powder! Never mind if they got to smell of salted fish, some of that went in too.

Sita was so busy packing the trunk that she paid no attention to the lick of cold water at her heels. She locked the trunk, placed the key high on the rock wall, and turned to give her attention to the lentils. It was only then that she discovered that she was walking about on a watery floor.

She stood still, horrified by what she saw. The water was oozing over the threshold, pushing its way into the room.

Sita was filled with panic. She forgot about her meal and everything else. Darting out of the hut, she ran splashing through ankle-deep water towards the safety of the peepul tree. If the tree hadn't been there, such a well-known landmark, she might have floundered into deep water, into the river.

She climbed swiftly into the strong arms of the tree, made herself secure on a familiar branch, and thrust the wet hair away from her eyes.

― ∞ ―

She was glad she had hurried. The hut was now surrounded by water. Only the higher parts of the island could still be seen—a few rocks, the big rock on which the hut was built, a hillock on which some thorny bilberry bushes grew.

The hens hadn't bothered to leave the hut. They were probably perched on the cot now.

Would the river rise still higher? Sita had never seen it like this before. It swirled around her, stretching in all directions.

More drowned cattle came floating down. The most unusual things went by on the water—an aluminium kettle, a cane chair, a tin of tooth powder, an empty cigarette packet, a wooden slipper, a plastic doll...

A doll!

With a sinking feeling, Sita remembered Mumta.

Poor Mumta! She had been left behind in the hut. Sita, in her hurry, had forgotten her only companion.

Well, thought Sita, if I can be careless with someone I've made, how can I expect the Gods to notice me, alone in the middle of the river?

The waters were higher now, the island fast disappearing.

Something came floating out of the hut.

It was an empty kerosene tin, with one of the hens perched on top. The tin came bobbing along on the water, not far from the tree, and was then caught by the current and swept into the river. The hen still managed to keep its perch.

A little later, the water must have reached the cot because the remaining hens flew up to the rock ledge and sat huddled there in the small recess.

The water was rising rapidly now, and all that remained of the island was the big rock that supported the hut, the top of the hut itself and the peepul tree.

It was a tall tree with many branches and it seemed unlikely that the water could ever go right over it. But how long would Sita have to remain there? She climbed a little higher, and as she did so, a jet-black jungle crow settled in the upper branches, and Sita saw that there was a nest in them—a crow's nest, an untidy platform of twigs wedged in the fork of a branch.

In the nest were four blue-green, speckled eggs. The crow sat on them and cawed disconsolately. But though the crow was miserable, its presence brought some cheer to Sita. At least she was not alone. Better to have a crow for company than no one at all.

Other things came floating out of the hut—a large pumpkin; a red turban belonging to Grandfather, unwinding in the water like a long snake; and then—Mumta! The doll, being filled with straw and wood shavings, moved quite swiftly on the water and passed close to the peepul tree. Sita saw it and wanted to call out, to urge her friend to make for the tree, but she knew that Mumta could not swim—the doll could only float, travel with the river, and perhaps be washed ashore many miles downstream.

The tree shook in the wind and the rain. The crow cawed and flew up, circled the tree a few times and returned to the nest. Sita clung to her branch.

The tree trembled throughout its tall frame. To Sita it felt like an earthquake tremor; she felt the shudder of the tree in her own bones.

The river swirled all around her now. It was almost up to the roof of the hut. Soon the mud walls would crumble and vanish. Except for the big rock and some trees far, far away, there was only water to be seen.

For a moment or two Sita glimpsed a boat with several people in it moving sluggishly away from the ruins of a flooded village, and she thought she saw someone pointing towards her, but the river swept them on, and the boat was lost to view.

The river was very angry; it was like a wild beast, a dragon on the rampage, thundering down from the hills, and sweeping across the plain, bringing with it dead animals, uprooted trees, household goods and huge fish choked to death by the swirling mud.

The tall, old peepul tree groaned. Its long, winding roots clung tenaciously to the earth from which the tree had sprung many, many years ago. But the earth was softening; the stones were being washed away. The roots of the tree were rapidly losing their hold.

The crow must have known that something was wrong, because it kept flying up and circling the tree, reluctant to settle in it and reluctant to fly away. As long as the nest was there, the crow would remain, flapping about and cawing in alarm.

Sita's wet cotton dress clung to her thin body. The rain ran down from her long black hair. It poured from every leaf of the tree. The crow, too, was drenched and groggy.

The tree groaned and moved again. It had seen many monsoons. Once before, it had stood firm while the river had swirled around its massive trunk. But it had been young then. Now, old in years and tired of standing still, the tree was ready to join the river.

With a flurry of its beautiful leaves, and a surge of mud from below, the tree left its place in the earth, and, tilting, moved slowly forward, turning a little from side to side, dragging its roots along the ground. To Sita, it seemed as though the river was rising to meet the sky.

Then the tree moved into the main current of the river, and went a little faster, swinging Sita from side to side. Her feet were in the water but she clung tenaciously to her branch.

∞

The branches swayed, but Sita did not lose her grip. The water was very close now. Sita was frightened. She could not see the extent of the flood or the width of the river. She could only see the immediate danger—the water surrounding the tree.

The crow kept flying around the tree. The bird was in a terrible rage. The nest was still in the branches, but not for long... The tree lurched and twisted slightly to one side, and the nest fell into the water. Sita saw the eggs go one by one.

The crow swooped low over the water, but there was nothing it could do. In a few moments, the nest had disappeared.

The bird followed the tree for about fifty yards, as though hoping that something still remained in the tree. Then, flapping its wings, it rose high into the air and flew across the river until it was out of sight.

Sita was alone once more. But there was no time for feeling lonely. Everything was in motion—up and down and sideways and forwards. 'Any moment,' thought Sita, 'the tree will turn right over and I'll be in the water!'

She saw a turtle swimming past—a great river turtle, the kind that feeds on decaying flesh. Sita turned her face away. In the distance she saw a flooded village and people in flat-bottomed boats but they were very far away.

Because of its great size, the tree did not move very swiftly on the river. Sometimes, when it passed into shallow water, it stopped, its roots catching in the rocks; but not for long—the river's momentum soon swept it on. At one place, where there was a bend in the river, the tree struck a sandbank and was still.

Sita felt very tired. Her arms were aching and she was no longer upright. With the tree almost on its side, she had to cling tightly to her branch to avoid falling off.

The grey, weeping sky was like a great shifting dome. She knew she could not remain much longer in that position. It might be better to try swimming to some distant rooftop or tree. Then she heard someone calling.

Craning her neck to look upriver, she was able to make out a small boat coming directly towards her.

The boat approached the tree. There was a boy in the boat who held on to one of the branches to steady himself, giving his free hand to Sita. She grasped it, and slipped into the boat beside him. The boy placed his bare foot against the tree trunk and pushed away. The little boat moved swiftly down the river. The big tree was left far behind. Sita would never see it again.

She lay stretched out in the boat, too frightened to talk. The boy looked at her, but he did not say anything, he did not even smile. He lay on his two small oars, stroking smoothly, rhythmically, trying to keep from going into the middle of the river. He wasn't strong enough to get the boat right out of the swift current, but he kept trying.

A small boat on a big river—a river that had no boundaries but which reached across the plains in all directions. The boat moved swiftly on the wild waters, and Sita's home was left far behind.

The boy wore only a loincloth. A sheathed knife was knotted into his waistband. He was a slim, wiry boy, with a hard, flat belly; he had high cheekbones, strong white teeth. He was a little darker than Sita.

'You live on the island,' he said at last, resting on his oars, and allowing the boat to drift a little, for he had reached a broader, more placid stretch of the river.

'I have seen you sometimes. But where are the others?'

'My grandmother was sick,' said Sita, 'so Grandfather took her to the hospital in Shahganj.'

'When did they leave?'

'Early this morning.'

Only that morning—and yet it seemed to Sita as though it had been many mornings ago.

'Where have you come from?' she asked. She had never seen the boy before.

'I come from...' he hesitated, '...near the foothills. I was in my boat, trying to get across the river with the news that one of the villages was badly flooded, but the current was too strong. I was swept down past your island. We cannot fight the river, we must go wherever it takes us.'

'You must be tired. Give me the oars.'

'No. There is not much to do now, except keep the boat steady.'

He brought in one oar, and with his free hand he felt under the seat where there was a small basket. He produced two mangoes, and gave one to Sita.

They bit deep into the ripe, fleshy mangoes, using their teeth to tear the skin away. The sweet juice trickled down their chins. The flavour of the fruit was heavenly—truly this was the nectar of the Gods!

Sita hadn't tasted a mango for over a year. For a few moments she forgot about the flood—all that mattered was the mango!

The boat drifted, but not so swiftly now, for as they went further away across the plains, the river lost much of its tremendous force.

'My name is Krishan,' said the boy. 'My father has many cows and buffaloes, but several have been lost in the flood.'

'I suppose you go to school,' said Sita.

'Yes, I am supposed to go to school. There is one not far from our village. Do you have to go to school?'

'No, there is too much work at home.'

It was no use wishing she was at home—home wouldn't be

there any more—but she wished, at that moment, that she had another mango.

Towards evening, the river changed colour. The sun, low in the sky, emerged from behind the clouds, and the river changed slowly from grey to gold, from gold to a deep orange, and then, as the sun went down, all these colours were drowned in the river, and the river took on the colour of the night.

The moon was almost at the full and Sita could see across the river, to where the trees grew on its banks.

'I will try to reach the trees,' said the boy, Krishan.

'We do not want to spend the night on the water, do we?'

And so he pulled for the trees. After ten minutes of strenuous rowing, he reached a turn in the river and was able to escape the pull of the main current. Soon they were in a forest, rowing between tall evergreens.

They moved slowly now, paddling between the trees, and the moon lighted their way, making a crooked silver path over the water.

'We will tie the boat to one of these trees,' said Krishan. 'Then we can rest. Tomorrow we will have to find our way out of the forest.'

He produced a length of rope from the bottom of the boat, tied one end to the boat's stern, and threw the other end over a stout branch which hung only a few feet above the water. The boat came to rest against the trunk of the tree.

It was a tall, sturdy toon tree—the Indian mahogany—and it was quite safe, for there was no rush of water here; besides, the trees grew close together, making the earth firm and unyielding.

But the denizens of the forest were on the move.

ANGRY RIVER

The animals had been flooded out of their holes, caves and lairs, and were looking for shelter and dry ground.

Sita and Krishan had barely finished tying the boat to the tree when they saw a huge python gliding over the water towards them. Sita was afraid that it might try to get into the boat; but it went past them, its head above water, its great awesome length trailing behind, until it was lost in the shadows.

Krishan had more mangoes in the basket, and he and Sita sucked hungrily on them while they sat in the boat.

A big sambar stag came thrashing through the water. He did not have to swim; he was so tall that his head and shoulders remained well above the water. His antlers were big and beautiful.

'There will be other animals,' said Sita. 'Should we climb into the tree?'

'We are quite safe in the boat,' said Krishan.

'The animals are interested only in reaching dry land. They will not even hunt each other. Tonight, the deer are safe from the panther and the tiger. So lie down and sleep, and I will keep watch.'

Sita stretched herself out in the boat and closed her eyes, and the sound of the water lapping against the sides of the boat soon lulled her to sleep. She woke once, when a strange bird called overhead. She raised herself on one elbow, but Krishan was awake, sitting in the prow, and he smiled reassuringly at her.

He looked blue in the moonlight, the colour of the young god Krishna, and for a few moments Sita was confused and wondered if the boy was indeed Krishna; but when she thought about it, she decided that it wasn't possible. He was just a village boy and she had seen hundreds like him—well, not exactly like him; he was different, in a way she couldn't explain to herself...

And when she slept again, she dreamt that the boy and Krishna were one, and that she was sitting beside him on a great white bird which flew over mountains, over the snowy peaks of the Himalayas, into the cloudland of the Gods. There was a great rumbling sound, as though the Gods were angry about the whole thing, and she woke up to this terrible sound and looked about her, and there in the moonlit glade, up to his belly in water, stood a young elephant, his trunk raised as he trumpeted his predicament to the forest—for he was a young elephant, and he was lost, and he was looking for his mother.

He trumpeted again, and then lowered his head and listened. And presently, from far away, came the shrill trumpeting of another elephant. It must have been the young one's mother, because he gave several excited trumpet calls, and then went stamping and churning through the flood water towards a gap in the trees. The boat rocked in the waves made by his passing.

'It's all right now,' said Krishan. 'You can go to sleep again.'

'I don't think I will sleep now,' said Sita.

'Then I will play my flute for you,' said the boy, 'and the time will pass more quickly.'

From the bottom of the boat he took a flute, and putting it to his lips, he began to play. The sweetest music that Sita had ever heard came pouring from the little flute, and it seemed to fill the forest with its beautiful sound. And the music carried her away again, into the land of dreams, and they were riding on the bird once more, Sita and the blue god, and they were passing through clouds and mist, until suddenly the sun shot out through the clouds. And at the same moment, Sita opened her eyes and saw the sun streaming through the branches of the toon tree, its bright green leaves making a dark pattern against the blinding blue of the sky.

Sita sat up with a start, rocking the boat. There were hardly any clouds left. The trees were drenched with sunshine.

The boy Krishan was fast asleep at the bottom of the boat.

ANGRY RIVER

His flute lay in the palm of his half-opened hand. The sun came slanting across his bare brown legs. A leaf had fallen on his upturned face, but it had not woken him, it lay on his cheek as though it had grown there.

Sita did not move again. She did not want to wake the boy. It didn't look as though the water had gone down, but it hadn't risen, and that meant the flood had spent itself.

The warmth of the sun, as it crept up Krishan's body, woke him at last. He yawned, stretched his limbs, and sat up beside Sita.

'I'm hungry,' he said with a smile.

'So am I,' said Sita.

'The last mangoes,' he said, and emptied the basket of its last two mangoes.

After they had finished the fruit, they sucked the big seeds until they were quite dry. The discarded seeds floated well on the water. Sita had always preferred them to paper boats.

'We had better move on,' said Krishan.

He rowed the boat through the trees, and then for about an hour they were passing through the flooded forest, under the dripping branches of rain-washed trees.

Sometimes they had to use the oars to push away vines and creepers. Sometimes drowned bushes hampered them. But they were out of the forest before noon.

Now the water was not very deep and they were gliding over flooded fields. In the distance they saw a village. It was on high ground. In the old days, people had built their villages on hilltops, which gave them a better defence against bandits and invading armies.

This was an old village, and though its inhabitants had long ago exchanged their swords for pruning forks, the hill on which it stood now protected it from the flood.

The people of the village—long-limbed, sturdy Jats—were

generous, and gave the stranded children food and shelter. Sita was anxious to find her grandparents, and an old farmer who had business in Shahganj offered to take her there. She was hoping that Krishan would accompany her, but he said he would wait in the village, where he knew others would soon be arriving, his own people among them.

'You will be all right now,' said Krishan. 'Your grandfather will be anxious for you, so it is best that you go to him as soon as you can. And in two or three days, the water will go down and you will be able to return to the island.'

'Perhaps the island has gone forever,' said Sita.

As she climbed into the farmer's bullock cart, Krishan handed her his flute.

'Please keep it for me,' he said. 'I will come for it one day.'

And when he saw her hesitate, he added, his eyes twinkling, 'It is a good flute!'

∞

It was slow going in the bullock cart. The road was awash, the wheels got stuck in the mud, and the farmer, his grown son and Sita had to keep getting down to heave and push in order to free the big, wooden wheels.

They were still in a foot or two of water. The bullocks were bespattered with mud, and Sita's legs were caked with it. They were a day and a night in the bullock cart before they reached Shahganj; by that time, Sita, walking down the narrow bazaar of the busy market town, was hardly recognizable.

Grandfather did not recognize her. He was walking stiffly down the road, looking straight ahead of him, and would have walked right past the dusty, dishevelled girl if she had not charged straight at his thin, shaky legs and clasped him around the waist.

'Sita!' he cried, when he had recovered his wind and his balance.

'But how are you here? How did you get off the island? I was so worried—it has been very bad these last two days...'

'Is Grandmother all right?' asked Sita.

But even as she spoke, she knew that Grandmother was no longer with them. The dazed look in the old man's eyes told her as much. She wanted to cry, not for Grandmother, who could suffer no more, but for Grandfather, who looked so helpless and bewildered; she did not want him to be unhappy. She forced back her tears, took his gnarled and trembling hand, and led him down the crowded street. And she knew, then, that it would be on her shoulder that Grandfather would have to lean in the years to come.

They returned to the island after a few days, when the river was no longer in spate. There was more rain, but the worst was over. Grandfather still had two of the goats; it had not been necessary to sell more than one.

He could hardly believe his eyes when he saw that the tree had disappeared from the island—the tree that had seemed as permanent as the island, as much a part of his life as the river itself. He marvelled at Sita's escape.

'It was the tree that saved you,' he said.

'And the boy,' said Sita.

Yes, and the boy.

She thought about the boy, and wondered if she would ever see him again. But she did not think too much, because there was so much to do.

For three nights they slept under a crude shelter made out of jute bags. During the day she helped Grandfather rebuild the mud hut. Once again, they used the big rock as a support.

The trunk, which Sita had packed so carefully, had not been

swept off the island, but the water had got into it, and the food and clothing had been spoilt. But Grandfather's hookah had been saved, and, in the evenings, after their work was done and they had eaten the light meal which Sita prepared, he would smoke with a little of his old contentment, and tell Sita about other floods and storms which he had experienced as a boy.

Sita planted a mango seed in the same spot where the peepul tree had stood. It would be many years before it grew into a big tree, but Sita liked to imagine sitting in its branches one day, picking the mangoes straight from the tree, and feasting on them all day. Grandfather was more particular about making a vegetable garden and putting down peas, carrots, gram, and mustard.

One day, when most of the hard work had been done and the new hut was almost ready, Sita took the flute which had been given to her by the boy, and walked down to the water's edge and tried to play it.

But all she could produce were a few broken notes, and even the goats paid no attention to her music.

Sometimes Sita thought she saw a boat coming down the river and she would run to meet it; but usually there was no boat, or if there was, it belonged to a stranger or to another fisherman. And so she stopped looking out for boats. Sometimes she thought she heard the music of a flute, but it seemed very distant and she could never tell where the music came from.

Slowly, the rains came to an end. The flood waters had receded, and in the villages, people were beginning to till the land again, and sow crops for the winter months. There were cattle fairs and wrestling matches. The days were warm and sultry. The water in the river was no longer muddy, and one evening Grandfather brought home a huge mahseer fish and Sita made it into a delicious curry.

ANGRY RIVER

Grandfather sat outside the hut, smoking his hookah. Sita was at the far end of the island, spreading clothes on the rocks to dry.

One of the goats had followed her. It was the friendlier of the two, and often followed Sita about the island. She had made it a necklace of coloured beads.

She sat down on a smooth rock, and, as she did so, she noticed a small, bright object in the sand near her feet. She stooped and picked it up. It was a little wooden toy—a coloured peacock—that must have come down on the river and been swept ashore on the island. Some of the paint had rubbed off, but for Sita, who had no toys, it was a great find. Perhaps it would speak to her, as Mumta had spoken to her.

As she held the toy peacock in the palm of her hand, she thought she heard the flute music again, but she did not look up. She had heard it before, and she was sure that it was all in her mind. But this time the music sounded nearer, much nearer. There was a soft footfall in the sand. And, looking up, she saw the boy, Krishan, standing over her.

'I thought you would never come,' said Sita.

'I had to wait until the rains were over. Now that I am free, I will come more often. Did you keep my flute?'

'Yes, but I cannot play it properly. Sometimes it plays by itself, I think, but it will not play for me!'

'I will teach you to play it,' said Krishan.

He sat down beside her, and they cooled their feet in the water, which was clear now, reflecting the blue of the sky. You could see the sand and the pebbles of the riverbed.

'Sometimes the river is angry, and sometimes it is kind,' said Sita.

'We are part of the river,' said the boy. 'We cannot live without it.'

It was a good river, deep and strong, beginning in the

mountains and ending in the sea. Along its banks, for hundreds of miles, lived millions of people, and Sita was only one small girl among them, and no one had ever heard of her, no one knew her—except for the old man, the boy, and the river.

KOKI PLAYS THE GAME

'There's a cricket match on Saturday, isn't there?' asked Koki.
'That's right,' said Ranji. 'We're playing the Public School team.'
'I might come and watch,' said Koki.
'As you like. It won't be much of a game. We'll beat them easily.'

Ranji's own cricket team was quite different from his school team. It consisted of boys big and small, long and short, from various walks of life. Even Koki, a girl, was allowed honorary membership, and had sometimes been 'twelfth man'—an extra. She knew the game well, and often bowled to Ranji in the mornings when he wanted batting practice. Only a couple of the teammates could afford to go to private schools like Ranji's; most of them went to the local government school, and two or three had stopped going to school altogether.

There was Bhartu, who delivered newspapers in the mornings; the brothers Mukesh and Rakesh, whose father kept a sweet shop; and a tailor's son, Amir Ali. There was Billy Jones, an Anglo-Indian boy; 'Lumboo', the Tall One; Sitaram, the washerman's son, and several others. And there was also Bhim, who couldn't play at all, but who made a good umpire (when his glasses weren't steamed over) and who accompanied the team wherever it went.

This Saturday they were playing on their 'home' ground, a patch of wasteland behind a new cinema called the Apsara ('Heavenly Dancer').

The Public School boys had all arrived first, which was only natural since they lived together in the same boarding school. The members of Ranji's team came from different directions, so it was some time before they had all assembled. Even then, they were two short. But Ranji won the toss and decided to bat, hoping that the missing team members would arrive in time to take their turn at the wicket.

'If Mukesh and Rakesh aren't here in time, we won't have them in the team,' said Ranji sternly.

'Don't sack them,' said Lumboo. 'They always bring us sweets and snacks from their father's shop. We need them in the team even if they don't score any runs.'

'Well, if they turn up *without* refreshments, they'll be sacked,' said Ranji, always ready to be fair.

The two umpires had gone out to set up the stumps—Bhim, on behalf of Ranji's team, and a teacher from the Public School.

'I don't like the look of that teacher,' said Amir Ali.

'Well, we won't take any risks.'

Billy Jones and Lumboo always opened the batting. Lumboo's height helped him to deal with the fast-rising ball. He took the first ball.

The Public School's opening bowler was speedy but inaccurate. This was because he was trying to bowl too fast. His first ball went for a wide, which gave Ranji's team its first run. The second ball wasn't quite so wide, but it was still about a foot from the leg stump. Lumboo took a swipe at it and missed. The third ball pitched halfway down the wicket and kept low. It struck Lumboo on the pads.

'How's that!' shouted the bowler, wicketkeeper, and slip-fielders in unison.

The Public School's umpire did not hesitate. Up went his finger. Lumboo was given out leg-before-wicket (LBW). Lumboo stood aghast. He looked down at where his feet were placed, then back at his stumps.

'I'm not in front of the wicket,' he complained, to no one in particular.

KOKI PLAYS THE GAME

'The umpire's word is law,' said the wicketkeeper.

Lumboo slowly walked back to where his teammates reclined against a pile of bricks.

'I wasn't out!' he protested.

'Never mind,' said Ranji, whose turn it was to bat. 'You'll get your chance when you come on to bowl.'

He walked to the wicket with a confident air, his bat resting on his shoulder. He took guard carefully and, tapping his bat on the ground, faced the bowler. He received a straight ball, fast, and met it on the half-volley, driving it straight back past the bowler. It sped to the boundary, amidst delighted cries from Ranji's teammates. Four runs.

The next ball was short, just outside the off stump. Ranji stepped back and square-cut it past point. Another four! There were more cheers, and this time Ranji distinctly heard a girl's voice shouting: 'Good shot, Ranji!'

He looked back to where his teammates were gathered. There was no girl among them. He turned and looked toward the opposite boundary, and there, under the giant cinema hoarding, stood Koki. She waved to him.

Ranji did not wave back. He felt acutely self-conscious. Settling down to face the bowler again, he was aware of two things at once—of the bowler making faces and charging up to bowl, and of Koki standing on the boundary and waiting for him to hit another four.

This loss of concentration caused him to misjudge the next ball. Instead of playing forward, he played back.

The ball took the edge of his bat and flew straight into the wicketkeeper's gloves.

'How's that!' shouted all the fielders, appealing for a catch.

Ranji did not wait for the umpire—in this case, Bhim, to give him out. He knew he'd touched the ball. Scowling, he walked back to his team. It was all Koki's fault!

Now, there was a good partnership between Sitaram and Bhartu. Sitaram, who helped his father with the town's washing on Sundays, was in the habit of laying out clothes on a flat stone and pounding them with a stout stick—the method followed by most washermen.

He dealt with the cricket ball in much the same way—clouting it hard, and sending it to various points of the compass. He hit up 25 valuable runs before he was out, caught off a big hit. Bhartu pushed and prodded, merely keeping one end going, until he too was out to an LBW decision. Billy Jones had gone the same way, taking the ball on his pads. No one was happy with the LBW decisions.

'We must have neutral umpires,' said Amir Ali.

'But who wants to be an umpire?' said Ranji. 'We won't find anyone. We'll have to use our own team members—or let the other side provide *both* umpires!'

'Not after today,' said Lumboo.

Meanwhile, Mukesh and Rakesh had arrived, carrying paper bags full of samosas and jalebis. As a result, everyone cheered up. Wickets fell almost as rapidly as the snacks and sweets were consumed. Mukesh and Rakesh, who were the last men in, held out for several overs until Rakesh was given out—LBW! Ranji's team was all out for 87 runs—not really a match-winning score, except on a tricky wicket.

It was the Public School team's turn to bat. One of their opening batsmen was bowled by Lumboo for naught. The other batsman was twice rapped on the pads by balls from Ranji, but his loud appeals for LBW were turned down—by the Public School's umpire, naturally! Muttering to himself, Ranji hurled down a thunderbolt of a ball. It rose sharply and struck the batsman on the hand. Howling with pain, he dropped his bat and wrung his hand. Then he showed everyone a swollen finger and decided to 'retire hurt'.

'There's more than one way of getting them out,' muttered Ranji, as he passed the umpire.

The next two batsmen were good players, not as nervous as the openers. One of them got what might have been a faint tickle to an out-swinger from Lumboo, but he was given the benefit of the doubt by Bhim—who, as umpires went, was as impartial as a star. He showed no favours to his own team, no matter what the other umpire did. It just isn't fair, thought Ranji.

The number three and four batsmen put on 40 runs between them, and by mid-afternoon Ranji's players were feeling tired and hungry. Then three quick wickets fell to Sitaram's spinners. Three wickets remained, and 20 runs were needed by the Public School for victory.

This was when Bhartu, running to take a catch, collided with chubby Mukesh. Both of them went sprawling on the grass, and when they got up the ball was found lodged in the back of Mukesh's pants. How it got there no one could tell, but after much discussion the umpires had to agree that it qualified as a catch and the batsman was given out. But Bhartu had to leave the ground with a bleeding nose.

Ranji looked around for a replacement. There was no one in sight except Koki.

'Come and field,' said Ranji brusquely.

Koki needed no persuading. She slipped off her sandals and dashed barefoot on to the field, taking up Bhartu's position near the boundary.

The tail-end batsmen were now swinging at the ball in a desperate attempt to hit the remaining runs. A hard-hit drive sped past Koki and went for four runs. Ranji gave her a hard look. Then the two batsmen got into a muddle while trying to take a quick run, and one of them was run out.

The last man came in. The Public School was 8 runs behind. But a couple of boundaries would take care of that.

The batsmen ran two. And then one of them, over confident and sure of victory, swung out at a slow, tempting ball from Sitaram, and the ball flew towards Koki in a long, curving arc.

Koki had to run a few yards to her left. Then she leapt like a gazelle and took the ball in both hands. Ranji's team had won, and Koki had made the winning catch.

It was her last appearance as 'twelfth man'. From that day onwards she was a regular member of the team.

THE LOST RUBY

Once upon a time there lived a king, who was a great and powerful monarch. One day he was very sad, and as he sat in his council hall surrounded by his ministers, the chief minister, who was a good and wise man, asked him: 'Defender of the World! Why is your spirit sad today? Your Majesty ought not to allow grief to trouble your mind.'

The king would not tell him his grief. On the contrary, he resented his good minister's concern for him. 'It is all very well for you to talk,' he said. 'But if you had reason to be sad, I am sure you would find it impossible to practise what you have just suggested.' And the king decided to put his chief minister to the test, and told him to wait at the royal palace after the council was dismissed.

The minister accordingly made his way to the royal apartments and awaited further orders. The king took out a ruby of great price from a beautiful ivory casket, and placing it in the minister's hand, told him to look after it with great care.

When the minister got home, he found his wife reclining on cushions, chewing scented *paan*. He gave her the ruby to keep. She dropped it in a partition of her cash box and thought no more about it.

No sooner had the wily king delivered the ruby to his minister than he employed female spies to follow him up and mark where he kept the jewel. After a few days he bribed the steward of the minister's household to steal it for him. The king was sitting on the balcony of his palace overlooking the river, when the jewel was brought to him. Taking it from the hands of the steward, he deliberately threw it into the river.

The next morning, after dismissing his court, he asked the chief minister: 'Where is the ruby which I gave you to keep the other day?' The minister replied: 'I have got it, Defender of the World.'

'Well then,' said the king, 'go and fetch it, for I want it right now.'

Imagine the poor minister's amazement when, on going home, he understood that the ruby was nowhere to be found. He hurried back to the king and reported the loss. 'Your Majesty,' he said, 'if you will allow me a few days grace, I hope to find it and bring it back to you.'

'Very well,' said the king, laughing to himself. 'I give you three days in which to find the ruby. If, at the end of that time, you fail to find it, your life and the lives of all who are dear to you will be forfeit. And your house will be razed to the ground and ploughed up by donkeys!'

The minister left the palace with a heavy heart. He searched everywhere for the lost jewel, but because of its mysterious disappearance he did not have much hope of finding it.

I have no one, he thought, to whom I can leave my riches and possessions. My wife is the only soul on earth who is dear to me, and it seems we must both die after three days. What could be better than for us to enjoy ourselves during this period? We'll make the most of the time that's left to us.

In this mood he reached home and told his wife about the king's decision.

'Let us spend our wealth liberally and freely,' he said, 'for soon, we must die.'

His wife sighed deeply and only said, 'As you wish. Fate has dealt us a cruel blow. Let us take it with dignity and good cheer.'

That day saw the commencement of a period of great revelry

THE LOST RUBY

in the chief minister's house. Musicians of all kinds were engaged, and the halls were filled with guests, who came wondering what great luck had come the way of the chief minister. Rich food was served, and night and day the sound of music and laughter filled the house...

In addition, large quantities of food were prepared and given to the poor. No one who came to the house was allowed to leave empty-handed. Tradesmen, when they brought their customary presents of fresh fruit, were rewarded with gold coins, and went away rejoicing.

In a village near by there lived a poor flower-seller and a fisherwoman: the two women were neighbours and close friends. The flower-seller happened to be visiting the bazaar, where she heard of the grand doings at the minister's house. So she hurried there, with a present of vegetables and garlands, and received a gold coin. Then she walked across to her friend's house and advised her to take a present of fish to the minister, who would reward her in the same manner.

The fisherwoman was very poor. Her husband used to go fishing daily, but he seldom was able to catch large fish; those that he caught were so small that they rarely fetched more than a few pice in the bazaar. So the fisherwoman said to herself: 'Those miserable fish that my husband brings home are hardly worth presenting to the minister—he'll only feel insulted', and she thought no more about it.

But the following morning, as good luck would have it, her husband caught a large Rohu, the most delicious of Indian fresh-water fish. Delighted at his good fortune, he took it home to show his wife, who immediately placed the fish in a basket, covered it with a clean cloth, and hurried to the minister's house. The minister was really pleased to see such a fine large Rohu fish, and instead of giving her one gold coin, he gave her two.

The fisherwoman was overjoyed. She ran home with her prize, which was enough to keep herself and her husband in comfort for many a month.

This happened on the third and last day of the minister's life; the next day he and his wife were to be executed. Being very fond of fish curry, he said to his wife: 'Let's have one of your delightful fish curries for lunch today. We will never be able to enjoy it again. Now here's a fine Rohu. Let's take it to the kitchen and have it cleaned.'

He and his wife sat together to see the fish cut. The cook took out his kitchen knife and set to work.

As the cook thrust his knife into the fish's belly, out dropped the ruby which had been thrown into the river.

The minister and his wife were overcome with astonishment and joy. They washed the ruby in perfumed water, and then the

THE LOST RUBY

minister hastened to restore it to the king.

The king was equally amazed to see the ruby which he had thrown into the river. He at once demanded an explanation for its recovery. The minister told him how he had decided to spend all his riches, and how he had received the present of a fish which, when it was cut, gave up the lost ruby.

The king then acknowledged the part he had played in the loss of the ruby, 'But I see that you took your own advice to me,' he said. 'Endure sorrow cheerfully!' He bestowed high honours on his minister, and commended his wisdom and understanding before all his courtiers and ministers.

And so the minister's evil fortune was changed to good.

'And may the Eternal Dispenser of all Good thus deal with his servants.'

SEVEN BRIDES FOR SEVEN PRINCES

A long time ago there was a king who had seven sons—all of them brave, handsome and clever. The old king loved them equally, and the princes dressed alike and received the same amounts of pocket money. When they grew up they were given separate palaces, but the palaces were built and furnished alike, and if you had seen one palace you had seen the others.

When the princes were old enough to marry, the king sent his ambassadors all over the country to search out seven brides of equal beauty and talent. The ambassadors travelled everywhere and saw many princesses but could not find seven equally suitable brides. They returned to the king and reported their failure.

The king now became so despondent and gloomy that his chief minister decided that something had to be done to solve his master's problem.

'Do not be so downcast, Your Majesty,' he said. 'Surely it is impossible to find seven brides as accomplished as your seven sons. Let us trust to chance, and then perhaps we shall find the ideal brides.'

The minister had thought out a scheme, and when the princes agreed to it, they were taken to the highest tower of the fort, which overlooked the entire city as well as the surrounding countryside. Seven bows and seven arrows were placed before them, and they were told to shoot in any direction they liked. Each prince had agreed to marry the girl upon whose house the arrow fell, be she daughter of prince or peasant.

The seven princes took up their bows and shot their arrows in

SEVEN BRIDES FOR SEVEN PRINCES

different directions, and all the arrows except that of the youngest prince fell on the houses of well-known and highly- respected families. But the arrow shot by the youngest brother went beyond the city and out of sight.

Servants ran in all directions looking for the arrow and, after a long search, found it embedded in the trunk of a great banyan tree, in which sat a monkey.

Great was the dismay and consternation of the king when he discovered that his youngest son's arrow had made such an unfortunate descent. The king and his courtiers and his minister held a hurried conference. They decided that the youngest prince should be given another chance with his arrow. But to everyone's surprise, the prince refused a second chance.

'No,' he said. 'My brothers have found beautiful and good

brides, and that is their good fortune. But do not ask me to break the pledge I took before shooting my arrow. I know I cannot marry this monkey. But I will not marry anyone else! Instead I shall take the monkey home and keep her as a pet.'

The six lucky princes were married with great pomp. The city was ablaze with lights and fireworks, and there was music and dancing in the streets. People decorated their houses with the leaves of mango and banana trees. There was great rejoicing everywhere, except in the palace of the youngest prince. He had placed a diamond collar about the neck of his monkey and seated her on a chair cushioned with velvet. They both looked rather melancholy.

'Poor monkey,' said the prince. 'You are as lonely as I am on this day of rejoicing. But I shall make your stay here a happy one! Are you hungry?' And he placed a bowl of grapes before her, and persuaded her to eat a few. He began talking to the monkey and spending all his time with her. Some called him foolish, or obstinate; others said he wasn't quite right in the head.

The king was worried and discussed the situation with his minister and his other sons, in a bid to find some way of bringing the prince to his senses and marrying him into a noble family. But he refused to listen to their advice and entreaties.

As the months passed, the prince grew even more attached to his monkey, and could be seen walking with her in the gardens of his palace.

Then one day the king called a meeting of all seven princes and said, 'My sons, I have seen you all settled happily in life. Even you, my youngest, appear to be happy with your strange companion. The happiness of a father consists in the happiness of his sons and daughters. Therefore I wish to visit my daughters-in-law and give them presents.'

The eldest son immediately invited his father to dine at his palace, and the others did the same. The king accepted all their invitations, including that of the youngest prince. The receptions were very grand, and the king presented his daughters-in-law with precious jewels and costly dresses. Eventually it was the turn of the youngest son to entertain the king.

The youngest prince was very troubled. How could he invite his father to a house in which he lived with a monkey? He knew his monkey was more gentle and affectionate than some of the greatest ladies in the land; and he was determined not to hide her away as though she were someone to be ashamed of.

Walking beside his pet in the palace gardens, he said, 'What shall I do now, my friend? I wish you had a tongue with which to comfort me. All my brothers have shown their homes and wives to my father. They will ridicule me when I present you to him.'

The monkey had always been a silent and sympathetic listener when the prince spoke to her. Now he noticed that she was gesturing to him with her hands. Bending over her, he saw that she held a piece of broken pottery in her hand. The prince took the shard from her and saw that something was written on it. These were the words he read:

'Do not worry, sweet prince, but go to the place where you found me, and throw this piece of pottery into the hollow trunk of the banyan tree, and wait for a reply.'

The prince did as he was told. Going to the ancient banyan tree, he threw the shard of pottery into the hollow, and then stood back to see if anything would happen.

He did not have to wait long.

A beautiful fairy dressed in green stepped out of the hollow, and asked the prince to follow her. She told him that the queen of the fairies wished to see him in person.

The prince climbed the tree, entered the hollow, and after groping about in the dark was suddenly led into a spacious and wonderful garden, at the end of which stood a beautiful palace. Between an avenue of trees flowed a crystal-clear stream, and on the bed of the stream, instead of pebbles, there were rubies and diamonds and sapphires. Even the light which lit up this new world was warmer and less harsh than the light of the world outside. The prince was led past a fountain of silver water, up steps of gold, and in through the mother-of-pearl doors of the palace. But the splendour of the room into which he was led seemed to fade before the exquisite beauty of the fairy princess who stood before him.

'Yes, prince, I know your message,' said the princess. 'Do not be anxious, but go home and prepare to receive your father the king and your royal guests tomorrow evening. My servants will see to everything.'

Next morning, when the prince awoke in his palace, an amazing sight met his eyes. The palace grounds teemed with life. The gardens were full of pomegranate trees, laden with fruit, and under the trees were gaily decorated stalls serving sweets, scented-water and cooling sherbets. Children were playing on the lawns, and men and women were dancing or listening to music.

The prince was bewildered by what he saw, and he was even more amazed when he entered his banquet hall and found it full of activity. Tables groaned under the weight of delicious pulaos, curries and biryanis. Great chandeliers hung from the ceiling, bunches of roses filled the room with their perfume.

A servant came running to announce that the king and his courtiers were arriving. The prince hurried out to meet them. After dinner was served, everyone insisted on seeing the companion the prince had chosen for himself. They thought the monkey would make excellent entertainment after such a magnificent feast.

The prince could not refuse this request, and passed gloomily through his rooms in search of his monkey. He feared the ridicule that would follow. This, he knew, was his father's way of trying to cure him of his obstinacy.

He opened the door of his room and was almost blinded by a blaze of light. There, on a throne in the middle of the room, sat the fairy princess.

'Come, prince,' she said. 'I have sent away the monkey and I am here to offer you my hand.'

On hearing that his pet had gone, the prince burst into tears. 'What have you done?' he cried. 'It was cruel of you to take away my monkey. Your beauty will not compensate me for the loss of my companion.'

'If my beauty does not move you,' said the princess with a smile, 'let gratitude help you take my hand. See what pains I have taken to prepare this feast for your father and brothers. As my husband, you shall have all the riches and pleasures of the world at your command.'

The prince was indignant. 'I did not ask these things of you—nor do I know what plot has been afoot to deprive me of my monkey. Restore her to me, and I will be your slave!'

Then the fairy princess came down from her throne, and taking the prince by the hand, spoke to him with great love and respect.

'You see in me your friend and companion,' she said. 'Yes, it was I who took the form of a monkey, to test your faith and sincerity. See, my monkey's skin lies there in the corner.'

The prince looked, and saw in a corner of the room the skin of his monkey.

He joined the fairy princess on her throne, and when she said 'Arise, arise, arise,' the throne rose in the air and floated into the hall where the guests had gathered.

The prince presented his bride to his father, who was of

course, delighted. The guests were a little disappointed to find that their hostess was not, after all, a monkey. But they had to admit that the prince and the princess made a most handsome couple.

THE UGLY PRINCE AND
THE HEARTLESS PRINCESS

In the kingdom of Malla there was once a young prince named Kusa, who was famed for his great kindness and wisdom; but unfortunately he was very ugly.

In spite of his ugliness, everyone in the kingdom was extremely fond of the prince; but Kusa himself was sensitive about his appearance, and when his father, King Okkaka, urged him to marry, he said: 'Don't ask me to get married. How could a beautiful princess love such an ugly fellow?'

But the king insisted, and at last Kusa grew so tired of refusing to choose a bride, that he hit upon a scheme by which he hoped to free himself for ever from the problem of his marriage. He was very skilful with his hands, and he fashioned a golden image, and showing the king his handiwork, he said: 'If a princess as beautiful as this image can be found for me, I will make her my bride. Otherwise I will remain single.'

Kusa felt sure that there was no princess who could compare with his statue; but the king was determined to find such a beauty, and he sent messengers far and wide.

The messengers visited many kingdoms, carrying the statue with them. Whenever they arrived at a city or a village, they asked the inhabitants whether they knew of anyone who resembled the golden image. But nowhere was such a beauty to be found until the messengers reached the kingdom of Madda.

The King of Madda had eight lovely daughters, and the eldest of them, Pabhavati, bore an extraordinary resemblance to the golden image. When the messengers saw her, they went straight to the king and said that they had come to ask the hand of Princess Pabhavati for Prince Kusa, the son of King Okkaka.

The King of Madda knew that Okkaka was a rich and powerful king, and he was pleased at the idea of being allied to him through marriage.

'If King Okkaka will visit me,' he said, 'I will give him the hand of Princess Pabhavati for his son, Prince Kusa.'

The messengers hurried back to Malla with the good news, and King Okkaka was delighted at the outcome of their mission; but poor Kusa was dismayed.

'But my dear Father,' he said to the king, 'how will such a beautiful princess behave when she sees how ugly I am? She will surely flee from me at once.'

'Do not worry, my son,' said King Okkaka. 'I will revive an ancient custom in order to protect you. According to this custom, a bride may not look upon the face of her husband until one year after the marriage. Therefore, for one whole year, you must only meet your bride in a darkened room.'

'But how will that help me in the end?' asked Kusa doubtfully. 'My looks will not have improved by the end of the year. She will have to see me some day.'

'True, but during that year your bride will have learned to love you so much that, when she sees you at last, you will not be ugly in her eyes!'

Prince Kusa still had his doubts, but the king was insistent and wasted no time in visiting the kingdom of Madda and returning with the beautiful Princess Pabhavati. Soon after, the marriage ceremony was performed in a darkened chamber, by order of the king.

Princess Pabhavati was surprised to discover that she was not to look upon the face of her husband for one year after the marriage had taken place.

THE UGLY PRINCE AND THE HEARTLESS PRINCESS

This is a strange custom, she thought, but she accepted the condition without protest, and settled down in a magnificent suite of apartments, one room of which was always to be kept in complete darkness.

Kusa came daily to this room to visit his bride, and as his voice and manners were kind and gentle, Pabhavati soon grew to love him, although she did not get a glimpse of his face. He spent many hours playing to her upon his *sitar*, and she would listen to him, enthralled.

Was there ever a prince like this husband of mine? she thought. *How I long for the day when I shall see his face! Surely he must be as handsome as he is kind and wise.*

All might have been well if Pabhavati had been content to wait for a year; but, after she had been married for only a month, she grew impatient and found herself constantly wondering about Prince Kusa's appearance. During the second month she could conceal her curiosity no longer. One day, when Kusa was with her in the darkened room, she said: 'Dear husband, it makes me sad that I must wait so long before I can look upon your face. I beg you to meet me in the light of day.'

'No, Pabhavati, that is impossible,' said the prince. 'I cannot disobey my father, the king. Be patient a little longer. The months will pass quickly.'

But the quality of patience was absent in the princess, and soon she began to question the maidservants and others about her husband's appearance. As she never received a clear answer, she became even more curious. Finally she bribed one of her attendants to help her obtain a glimpse of Kusa.

One day, when the prince was due to ride through the city at the head of a procession, the waiting-woman concealed the princess in a corner room of the palace, a window of which looked out upon the highway.

When the procession came by, Pabhavati hurried to the window. She heard the sound of music and shouting, and saw gay banners and garlands thrown at the feet of the elephant upon which Prince Kusa was riding in state.

'Long live Kusa, our noble prince!' cried the people on the streets.

As the elephant passed beneath the window, Pabhavati caught a glimpse of the prince's face. She shrank back in horror.

'Oh, no!' she cried. 'Can that hideous creature be my husband? No, that is not Kusa!'

Her attendant assured her that it was indeed the prince, whereupon Pabhavati decided that she would flee instantly from such an ugly husband. She demanded that an escort be provided for her return to the kingdom of Madda, declaring that she would not be bound by marriage to a husband who was so different from the man she had imagined!

King Okkaka could have forced the princess to remain in the palace, but Kusa shook his head sadly and said, 'No, let her do as she wishes.'

Then, forgetful of all the love and tenderness that she had received from Kusa, and thinking only of his ugly face, Pabhavati left the palace and returned to her father's kingdom.

Prince Kusa was terribly unhappy; but one day the thought occurred to him that if he were to visit Pabhavati in her own land, he might find that her attitude had changed. He changed his princely robes for simple clothes, and, taking his *sitar*, he set out on foot for the kingdom of Madda.

After a journey of several days, Kusa arrived one evening at the chief city of Madda.

It was midnight when he reached the royal palace. He crept beneath the walls, then began playing softly upon his *sitar*. He played so sweetly that the sleepers in the palace stirred and

THE UGLY PRINCE AND THE HEARTLESS PRINCESS

smiled in their dreams. But Pabhavati wakened with a start and tensed as she listened to the familiar music.

That is Kusa below, she thought, afraid and angry at the same time. If my father knows that he is here, I will be forced to return to that hideous husband.

But Kusa had no intention of appealing to the king. He would rather lose Pabhavati for ever than have her return against her will. He was determined to keep his presence in the city a secret from everyone except the princess.

When morning came he went to the chief potter in the city and asked to become his apprentice.

'If I do good work for you, will you display my wares in the palace?' asked Kusa.

'Certainly,' said the potter. 'But show me what you can do.'

Kusa set to work at the potter's wheel, and the bowls he produced were so beautifully formed that the potter was delighted.

'I am sure the king will purchase such dainty bowls for his daughters,' he said; and taking some of the bowls made by Kusa, he went straight to the palace.

The King took a great fancy to the potter's new wares. When he learned that they had been made by a new apprentice, he said: 'Give the young man a thousand gold pieces, and tell him that from now on he must work only for my daughters. Now take eight of these beautiful bowls to the princesses as my gifts to them.'

The potter did as he was told, and the king's daughters were thrilled with their presents; but Pabhavati knew in her heart that they had been fashioned by Kusa. She returned her bowl to the potter and said, 'Take this bowl back to your apprentice and tell him that it is as ugly as he is.'

When the potter passed on these remarks to Kusa, the prince

sighed and thought: *How can I touch her hard heart? If I could speak to her, it might make a difference. Tomorrow I will seek service in the palace.*

He gave the potter the king's gold pieces and said goodbye; then, hearing that the palace cook needed an assistant, he presented himself at the royal kitchens.

The cook took Kusa into his service, and the prince proved to be as good a cook as he was a potter—so much so, that a dish specially prepared by him was sent straight to the king.

The king thoroughly enjoyed the dish, and when he heard that it had been prepared by the cook's new assistant, he said: 'Give him a thousand pieces of gold, and from now on let him prepare and serve all the food for myself and my daughters.'

THE UGLY PRINCE AND THE HEARTLESS PRINCESS

Kusa was happy to give the king's gold piece to the chief cook, then set to work to prepare a delicious meal.

At dinner, Pabhavati was horrified to see her husband, disguised as a cook, stagger into the banquet hall with a heavy load of dishes. He gave no sign of recognition; but the princess was angry and, staring at him with contempt, said: 'I do not care for these dishes. Bring me food that someone else has prepared.'

Her sisters protested, crying out that they had never tasted such delicious cooking. But although Kusa came day after day, serving a variety of tasty dishes, Pabhavati would not touch any of them.

At last the prince decided that there was no way in which he could touch the heart of the princess.

Nothing that I do pleases her, he thought. Now I must leave her for ever.

While he was preparing to leave the palace, he heard that the King of Madda was greatly troubled. The king had received news that seven kings were riding towards the city with seven armies, and that each of these kings, having heard of the beauty of Pabhavati, was anxious to make her his wife.

The king was in a quandary, because he felt sure that if he chose one of these kings as the husband of Pabhavati, the other six would attack his kingdom in revenge.

If only Pabhavati had not left her rightful husband, thought the king, *these troubles would not have arisen.*

Realizing that it was useless to spend his time in regrets, the king summoned his advisers and asked them which king he should choose for the princess.

'Not one of them alone,' declared the wise men. 'The princess has endangered the kingdom. Therefore she must suffer the consequences. She must be executed, her body divided into seven pieces, and one portion presented to each of the seven kings.

Only in this way can a terrible war be avoided.'

The king was horrified by this advice from his men of wisdom; but while he was sitting alone, deep in thought, Kusa, still in the guise of a cook, came to him and said: 'Your majesty, let me deal with these kings. Give me your army, and I will crush them or die in the attempt.'

'What!' cried the astonished king. 'Shall a cook do battle with kings?'

'If a cook knows how to fight, why not? But I must confess that I am not really a servant, but Prince Kusa, to whom you once entrusted your daughter. Although she has rejected me, I still love her, and it is only right that I should deal with these suitors.'

The king could hardly believe that it was Kusa who stood before him. He had Pabhavati brought to him, and when she admitted that the cook's apprentice was her royal husband, he cried: 'You should be ashamed, daughter, for allowing your husband to be treated as a servant in the palace.'

He dismissed Pabhavati from his presence, and begged Kusa's pardon for the way in which he had been insulted.

Kusa replied that all he wanted was freedom to deal with the seven invading kings, and the king immediately placed him at the head of an army. The fate of the kingdom lay in Kusa's hands.

The seven kings were taken by surprise when they saw Kusa and his forces advancing towards them, for they had not expected any resistance. In spite of their superior numbers, they were soon routed by an inspired force under Kusa's command. They laid down their arms and surrendered, and the prince led them as captives to the king.

'Deal with these prisoners as you will,' said Kusa.

'They are your captives,' said the king. 'It is for you to decide their fate.'

THE UGLY PRINCE AND THE HEARTLESS PRINCESS

'Then,' said the prince, 'since each of these kings wishes to marry a beautiful princess, why do you not marry them all to the sisters of Pabhavati?'

The king was delighted with this solution to his problem; it would guarantee the safety of his kingdom for ever. The seven kings were bowled over by the beauty and grace of Pabhavati's sisters. And the seven sisters thought their prospective husbands looked very handsome indeed.

But Pabhavati sat alone, weeping bitter tears. She now realized how heartlessly she had treated Kusa, and what a noble man and lover she had scorned.

He will never forgive me, she thought sadly.

She went to him, and threw herself at his feet, crying: 'Forgive me, my husband, and take me back, even if you decide to treat me as a slave.'

Kusa raised her gently from the ground.

'Do you really wish to return to me?' he asked. 'Look at me, Pabhavati. I am still as ugly as when you ran away from me.'

Pabhavati gazed at him steadfastly; and instead of the loathing which Kusa had seen in her eyes before, he now saw only wonder and tenderness.

'You have changed!' she cried. 'You are no longer ugly!'

'No,' said Kusa. 'I haven't changed. It is you who have changed.'

THE TUNNEL

It was almost noon, and the jungle was very still, very silent. Heat waves shimmered along the railway embankment where it cut a path through the tall evergreen trees. The railway lines were two straight black serpents disappearing into the tunnel in the hillside.

Suraj stood near the cutting, waiting for the midday train. It wasn't a station, and he wasn't catching a train. He was waiting so that he could watch the steam engine come roaring out of the tunnel.

He had cycled out of the town and taken the jungle path until he had come to a small village. He had left the cycle there, and walked over a low, scrub-covered hill and down to the tunnel exit.

Now he looked up. He had heard, in the distance, the shrill whistle of the engine. He couldn't see anything, because the train was approaching from the other side of the hill; but presently a sound like distant thunder issued from the tunnel, and he knew the train was coming through.

A second or two later, the steam engine shot out of the tunnel, snorting and puffing like some green, black and gold dragon—some beautiful monster out of Suraj's dreams. Showering sparks left and right, it roared a challenge to the jungle.

Instinctively, Suraj stepped back a few paces. And then the train had gone, leaving only a plume of smoke to drift lazily over tall shisham trees.

The jungle was still again. No one moved. Suraj turned from his contemplation of the drifting smoke and began walking along the embankment towards the tunnel.

THE TUNNEL

The tunnel grew darker as he walked further into it. When he had gone about twenty yards, it became pitch black. Suraj had to turn and look back at the opening to reassure himself that there was still daylight outside. Ahead of him, the tunnel's other opening was just a small round circle of light.

The tunnel was still full of smoke from the train, but it would be several hours before another train came through. Till then, it belonged to the jungle again.

Suraj didn't stop, because there was nothing to do in the tunnel and nothing to see. He had simply wanted to walk through, so that he would know what the inside of a tunnel was really like. The walls were damp and sticky. A bat flew past. A lizard scuttled between the lines.

Coming straight from the darkness into the light, Suraj was dazzled by the sudden glare. He put a hand up to shade his eyes and looked up at the tree-covered hillside. He thought he saw something moving between the trees.

It was just a flash of orange and gold, and a long swishing tail. It was there between the trees for a second or two, and then it was gone.

About fifty feet from the entrance to the tunnel stood the watchman's hut. Marigolds grew in front of the hut, and at the back there was a small vegetable patch. It was the watchman's duty to inspect the tunnel and keep it clear of obstacles. Every day, before the train came through, he would walk the length of the tunnel. If all was well, he would return to his hut and take a nap. If something was wrong, he would walk back up the line and wave a red flag and the engine driver would slow down. At night, the watchman lit an oil lamp and made a similar inspection of the tunnel. Of course, he could not stop the train if there was a porcupine on the line. But if there was any danger to the train, he'd go back up the line and wave his lamp to the approaching engine. If all was well, he'd hang his lamp at the door of the hut and go to sleep.

He was just settling down on his cot for an afternoon nap when he saw the boy emerge from the tunnel. He waited until Suraj was only a few feet away and then said, 'Welcome, welcome, I don't often have visitors. Sit down for a while, and tell me why you were inspecting my tunnel.'

'Is it your tunnel?' asked Suraj.

'It is,' said the watchman. 'It is truly my tunnel, since no one else will have anything to do with it. I have only lent it to the government.'

Suraj sat down on the edge of the cot.

'I wanted to see the train come through,' he said. 'And then, when it had gone, I thought I'd walk through the tunnel.'

'And what did you find in it?'

'Nothing. It was very dark. But when I came out, I thought I saw an animal—up on the hill—but I'm not sure, it moved away very quickly.'

'It was a leopard you saw,' said the watchman. 'My leopard.'

'Do you own a leopard too?'

'I do.'

'And do you lend it to the government?'

'I do not.'

'Is it dangerous?'

'No, it's a leopard that minds its own business. It comes to this range for a few days every month.'

'Have you been here a long time?' asked Suraj.

'Many years. My name is Sunder Singh.'

'My name's Suraj.'

'There's one train during the day. And another during the night. Have you seen the night mail come through the tunnel?'

'No. At what time does it come?'

'About nine o'clock, if it isn't late. You could come and sit here with me, if you like. And after it has gone, I'll take you home.'

'I shall ask my parents,' said Suraj. 'Will it be safe?'

'Of course. It's safer in the jungle than in the town. Nothing happens to me out here, but last month when I went into the town, I was almost run over by a bus.'

Sunder Singh yawned and stretched himself out on the cot. 'And now I'm going to take a nap, my friend. It is too hot to be up and about in the afternoon.'

'Everyone goes to sleep in the afternoon,' complained Suraj. 'My father lies down as soon as he's had his lunch.'

'Well, the animals also rest in the heat of the day. It is only the tribe of boys who cannot, or will not, rest.'

Sunder Singh placed a large banana leaf over his face to keep away the flies, and was soon snoring gently. Suraj stood up, looking up and down the railway tracks. Then he began walking back to the village.

The following evening, towards dusk, as the flying foxes swooped silently out of the trees, Suraj made his way to the watchman's hut.

It had been a long hot day, but now the earth was cooling, and a light breeze was moving through the trees. It carried with it a scent of mango blossoms, the promise of rain.

Sunder Singh was waiting for Suraj. He had watered his small garden, and the flowers looked cool and fresh. A kettle was boiling on a small oil stove.

'I'm making tea,' he said. 'There's nothing like a glass of hot tea while waiting for a train.'

They drank their tea, listening to the sharp notes of the tailorbird and the noisy chatter of the seven sisters. As the brief twilight faded, most of the birds fell silent. Sunder Singh lit his oil lamp and said it was time for him to inspect the tunnel. He moved off towards the tunnel, while Suraj sat on the cot, sipping his tea. In the dark, the trees seemed to move closer to him. And the night life of the forest was conveyed on the breeze—the sharp call of a barking deer, the cry of a fox, the quaint *tonk tonk* of a nightjar. There were some sounds that Suraj couldn't recognize—sounds that came from the trees, creakings and whisperings, as though the trees were coming alive, stretching their limbs in the dark, shifting a little, flexing their fingers.

Sunder Singh stood inside the tunnel, trimming his lamp. The night sounds were familiar to him and he did not give them much thought; but something else—a padded footfall, a rustle of dry leaves—made him stand alert for a few seconds, peering into the darkness. Then, humming softly to himself, he returned to where Suraj was waiting. Another ten minutes remained for the night mail to arrive.

As Sunder Singh sat down on the cot beside Suraj, a new sound reached both of them quite distinctly—a rhythmic sawing sound, as if someone was cutting through the branch of a tree.

'What's that?' whispered Suraj.

'It's the leopard,' said Sunder Singh. 'I think it's in the tunnel.'

'The train will soon be here,' reminded Suraj.

'Yes, my friend. And if we don't drive the leopard out of the tunnel, it will be run over and killed. I can't let that happen.'

'But won't it attack us if we try to drive it out?' asked Suraj, beginning to share the watchman's concern.

'Not this leopard. It knows me well. We have seen each other many times. It has a weakness for goats and stray dogs, but it won't harm us. Even so, I'll take my axe with me. You stay here, Suraj.'

'No, I'm going with you. It'll be better than sitting here alone in the dark!'

'All right, but stay close behind me. And remember, there's nothing to fear.'

THE TUNNEL

Raising his lamp high, Sunder Singh advanced into the tunnel, shouting at the top of his voice to try and scare away the animal. Suraj followed close behind, but he found he was unable to do any shouting. His throat was quite dry.

They had gone just about twenty paces into the tunnel when the light from the lamp fell upon the leopard. It was crouching between the tracks, only fifteen feet away from them. It was not a very big leopard, but it looked lithe and sinewy. Baring its teeth and snarling, it went down on its belly, tail twitching.

Suraj and Sunder Singh both shouted together. Their voices rang through the tunnel. And the leopard, uncertain as to how many terrifying humans were there in the tunnel with him, turned swiftly and disappeared into the darkness.

To make sure that it had gone, Sunder Singh and Suraj walked the length of the tunnel. When they returned to the entrance, the rails were beginning to hum. They knew the train was coming.

Suraj put his hand to the rails and felt its tremor. He heard the distant rumble of the train. And then the engine came round the bend, hissing at them, scattering sparks into the darkness, defying the jungle as it roared through the steep sides of the cutting. It charged straight at the tunnel, and into it, thundering past Suraj like the beautiful dragon of his dreams.

And when it had gone, the silence returned and the forest seemed to breathe, to live again. Only the rails still trembled with the passing of the train.

And they trembled to the passing of the same train, almost a week later, when Suraj and his father were both travelling in it.

Suraj's father was scribbling in a notebook, doing his accounts. Suraj sat at an open window staring out at the darkness. His father was going to Delhi on a business trip and had decided to take the boy along. 'I don't know where he gets to most of the time,' he'd complained. 'I think it's time he learnt something about my business.'

The night mail rushed through the forest with its hundreds of passengers. Tiny flickering lights came and went, as they passed small villages on the fringe of the jungle.

Suraj heard the rumble as the train passed over a small bridge. It was too dark to see the hut near the cutting, but he knew they must be approaching the tunnel. He strained his eyes looking out into the night; and then, just as the engine let out a shrill whistle, Suraj saw the lamp.

He couldn't see Sunder Singh, but he saw the lamp, and he knew that his friend was out there.

THE TUNNEL

The train went into the tunnel and out again; it left the jungle behind and thundered across the endless plains; and Suraj stared out at the darkness, thinking of the lonely cutting in the forest, and the watchman with the lamp who would always remain a firefly for those travelling thousands, as he lit up the darkness for steam engines and leopards.

THE ELEPHANT AND THE CASSOWARY BIRD

The baby elephant wasn't out of place in our home in north India because India is where elephants belong, and in any case, our house was full of pets brought home by Grandfather, who was in the Forest Service. But the cassowary bird was different. No one had ever seen such a bird before—not in India, that is. Grandfather had picked it up on a voyage to Singapore, where he'd been given the bird by a rubber planter who'd got it from a Dutch trader who'd got it from a man in Indonesia.

Anyway, it ended up at our home in Dehra, and seemed to do quite well in the subtropical climate. It looked like a cross between a turkey and an ostrich, but bigger than the former and smaller than the latter—about five feet in height. It was not a beautiful bird, nor even a friendly one, but it had come to stay, and everyone was curious about it, especially the baby elephant.

Right from the start, the baby elephant took a great interest in the cassowary, a bird unlike any found in the Indian jungles. He would circle round the odd creature, and diffidently examine with his trunk the texture of its stumpy wings. Of course he suspected no evil, and his childlike curiosity encouraged him to take liberties which resulted in an unpleasant experience.

Noticing the baby elephant's attempts to make friends with the rather morose cassowary, we felt a bit apprehensive. Self-contained and sullen, the big bird responded only by slowly and slyly raising one of its powerful legs, in the meantime gazing into space with an innocent air. We knew what the gesture meant;

THE ELEPHANT AND THE CASSOWARY BIRD

we had seen that treacherous leg raised on many an occasion, and suddenly shooting out with a force that would have done credit to a vicious camel. In fact, camel and cassowary kicks are delivered on the same plan, except that the camel kicks backward like a horse and the bird forward.

We wished to spare our baby elephant a painful experience, and led him away from the bird. But he persisted in his friendly overtures and, one morning, he received an ugly reward. Rapid as lightning, the cassowary hit straight from the hip and knee joints, and the elephant ran squealing to Grandfather.

For several days he avoided the cassowary, and we thought he had learnt his lesson. He crossed and recrossed the compound and the garden, swinging his trunk, thinking furiously. Then, a week later, he appeared on the verandah at breakfast time in

his usual cheery, childlike fashion, sidling up to the cassowary as if nothing had happened.

We were struck with amazement at this and so, it seemed, was the bird. Had the painful lesson already been forgotten? And by a member of the elephant tribe noted for its ability to never forget? Another dose of the same medicine would serve the booby right.

The cassowary once more began to draw up its fighting leg with sinister determination. It was nearing the true position for the master kick, kung fu style, when all of a sudden the baby elephant seized with his trunk the cassowary's other leg and pulled it down. There was a clumsy flapping of wings, a tremendous swelling of the bird's wattle, and an undignified getting up, as if it were a floored boxer doing its his best to beat the count of ten. The bird then marched off with an attempt to look stately and unconcerned, while we at the breakfast table were convulsed with laughter.

After this, the cassowary bird gave the baby elephant as wide a berth as possible. But they were not forced to coexist for very long. The baby elephant, getting bulky and cumbersome, was sold and now lives in a zoo where he is a favourite with young visitors who love to take rides on his back.

As for the cassowary, he continued to grace our verandah for many years, gaped at but not made much of, while entering on a rather friendless old age.

THE PARROT WHO WOULDN'T TALK

'You're no beauty! Can't talk, can't sing, can't dance!'
With these words Aunt Ruby would taunt the unfortunate parakeet who glared morosely at everyone from his ornamental cage at one end of the long verandah of Granny's bungalow in north India.

In those distant days, almost everyone—Indian or European—kept a pet parrot or parakeet, or 'lovebird' as some of the smaller ones were called. Sometimes these birds became great talkers, or rather mimics, and would learn to recite entire mantras (religious chants), or admonitions to the children of the house, such as *'Paro, beta, paro!'* ('Study, child, study!') or, for the benefit of boys like me—'Don't be greedy, don't be greedy.'

These expressions were, of course, picked up by the parrot over a period of time, after many repetitions by whichever member of the household had taken on the task of teaching the bird to talk.

But our parrot refused to talk.

He'd been bought by Aunt Ruby from a birdcatcher who'd visited all the houses on our road, selling caged birds ranging from colourful budgerigars to chirpy little munnias and even common sparrows that had been dabbed with paint and passed off as some exotic species. Neither Granny nor Grandfather were keen on keeping caged birds as pets, but Aunt Ruby threatened to throw a tantrum if she did not get her way—and Aunt Ruby's tantrums were dreadful to behold.

Anyway, she insisted on keeping the parrot and teaching

him to talk. But the bird took an instant dislike to my aunt and resisted all her blandishments.

'Kiss, kiss,' Aunt Ruby would coo, putting her face close to the barge of the cage. But the parrot would back away, his beady little eyes getting even smaller with anger at the prospect of being kissed by Aunt Ruby. And, on one occasion, he lunged forward without warning and knocked my aunt's spectacles off her nose.

After that, Aunt Ruby gave up her endearments and became quite hostile towards the poor bird, making faces at him and calling out, 'Can't talk, can't sing, can't dance!' and other nasty comments.

It fell upon me, then ten years old, to feed the parrot, and he seemed quite happy to receive green chillies and ripe tomatoes from my hands, these delicacies being supplemented by slices of mango, for it was then the mango season. It also gave me an opportunity to consume a couple of mangoes while feeding the parrot.

One afternoon, while everyone was indoors enjoying a siesta, I gave the parrot his lunch and then deliberately left the cage door open. Seconds later, the bird was winging his way to the freedom of the mango orchard.

At the same time Grandfather came on to the veranda, and remarked, 'I see your aunt's parrot has escaped.'

'The door was quite loose,' I said with a shrug. 'Well, I don't suppose we'll see it again.'

Aunt Ruby was upset at first, and threatened to buy another bird. We put her off by promising to buy her a bowl of goldfish.

'But goldfish don't talk,' she protested.

'Well, neither did your bird,' said Grandfather. 'So we'll get you a gramophone. You can listen to Clara Cluck all day. They say she sings like a nightingale.'

I thought we'd never see the parrot again, but he probably

THE PARROT WHO WOULDN'T TALK

missed his green chillies, because a few days later, I found the bird sitting on the verandah railing, looking expectantly at me with his head cocked to one side. Unselfishly, I gave the parrot half of my mango.

While the bird was enjoying the mango, Aunt Ruby emerged from her room and, with a cry of surprise, called out, 'Look, my parrot's come back! He must have missed me!'

With a loud squawk, the parrot flew out of her reach and, perching on the nearest rose bush, glared at Aunt Ruby and shrieked at her in my aunt's familiar tones, 'You're no beauty! Can't talk, can't sing, can't dance!'

Aunt Ruby went ruby red and dashed indoors. But that wasn't the end of the affair. The parrot became a frequent visitor to

the garden and verandah and whenever he saw Aunt Ruby he would call out, 'You're no beauty, you're no beauty! Can't sing, can't dance!'

The parrot had learnt to talk after all.

A RUPEE GOES A LONG WAY

Ranji had a one rupee coin. He'd had it since morning, and now it was afternoon—and that was far too long to keep a rupee. It was time he spent the money, or some of it, or most of it.

Ranji had made a list in his head of all the things he wanted to buy and all the things he wanted to eat. But he knew that with only one rupee in his pocket the list wouldn't get much shorter. His tummy, he decided, should be given first choice. So he made his way to the Jumna Sweet Shop, tossed the coin on the counter, and asked for a rupee's worth of jalebis—those spangled, golden sweets made of flour and sugar that are so popular in India.

The shopkeeper picked up the coin, looked at it carefully, and set it back on the counter. 'That coin's no good,' he said.

'Are you sure?' Ranji asked.

'Look,' said the shopkeeper, holding up the coin. 'It's got England's King George on one side. These coins went out of use long ago. If it was one of the older ones—like Queen Victoria's, made of silver—it would be worth something for the silver, much more than a rupee. But this isn't a silver rupee. So, you see, it isn't old enough to be valuable, and it isn't new enough to buy anything.'

Ranji looked from the coin to the shopkeeper to the chains of hot jalebis sizzling in a pan. He shrugged, took the coin back and turned on to the road. There was no one to blame for the coin.

Ranji wandered through the bazaar. He gazed after the passing balloon-man, whose long pole was hung with balloons of many colours. They were only twenty paise each—he could have had five for a rupee—but he didn't have any more change.

He was watching some boys playing marbles and wondering whether he should join them, when he heard a familiar voice behind him. 'Where are you going, Ranji?'

It was Mohinder Singh, Ranji's friend. Mohinder's turban was too big for him and was almost falling over his eyes. In one hand he held a home-made fishing rod, complete with hook and line.

'I'm not going anywhere,' said Ranji. 'Where are you going?'

'I'm not going, I've been,' Mohinder said. 'I was fishing in the canal all morning.'

Ranji stared at the fishing rod. 'Will you lend it to me?' he asked.

'You'll only lose it or break it,' Mohinder said. 'But I don't mind selling it to you. Two rupees. Is that too much?'

'I've got one rupee,' said Ranji, showing his coin. 'But it's an old one. The sweet-seller would not take it.'

'Please let me see it,' said Mohinder.

He took the coin and looked it over as though he knew all about coins. 'Hmmm…I don't suppose it's worth much, but my uncle collects old coins. Give it to me and I'll give you the rod.'

'All right,' said Ranji, only too happy to make the exchange. He took the fishing rod, waved goodbye to Mohinder and set off. Soon he was on the main road leading out of town.

After some time a truck came along. It was on its way to the quarries near the riverbed, where it would be loaded with limestone. Ranji knew the driver and waved and shouted to him until he stopped.

'Will you take me to the river?' Ranji asked. 'I'm going fishing.'

There was already someone sitting up in the front with the driver. 'Climb up in the back,' he said. 'And don't lean over the side.'

Ranji climbed into the back of the open truck. Soon he was

A RUPEE GOES A LONG WAY

watching the road slide away from him. They quickly passed bullock carts, cyclists and a long line of camels. Motorists honked their horns as dust from the truck whirled up in front of them.

Soon the truck stopped near the riverbed. Ranji got down, thanked the driver, and began walking along the bank. It was the dry season and the river was just a shallow, muddy stream. Ranji walked up and down without finding water deep enough for the smallest of fish.

'No wonder Mohinder let me have his rod,' he muttered. And with a shrug he turned back towards the town.

It was a long, hot walk back to the bazaar. Ranji walked slowly along the dusty road, swiping at bushes with his fishing rod. There were ripe mangoes on the trees, and Ranji tried to get at a few of them with the tip of the rod, but they were well out of reach. The sight of all those mangoes made his mouth water, and he thought again of the jalebis that he hadn't been able to buy.

He had reached a few scattered houses when he saw a barefoot boy playing a flute. In the stillness of the hot afternoon the cheap flute made a cheerful sound.

Ranji stopped walking. The boy stopped playing. They stood there, sizing each other up. The boy had his eye on Ranji's fishing rod; Ranji had his eye on the flute.

'Been fishing?' asked the flute player.

'Yes,' said Ranji.

'Did you catch anything?'

'No,' said Ranji. 'I didn't stay very long.'

'Did you see any fish?'

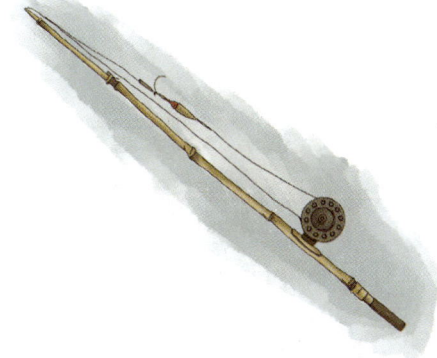

'The water was very muddy.'

There was a long silence. Then Ranji said, 'It's a good rod.'

'This is a good flute,' said the boy.

Ranji took the flute and examined it. He put it to his lips and blew hard. There was a shrill, squeaky noise, and a startled magpie flew out of a mango tree.

'Not bad,' said Ranji.

The boy had taken the rod from Ranji and was looking it over. 'Not bad,' he said.

Ranji hesitated no longer. 'Let's exchange.'

A trade was made, and the barefoot boy rested the fishing rod on his shoulder and went on his way, leaving Ranji with the flute. Ranji began playing the flute, running up and down the scale. The notes sounded lovely to him, but they startled people who were passing on the road.

After a while Ranji felt thirsty and drank water from a roadside tap. When he came to the clock tower, where the bazaar began, he sat on the low wall and blew vigorously on the flute. Several children gathered around, thinking he might be a snake charmer. When no snake appeared, they went away.

'I can play better than that,' said a boy who was carrying several empty milk cans.

'Let's see,' Ranji said.

A RUPEE GOES A LONG WAY

The boy took the flute and put it to his lips and played a lovely little tune.

'You can have it for a rupee,' said Ranji.

'I don't have any money to spare,' said the boy. 'What I get for my milk, I have to take home. But you can have this necklace.'

'He showed Ranji a pretty necklace of brightly coloured stones.'

'I'm not a girl,' said Ranji.

'I didn't say you have to wear it. You can give it to your sister.'

'I don't have a sister.'

'Then you can give it to your mother,' said the boy. 'Or your grandmother. The stones are very precious. They were found in the mountains near Tibet.'

Ranji was tempted. He knew the stones had little value, but they were pretty. And he was tired of the flute.

They made the exchange, and the boy went off playing the flute. Ranji was about to thrust the necklace into his pocket when he noticed a girl staring at him. Her name was Koki and she lived close to his house.

'Hello, Koki,' he said, feeling rather silly with the necklace still in his hands.

'What's that you've got, Ranji?'

'A necklace. It's pretty, isn't it? Would you like to have it?'

'Oh, thank you,' said Koki, clapping her hands with pleasure.

'One rupee,' said Ranji.

'Oh,' said Koki.

She made a face, but Ranji was looking the other way and

humming. Koki kept staring at the necklace. Slowly she opened a little purse, took out a shining new rupee, and held it out to Ranji.

Ranji handed her the necklace. The coin felt hot in his hand. It wasn't going to stay there for long. Ranji's stomach was rumbling. He ran across the street to the Jumna Sweet Shop and tossed the coin on the counter.

'Jalebis for a rupee,' he said.

The sweet seller picked up the coin, studied it carefully, then gave Ranji a toothy smile and said, 'Always at your service, sir.' He filled a paper bag with hot jalebis and handed them over.

When Ranji reached the clock tower, he found Koki waiting.

'Oh, I'm so hungry,' she said, giving him a shy smile.

So they sat side by side on the low wall, and Koki helped Ranji finish the jalebis.

THE FLUTE PLAYER

Down the main road passed big yellow buses, cars, pony-drawn tongas, motorcycles and bullock carts. This steady flow of traffic seemed, somehow, to form a barrier between the city on one side of the Trunk Road, and the distant sleepy villages on the other. It seemed to cut India in half—the India Kamla knew slightly, and the India she had never seen.

Kamla's grandmother lived on the outskirts of the city of Jaipur, and just across the road from the house there were fields and villages stretching away for hundreds of miles. But Kamla had never been across the main road. This separated the busy city from the flat green plains stretching endlessly towards the horizon.

Kamla was used to city life. In England, it was London and Manchester. In India, it was Delhi and Jaipur. Rainy Manchester was, of course, different in many ways from sun-drenched Jaipur, and Indian cities had stronger smells and more vibrant colours than their English counterparts. Nevertheless, they had much in common—busy people always on the move, money constantly changing hands, buses to catch, schools to attend, parties to go to, TV to watch. Kamla had seen very little of the English countryside, even less of India outside the cities.

Her parents lived in Manchester where her father was a doctor in a large hospital. She went to school in England. But this year, during the summer holidays, she had come to India to stay with her grandmother. Apart from a maidservant and a grizzled old nightwatchman, Grandmother lived quite alone in a small house on the outskirts of Jaipur. During the winter months, Jaipur's climate was cool and bracing but in the summer, a fierce sun poured down upon the city from a cloudless sky.

None of the other city children ventured across the main road into the fields of millet, wheat and cotton, but Kamla was determined to visit the fields before she returned to England. From the flat roof of the house she could see them stretching away for miles, the ripening wheat swaying in the hot wind. Finally, when there were only two days left before she went to Delhi to board a plane for London, she made up her mind and crossed the main road.

She did this in the afternoon, when Grandmother was asleep and the servants were in the bazaar. She slipped out of the back door and her slippers kicked up the dust as she ran down the path to the main road. A bus roared past and more dust rose from the road and swirled about her. Kamla ran through the dust, past the jacaranda trees that lined the road, and into the fields.

Suddenly, the world became an enormous place, bigger and more varied than it had seemed from the air, also mysterious and exciting—and just a little frightening.

The sea of wheat stretched away till it merged with the hot blinding blue of the sky. Far to her left, were a few trees and the low white huts of a village. To her right, lay hollow pits of red dust and a blackened chimney where bricks used to be made. In front, some distance away, Kamla could see a camel moving round a well, drawing up water for the fields. She set out in the direction of the camel.

Her grandmother had told her not to wander off on her own in the city; but this wasn't the city, and as far as she knew, camels did not attack people.

It took her a long time to get to the camel. It was about half a mile away, though it seemed much nearer. And when Kamla reached it, she was surprised to find that there was no one else in sight. The camel was turning the wheel by itself, moving round

THE FLUTE PLAYER

and round the well, while the water kept gushing up in little trays to run down the channels into the fields. The camel took no notice of Kamla, did not look at her even once, just carried on about its business.

There must be someone here, thought Kamla, walking towards a mango tree that grew a few yards away. Ripe mangoes dangled like globules of gold from its branches. Under the tree, fast asleep, was a boy.

All he wore was a pair of dirty white shorts. His body had been burnt dark by the sun; his hair was tousled, his feet chalky with dust. In the palm of his outstretched hand was a flute. He was a thin boy, with long bony legs, but Kamla felt that he was strong too, for his body was hard and wiry.

Kamla came nearer to the sleeping boy, peering at him with some curiosity, for she had not seen a village boy before. Her shadow fell across his face. The coming of the shadow woke the boy. He opened his eyes and stared at Kamla. When she did not say anything, he sat up, his head a little to one side, his hands clasping his knees, and stared at her.

'Who are you?' he asked a little gruffly. He was not used to waking up and finding strange girls staring at him.

'I'm Kamla. I've come from England, but I'm really from India. I mean I've come home to India, but I'm really from England.' This was going to be rather confusing, so she countered with an abrupt, 'Who are you?'

'I'm the strongest boy in the village,' said the boy, deciding to assert himself without any more ado. 'My name is Romi. I can wrestle and swim and climb any tree.'

'And do you sleep a lot?' asked Kamla innocently.

Romi scratched his head and grinned.

'I must look after the camel,' he said. 'It is no use staying awake for the camel. It keeps going round the well until it is tired, and then it stops. When it has rested, it starts going round again. It can carry on like that all day. But it eats a lot.'

Mention of the camel's food reminded Romi that he was hungry. He was growing fast these days and was nearly always hungry. There were some mangoes lying beside him, and he offered one to Kamla. They were silent for a few minutes. You cannot suck mangoes and talk at the same time. After they had finished, they washed their hands in the water from one of the trays.

'There are parrots in the tree,' said Kamla, noticing three or four green parrots conducting a noisy meeting in the topmost branches. They reminded her a bit of a pop group she had seen and heard at home.

THE FLUTE PLAYER

'They spoil most of the mangoes,' said Romi.

He flung a stone at them, missed, but they took off with squawks of protest, flashes of green and gold wheeling in the sunshine.

'Where do you swim?' asked Kamla. 'Down in the well?'

'Of course not. I'm not a frog. There is a canal not far from here. Come, I will show you!'

As they crossed the fields, a pair of blue jays flew out of a bush, rockets of bright blue that dipped and swerved, rising and falling as they chased each other.

Remembering a story that Grandmother had told her, Kamla said, 'They are sacred birds, aren't they? Because of their blue throats.' She told him the story of the God Shiva having a blue throat because he had swallowed a poison that would have destroyed the world; he had kept the poison in his throat and would not let it go further. 'And so his throat is blue, like the blue jay's.'

Romi liked this story. His respect for Kamla greatly increased. But he was not to be outdone, and when a small grey squirrel dashed across the path he told her that squirrels too, were sacred. Krishna, the god who had been born into a farmer's family like Romi's, had been fond of squirrels and would take them in his arms and stroke them. 'That is why squirrels have four dark lines down their backs,' said Romi. 'Krishna was very dark, as dark as I am, and the stripes are the marks of his fingers.'

'Can you catch a squirrel?' asked Kamla.

'No, they are too quick. But I caught a snake once. I caught it by its tail and dropped it in the old well. That well is full of snakes. Whenever we catch one, instead of killing it, we drop it in the well! They can't get out.'

Kamla shuddered at the thought of all those snakes swimming and wriggling about at the bottom of the deep well. She wasn't sure that she wanted to return to the well with him. But she forgot about the snakes when they reached the canal.

It was a small canal, about ten metres wide, and only waist-deep in the middle, but it was very muddy at the bottom. She had never seen such a muddy stream in her life.

'Would you like to get in?' asked Romi.

'No,' said Kamla. 'You get in.'

Romi was only too ready to show off his tricks in the water. His toes took a firm hold on the grassy bank, the muscles of his calves tensed, and he dived into the water with a loud splash, landing rather awkwardly on his belly. It was a poor dive, but Kamla was impressed.

Romi swam across to the opposite bank and then back again. When he climbed out of the water, he was covered with mud. It made him look quite fierce. 'Come on in,' he invited. 'It's not deep.'

'It's dirty,' said Kamla, but felt tempted all the same.

'It's only mud,' said Romi. 'There's nothing wrong with mud. Camels like mud. Buffaloes love mud.'

'I'm nor a camel—nor a buffalo.'

'All right. You don't have to go right in, just walk along the sides of the channel.'

After a moment's hesitation, Kamla slipped her feet out of her slippers, and crept cautiously down the slope till her feet were in the water. She went no further, but even so, some of the muddy water splashed on to her clean white skirt. What would she tell Grandmother? Her feet sank into the soft mud and she gave a little squeal as the water reached her knees. It was with some difficulty that she got each foot out of the sticky mud.

Romi took her by the hand, and they went stumbling along the side of the channel while little fish swam in and out of their legs, and a heron, one foot raised, waited until they had passed before snapping a fish out of the water. The little fish glistened

THE FLUTE PLAYER

in the sun before it disappeared down the heron's throat.

Romi gave a sudden exclamation and came to a stop. Kamla held on to him for support.

'What is it?' she asked, a little nervously.

'It's a tortoise,' said Romi. 'Can you see it?'

He pointed to the bank of the canal, and there, lying quite still, was a small tortoise. Romi scrambled up the bank and, before Kamla could stop him, had picked up the tortoise. As soon as he touched it, the animal's head and legs disappeared into its shell. Romi turned it over, but from behind the breastplate only the head and a spiky tail were visible.

'Look!' exclaimed Kamla, pointing to the ground where the tortoise had been lying. 'What's in that hole?'

They peered into the hole. It was about half a metre deep, and at the bottom were five or six white eggs, a little smaller than a hen's eggs.

'Put it back,' said Kamla. 'It was sitting on its eggs.'

Romi shrugged and dropped the tortoise back on its hole. It peeped out from behind its shell, saw the children were still present, and retreated into its shell again.

'I must go,' said Kamla. 'It's getting late. Granny will wonder where I have gone.'

They walked back to the mango tree, and washed their hands and feet in the cool clear water from the well; but only after Romi had assured Kamla that there weren't any snakes in the well—he had been talking about an old disused well on the far side of the village. Kamla told Romi she would take him to her house one day, but it would have to be next year, or perhaps the year after, when she came to India again.

'Is it very far, where you are going?' asked Romi.

'Yes, England is across the seas. I have to go back to my parents. And my school is there, too. But I will take the plane from Delhi. Have you ever been to Delhi?'

'I have not been further than Jaipur,' said Romi. 'What is England like? Are there canals to swim in?'

'You can swim in the sea. Lots of people go swimming in the sea. But it's too cold most of the year. Where I live, there are shops and cinemas and places where you can eat anything you like. And people from all over the world come to live there. You can see red faces, brown faces, black faces, white faces!'

'I saw a red face once,' said Romi. 'He came to the village to take pictures. He took one of me sitting on the camel. He said he would send me the picture, but it never came.'

Kamla noticed the flute lying on the grass. 'Is it your flute?' she asked.

'Yes,' said Romi. 'It is an old flute. But the old ones are best. I found it lying in a field last year. Perhaps it was the God Krishna's! He was always playing the flute.'

'And who taught you to play it?'

'Nobody. I learnt by myself. Shall I play it for you?'

Kamla nodded, and they sat down on the grass, leaning against the trunk of the mango tree, and Romi put the flute to his lips and began to play.

It was a slow, sweet tune, a little sad, a little happy, and the notes were taken up by the breeze and carried across the fields. There was no one to hear the music except the birds and the camel and Kamla. Whether the camel liked it or not, we shall never know; it just kept going round and round the well, drawing up water for the fields. And whether the birds liked it or not, we cannot say, although it is true that they were all suddenly silent when Romi began to play. But Kamla was charmed by the music, and she watched Romi while he played, and the boy smiled at her with his eyes and ran his fingers along the flute. When he stopped playing, everything was still, everything silent, except

THE FLUTE PLAYER

for the soft wind sighing in the wheat and the gurgle of water coming up from the well.

Kamla stood up to leave.

'When will you come again?' asked Romi.

'I will try to come next year,' said Kamla.

'That is a long time. By then you will be quite old. You may not want to come.'

'I will come,' said Kamla.

'Promise?'

'Promise.'

Romi put the flute in her hands and said, 'You keep it. I can get another one.'

'But I don't know how to play it,' said Kamla.

'It will play by itself,' said Romi.

She took the flute and put it to her lips and blew on it, producing a squeaky little note that startled a lone parrot out of the mango tree. Romi laughed, and while he was laughing, Kamla turned and ran down the path through the fields. And when she had gone some distance, she turned and waved to Romi with the flute. He stood near the well and waved back at her.

Cupping his hands to his mouth, he shouted across the fields, 'Don't forget to come next year!'

And Kamla called back, 'I won't forget.' But her voice was faint, and the breeze blew the words away and Romi did not hear them.

Was England home? wondered Kamla. *Or was this Indian city home? Or was her true home in that other India, across the busy Trunk Road?* Perhaps she would find out one day.

Romi watched her until she was just a speck in the distance, and then he turned and shouted at the camel, telling it to move faster. But the camel did not even glance at him; it just carried on as before, as India has carried on for thousands of years, round and round and round the well, while the water gurgled and splashed over the smooth stones.

THE KITEMAKER

There was but one tree in the street known as Gali Ram Nath—an ancient banyan that had grown through the cracks of an abandoned mosque—and little Ali's kite was caught in its branches. The boy, barefoot and clad only in a torn shirt, ran along the cobbled stones of the narrow street, to where his grandfather sat nodding dreamily in the sunshine in their back courtyard.

'Grandfather,' shouted the boy. 'My kite has gone!'

The old man woke from his daydream with a start and, raising his head, displayed a beard that would have been white had it not been dyed red with mehendi leaves.

'Did the twine break?' he asked. 'I know that kite twine is not what it used to be.'

'No, Grandfather, the kite is stuck in the banyan tree.'

The old man chuckled. 'You have yet to learn how to fly a kite properly, my child. And I am too old to teach you, that's the pity of it. But you shall have another.'

He had just finished making a new kite from bamboo, paper and thin silk, and it lay in the sun, firming up. It was a pale pink kite, with a small green tail. The old man handed it to Ali, and the boy raised himself on his toes and kissed his grandfather's hollowed-out cheek.

'I will not lose this one,' he said. 'This kite will fly like a bird.' And he turned on his heels and skipped out of the courtyard.

The old man remained dreaming in the sun. His kite shop was gone, the premises long since sold to a junk dealer; but he still made kites, for his own amusement and for the benefit of his grandson, Ali. Not many people bought kites these days. Adults disdained them, and children preferred to spend their money at the cinema. Moreover, there were not many open spaces left for the flying of kites. The city had swallowed up the open grassland that had stretched from the old fort's walls to the riverbank.

But the old man remembered a time when grown men flew kites, and great battles were fought, the kites swerving and swooping in the sky, tangling with each other until the string of one was severed. Then the defeated but liberated kite would float away into the blue unknown. There was a good deal of betting, and money frequently changed hands.

Kite flying was then the sport of kings, and the old man remembered how the Nawab himself would come down to the riverside with his retinue to participate in this noble pastime. There was time, then, to spend an idle hour with a gay, dancing strip of paper. Now everyone hurried, in a heat of hope, and delicate things like kites and daydreams were trampled underfoot.

He, Mehmood the kitemaker, had in the prime of his life been well-known throughout the city. Some of his more elaborate kites once sold for as much as three or four rupees each.

At the request of the Nawab he had once made a very special kind of kite, unlike any that had been seen in the district. It consisted of a series of small, very light paper discs trailing on a thin bamboo frame. To the end of each disc he fixed a sprig of grass, forming a balance on both sides. The surface of the foremost disc was slightly convex, and a fantastic face was painted on it, having two eyes made of small mirrors. The discs, decreasing in size from head to tail, assumed an undulatory form and gave the kite the appearance of a crawling serpent. It required great skill to raise this cumbersome device from the ground, and only Mehmood could manage it.

Everyone had heard of the 'Dragon Kite' that Mehmood

THE KITEMAKER

had built, and word went round that it possessed supernatural powers. A large crowd assembled in the open to watch its first public launching in the presence of the Nawab.

At the first attempt it refused to leave the ground. The discs made a plaintive, protesting sound, and the sun was trapped in the little mirrors, making the kite a living, complaining creature. Then the wind came from the right direction, and the Dragon Kite soared into the sky, wriggling its way higher and higher, the sun still glinting in its devil eyes. And when it went very high, it pulled fiercely at the twine, and Mehmood's young sons had to help him with the reel. Still the kite pulled, determined to be free, to break loose, to live a life of its own. And eventually it did so.

The twine snapped, the kite leaped away towards the sun, sailing on heavenward until it was lost to view. It was never found again, and Mehmood wondered afterwards if he had made too vivid, too living a thing of the great kite. He did not make another like it. Instead he presented to the Nawab a musical kite, one that made a sound like a violin when it rose into the air.

Those were more leisurely, more spacious days. But the Nawab had died years ago, and his descendants were almost as poor as Mehmood himself. Kitemakers, like poets, once had their patrons; but now no one knew Mehmood, simply because there were too many people in the Gali, and they could not be bothered with their neighbours.

When Mehmood was younger and had fallen sick, everyone in the neighbourhood had come to ask after his health; but now, when his days were drawing to a close, no one visited him. Most of his old friends were dead and his sons had grown up: one was working in a local garage and the other, who was in Pakistan at the time of the Partition, had not been able to rejoin his relatives.

The children who had bought kites from him ten years ago were now grown men, struggling for a living; they did not have time for the old man and his memories. They had grown up in a swiftly changing and competitive world, and they looked at the old kitemaker and the banyan tree with the same indifference.

Both were taken for granted—permanent fixtures that were of no concern to the raucous, sweating mass of humanity that surrounded them. No longer did people gather under the banyan tree to discuss their problems and their plans; only in the summer months did a few seek shelter from the fierce sun.

But there was the boy, his grandson. It was good that Mehmood's son worked close by, for it gladdened the old man's heart to watch the small boy at play in the winter sunshine, growing under his eyes like a young and well-nourished sapling putting forth new leaves each day. There is a great affinity between trees and men. We grow at much the same pace, if we are not hurt or starved or cut down. In our youth we are resplendent creatures, and in our declining years we stoop a little, we remember, we stretch our brittle limbs in the sun, and then, with a sigh, we shed our last leaves.

Mehmood was like the banyan, his hands gnarled and twisted like the roots of the ancient tree. Ali was like the young mimosa planted at the end of the courtyard. In two years, both he and the tree would acquire the strength and confidence of their early youth.

The voices in the street grew fainter, and Mehmood wondered if he was going to fall asleep and dream, as he so often did, of a kite so beautiful and powerful that it would resemble the great white bird of the Hindus—Garuda, God Vishnu's famous steed. He would like to make a wonderful new kite for little Ali. He had nothing else to leave the boy.

He heard Ali's voice in the distance, but did not realize that the boy was calling him. The voice seemed to come from very far away.

Ali was at the courtyard door, asking if his mother had as yet returned from the bazaar. When Mehmood did not answer, the boy came forward repeating his question. The sunlight was slanting across the old man's head, and a small white butterfly rested on his flowing beard. Mehmood was silent; and when Ali put his small brown hand on the old man's shoulder, he met with no response. The boy heard a faint sound, like the rubbing of marbles in his pocket.

Suddenly afraid, Ali turned and moved to the door, and then ran down the street, shouting for his mother. The butterfly left the old man's beard and flew to the mimosa tree, and a sudden gust of wind caught the torn kite and lifted it in the air, carrying it far above the struggling city into the blind blue sky.

THE LAST TIGER

On the left bank of the Ganga River, where it emerges from the Himalayan foothills, there is a long stretch of heavy forest. These are villages on the fringe of the forest, inhabited by bamboo cutters and farmers, but there are few signs of commerce or pilgrimage. Hunters, however, have found the area an ideal hunting ground during the last seventy years, and as a result the animals are not as numerous as they used to be. The trees, too, have been disappearing slowly; and, as the forest recedes, the animals lose their food and shelter and move on further into the foothills. Slowly, they are being denied the right to live.

Only the elephants can cross the river. And two years ago, when a large area of forest was cleared to make way for a refugee resettlement camp, a herd of elephants—finding their favourite food, the green shoots of the bamboo, in short supply—waded across the river. They crashed through the suburbs of Haridwar, knocked down a factory wall, pulled down several tin roofs, held up a train, and left a trail of devastation in their wake until they found a new home in a new forest which was still untouched. Here, they settled down to a new life—but an unsettled, wary life. They did not know when men would appear again, with tractors, bulldozers and dynamite.

There was a time when the forest on the banks of the Ganga had provided food and shelter for some thirty or forty tigers; but men in search of trophies had shot them all, and now there remained only one old tiger in the jungle. Many hunters had tried to get him, but he was a wise and crafty old tiger, who knew the ways of men, and he had so far survived all attempts on his life.

Although the tiger had passed the prime of his life, he had lost none of his majesty. His muscles rippled beneath the golden yellow of his coat, and he walked through the long grass with the confidence of one who knew that he was still a king, even though his subjects were fewer. His great head pushed through the foliage, and it was only his tail, swinging high, that showed occasionally above the sea of grass.

In late spring he would head for the large jheel, the only water in the forest (if you don't count the river, which was several miles away), which was almost a lake during the rainy season, but just a muddy marsh at this time of the year.

Here, at different times of the day and night, all the animals came to drink—the long-horned sambar, the delicate chital, the swamp deer, the hyenas and jackals, the wild boar, the panthers—and the lone tiger. Since the elephants had gone, the water was usually clear except when buffaloes from the nearest village came to wallow in it, and then it was very muddy. These buffaloes, though they were not wild, were not afraid of the panther or even of the tiger. They knew the panther was afraid of their massive horns and that the tiger preferred the flesh of the deer.

One day, there were several sambars at the water's edge; but they did not stay long. The scent of the tiger came with the breeze, and there was no mistaking its strong feline odour. The deer held their heads high for a few moments, their nostrils twitching, and then scattered into the forest, disappearing behind a screen of leaf and bamboo.

When the tiger arrived, there was no other animal near the water. But the birds were still there. The egrets continued to wade in the shallows, and a kingfisher darted low over the water, dived suddenly, a flash of blue and gold, and made off with a slim silver fish, which glistened in the sun like a polished gem.

THE LAST TIGER

A long brown snake glided in and out among the water lilies and disappeared beneath a fallen tree which lay rotting in the shallows.

The tiger waited in the shelter of a rock, his ears pricked up for the least unfamiliar sound; he knew that it was at that place that men sometimes sat up for him with guns, for they coveted his beauty—his stripes, the gold of his body, his fine teeth, his whiskers, and his noble head. They would have liked to hang his skin on a wall, with his head stuffed and mounted, and pieces of glass replacing his fierce eyes. Then they would have boasted of their triumph over the king of the jungle.

The tiger had encountered hunters before, so he did not usually show himself in the open during the day. But of late he had heard no guns, and if there were hunters around, you would have heard their guns (for a man with a gun cannot resist letting it off, even if it is only at a rabbit—or at another man). And, besides, the tiger was thirsty.

He was also feeling quite hot. It was March, and the shimmering dust haze of summer had come early. Tigers—unlike other cats—are fond of water, and on a hot day will wallow in it for hours.

He walked into the water, in amongst the water lilies, and drank slowly. He was seldom in a hurry when he ate or drank. Other animals might bolt down their food, but they are only other animals. A tiger is a tiger; he has his dignity to preserve even though he isn't aware of it!

He raised his head and listened, one paw suspended in the air. A strange sound had come to him on the breeze, and he was wary of strange sounds. So he moved swiftly into the shelter of the tall grass that bordered the jheel, and climbed a hillock until he reached his favourite rock. This rock was big enough both to hide him and to give him shade. Anyone looking up from the jheel would have thought it strange that the rock had a round bump on the top. The bump was the tiger's head. He kept it very still.

The sound he heard was only the sound of a flute, rendered thin and reedy in the forest. It belonged to Ramu, a slim brown boy who rode a buffalo. Ramu played vigorously on the flute. Shyam, a slightly smaller boy, riding another buffalo, brought up the rear of the herd.

There were about eight buffaloes in the herd, and they belonged to the families of the two friends Ramu and Shyam. Their people were Gujars, a nomadic community who earned a livelihood by keeping buffaloes and selling milk and butter. The boys were about twelve years old, but they could not have told you exactly because in their village nobody thought birthdays were important. They were almost the same age as the tiger, but he was old and experienced while they were still cubs.

The tiger had often seen them at the tank, and he was not worried by their presence. He knew the village people would do him no harm as long as he left their buffaloes alone. Once when he was younger and full of bravado, he had killed a buffalo—not because he was hungry, but because he was young and wanted to try out his strength—and after that the villagers had hunted him for days, with spears, bows and an old muzzle loader. Now, he left the buffaloes alone, even though the deer in the forest were not as numerous as before.

The boys knew that a tiger lived in the jungle, for they had often heard him roar; but they did not suspect that he was so near just then.

The tiger gazed down from his rock, and the sight of eight fat black buffaloes made him give a low, throaty moan. But the boys were there. Besides, a buffalo was not easy to kill.

He decided to move on and find a cool shady place in the heart of the jungle where he could rest during the warm afternoon

THE LAST TIGER

and be free of the flies and mosquitoes that swarmed around the jheel. At night he would hunt.

With a lazy, half-humorous roar—'A-oonh!'—he got up off his haunches and sauntered off into the jungle.

Even the gentlest of the tiger's roars can be heard half a mile away, and the boys, who were barely fifty yards away, looked up immediately.

'There he goes!' said Ramu, taking the flute from his lips and pointing it towards the hillocks. He was not afraid, for he knew that this tiger was not interested in humans. 'Did you see him?'

'I saw his tail, just before he disappeared. He's a big tiger!'

'Do not call him tiger. Call him uncle, or maharaja.'

'Oh, why?'

'Don't you know that it's unlucky to call a tiger a tiger? My father always told me so. But if you meet a tiger, and call him uncle, he will leave you alone.'

'I'll try and remember that,' said Shyam.

The buffaloes were now well inside the water, and some of them were lying down in the mud. Buffaloes love soft, wet mud and will wallow in it for hours. The slushier the mud the better. Ramu, to avoid being dragged down into the mud with his buffalo, slipped off its back and plunged into the water. He waded to a small islet covered with reeds and water lilies. Shyam was close behind him.

They lay down on their hard flat stomachs, on a patch of grass, and allowed the warm sun to beat down on their bare brown bodies.

Ramu was the more knowledgeable boy because he had been to Haridwar and Dehradun several times with his father. Shyam had never been out of the village.

Shyam said, 'The pool is not so deep this year.'

'We have had no rain since January,' said Ramu. 'If we do not get rain soon the jheel may dry up altogether.'

'And then what will we do?'

'We? I don't know. There is a well in the village. But even that may dry up. My father told me that it did once, just about the time I was born, and everyone had to walk ten miles to the river for water.'

'And what about the animals?'

'Some will stay here and die. Others will go to the river. But there are too many people near the river now—and temples, houses and factories—so the animals stay away. And the trees have been cut, so that between the jungle and the river there is no place to hide. Animals are afraid of the open—they are afraid of men with guns.'

'Even at night?'

'At night men come in jeeps, with searchlights. They kill the deer for meat, and sell the skins of tigers and panthers.'

'I didn't know a tiger's skin was worth anything.'

'It's worth more than our skins,' said Ramu knowingly. 'It will fetch six hundred rupees. Who would pay that much for one of us?'

'Our fathers would.'

'True, if they had the money.'

'If my father sold his fields, he would get more than six hundred rupees.'

'True, but if he sold his fields, none of you would have anything to eat. A man needs land as much as a tiger needs a jungle.'

'Yes,' said Shyam. 'And that reminds me, my mother asked me to take some roots home.'

'I will help you.'

They walked deeper into the jheel until the water was up to their waists, and began pulling up water lilies by the roots. The flower is beautiful but the villagers value the root more. When

THE LAST TIGER

it is cooked, it makes a delicious and nourishing dish. The plant multiplies multiplies rapidly and is always in good supply. In the year when the famine hit the village, it was only the root of the water lily that saved many from starvation.

When Shyam and Ramu had finished gathering roots, they emerged from the water and passed the time wrestling with each other, slipping about in the soft mud which soon covered them from head to toe.

To get rid of the mud, they dived into the water again and swam across to their buffaloes. Then, jumping on to their backs and digging their heels into the thick hides, the boys raced them across the jheel, shouting and hollering so much that all the birds flew away in fright, and the monkeys set up a shrill chattering of their own in the dhak trees.

In March, the flame of the forest, or dhak trees, are ablaze with bright scarlet and orange flowers.

It was evening, and the twilight was fading fast, when the buffalo herd finally wandered its way homeward, to be greeted outside the village by the barking of dogs, the gurgle of hookah pipes, and the homely smell of cow-dung smoke.

The tiger made a kill that night—a chital. He made his approach against the wind so that the unsuspecting spotted deer did not see him until it was too late. A blow on the deer's haunches from the tiger's paw brought it down, and then the great beast fastened his fangs on the deer's throat. It was all over in a few minutes. The tiger was too quick and strong, and the deer did not struggle much.

It was a violent end for so gentle a creature. But, you must not imagine that in the jungle the deer live in permanent fear of death. It is only man, with his imagination and his fear of the hereafter, who is afraid of dying. In the jungle it is different. Sudden death appears at intervals. Wild creatures do not have to think about it, and so the sudden killing of one of their number by some predator of the forest is only a fleeting incident soon forgotten by the survivors.

The tiger feasted well, growling with pleasure as he ate his way up the body, leaving the entrails. When he had had his night's fill he left the carcass for the vultures and jackals. The cunning old tiger never returned to the same carcass, even if there was still plenty left to eat. In the past, when he had gone back to a kill he had often found a man sitting in a tree waiting up for him with a rifle.

His belly filled, the tiger sauntered over to the edge of the forest and looked out across the sandy wasteland and the deep, singing river, at the twinkling lights of Rishikesh on the opposite bank, and raised his head and roared his defiance at mankind.

He was a lonesome bachelor. It was five or six years since he had a mate. She had been shot by the trophy hunters, and her two cubs had been trapped by men who do trade in wild animals. One went to a circus, where he had to learn tricks to amuse men and respond to the crack of a whip; the other, more fortunate, went first to a zoo in Delhi and was later transferred to a zoo in America.

Sometimes, when the old tiger was very lonely, he gave a great roar, which could be heard throughout the forest. The villagers thought he was roaring in anger, but the jungle knew that he was really roaring out of loneliness. When the sound of his roar had died away, he paused, standing still, waiting for an answering roar; but it never came. It was taken up instead by the shrill scream of a barbet high up in a sal tree.

It was dawn now, dew-fresh and cool, and jungle dwellers were on the move...

The black beady little eyes of a jungle rat were fixed on a brown hen who was pecking around in the undergrowth near her nest. He had a large family to feed, this rat, and he knew that in the hen's nest was a clutch of delicious fawn-coloured eggs. He waited patiently for nearly an hour before he had the satisfaction of seeing the hen leave her nest and go off in search of food.

As soon as she had gone, the rat lost no time in making his raid. Slipping quietly out of his hole, he slithered along among the leaves; but, clever as he was, he did not realize that his own movements were being watched.

A pair of grey mongooses scouted about in the dry grass. They, too, were hungry, and eggs usually figured large on their menu. Now, lying still on an outcrop of rock, they watched the rat sneaking along, occasionally sniffing at the air and finally vanishing behind a boulder. When he reappeared, he was struggling to roll an egg uphill towards his hole.

The rat was in difficulty, pushing the egg sometimes with his paws, sometimes with his nose. The ground was rough, and the egg wouldn't move straight. Deciding that he must have help, he scuttled off to call his spouse. Even now the mongooses did not descend on the tantalizing egg. They waited until the rat returned with his wife, and then watched as the male rat took the egg firmly between his forepaws and rolled over on to his back. The female rat then grabbed her mate's tail and began to drag him along.

Totally absorbed in the struggle with the egg, the rats did not hear the approach of the mongooses. When these two, large furry visitors suddenly bobbed up from behind a stone, the rats squealed with fright, abandoned the egg, and fled for their lives.

The mongooses wasted no time in breaking open the egg and making a meal of it. But just as, a few minutes ago, the rat had not noticed their approach, so now they did not notice the village boy, carrying a small bright axe and a net bag in his hands, creeping along.

Ramu, too, was searching for eggs, and when he saw the mongooses busy with one, he stood still to watch them, his eyes roving in search of the nest. He was hoping the mongooses would lead him to the nest; but, when they had finished their meal and made off into the undergrowth, Ramu had to do his own searching. He failed to find the nest, and moved further into the forest. The rat's hopes were just reviving when, to his disgust, the mother hen returned.

Ramu now made his way to a mahua tree.

The flowers of the mahua can be eaten by animals as well as by men. Bears are particularly fond of them and will eat large quantities of flowers which gradually start fermenting in their stomachs, with the result that the animals get quite drunk. Ramu had often seen a couple of bears stumbling home to their cave, bumping into each other or into the trunks of trees. They are short-sighted to begin with, and when drunk can hardly see at all. But their sense of smell and hearing are so good that in the end they find their way home.

Ramu decided he would gather some mahua flowers, and climbed up the tree, which is leafless when it blossoms. He began breaking the white flowers and throwing them to the ground. He had been on the tree for about five minutes when he heard the whining grumble of a bear, and presently a young sloth bear ambled into the clearing beneath the tree.

He was a small bear, little more than a cub, and Ramu was not frightened; but, because he thought the mother might be in the vicinity, he decided to take no chances, and sat very still, waiting to see what the bear would do. He hoped it wouldn't choose the mahua tree for a meal.

At first, the young bear put his nose to the ground and sniffed his way along until he came to a large anthill. Here he began huffing and puffing, blowing rapidly in and out of his nostrils, causing the dust from the anthill to fly in all directions. But he was a disappointed bear, because the anthill had been deserted long ago. And so, grumbling, he made his way across to a tall wild plum tree, and shinning rapidly up the smooth trunk, was soon perched on its topmost branches. It was only then that he saw Ramu.

The bear at once scrambled several feet higher up the tree, and laid himself out flat on a branch. It wasn't a very thick branch and left a large expanse of bear showing on either side. The bear tucked his head away behind another branch, and so long as he could not see Ramu, seemed quite satisfied that he was well-hidden, though he couldn't help grumbling with anxiety, for a bear, like most animals, is afraid of man.

Bears, however, are also very curious—and curiosity has often led them into trouble. Slowly, inch by inch, the young bear's black snout appeared over the edge of the branch; but immediately the eyes came into view and met Ramu's, he drew back with a jerk and the head was once more hidden. The bear did this two or three times, and Ramu, highly amused, waited until it wasn't looking, then moved some way down the tree. When the bear looked up again and saw that the boy was missing, he was so pleased with himself that he stretched right across to the next branch, to get a plum. Ramu chose this moment to burst into loud laughter. The startled bear tumbled out of the tree, dropped through the branches for a distance of some fifteen feet, and landed with a thud in a heap of dry leaves.

And then several things happened at almost the same time.

The mother bear came charging into the clearing. Spotting Ramu in the tree, she reared up on her hind legs, grunting fiercely. It was Ramu's turn to be startled. There are few animals more dangerous than a rampaging mother bear, and the boy knew that one blow from her clawed forepaws could rip his skull open.

But before the bear could approach the tree, there was a tremendous roar, and the old tiger bounded into the clearing. He had been asleep in the bushes not far away—he liked a good sleep after a heavy meal—and the noise in the clearing had woken him.

He was in a bad mood, and his loud 'A-oonh!' made his displeasure quite clear. The bears turned and ran from the clearing, the youngster squealing with fright.

The tiger then came into the centre of the clearing, looked up at the trembling boy, and roared again.

Ramu nearly fell out of the tree...

'Good day to you, Uncle,' he stammered, showing his teeth in a nervous grin.

Perhaps this was too much for the tiger. With a low growl, he turned his back on the mahua tree and padded off into the jungle, his tail twitching in disgust.

That night, when Ramu told his parents and his grandfather about the tiger and how it had saved him from a female bear, it started a round of tiger stories—about how some of them could be gentlemen, others rogues. Sooner or later the conversation came round to man-eaters, and Grandfather told two stories which he swore were true, although his listeners only half believed him.

The first story concerned the belief that a man-eating tiger is guided towards his next victim by the spirit of a human being previously killed and eaten by the tiger. Grandfather said that he actually knew three hunters who sat up in a machan over a human kill and when the tiger came, the corpse sat up and pointed with his right hand at the men in the tree. The tiger then went away. But the hunters knew he would return, and one man was brave enough to get down from the tree and tie the right arm of the corpse to its side. Later, when the tiger returned, the corpse sat up and this time pointed out the men with his left hand. The enraged tiger sprang into the tree and killed his enemies in the machan.

'And then there was a bania,' said Grandfather, beginning another story, 'who lived in a village in the jungle. He wanted to visit a neighbouring village to collect some money that was owed to him, but as the road lay through heavy forest in which lived a terrible man-eating tiger, he did not know what to do. Finally, he went to a sadhu who gave him two powders. By eating the first powder he could turn into a huge tiger, capable of dealing with any other tiger in the jungle, and by eating the second he would become a bania again.

'Armed with his two powders, and accompanied by his pretty, young wife, the bania set out on his journey. They had not gone far into the forest when they came upon the man-eater sitting in the middle of the road. Before swallowing the first powder, the bania told his wife to stay where she was, so that when he returned after killing the tiger, she could at once give him the second powder and enable him to resume his old shape.

'Well, the bania's plan worked, but only up to a point. He swallowed the first powder and immediately became a magnificent tiger. With a great roar, he bounded towards the man-eater, and after a brief, furious fight, killed his opponent. Then, with his jaws still dripping blood, he returned to his wife.

'The poor girl was terrified and spilt the second powder on the ground. The bania was so angry that he pounced on his wife and killed and ate her. And afterwards this terrible tiger was so enraged at not being able to become a human again that he killed and ate hundreds of people all over the country.

'The only people he spared,' added Grandfather, with a twinkle in his eyes, 'were those who owed him money. A bania never gives up a loan as lost, and the tiger still hoped that one day he might become a human again and be able to collect his dues.'

Next morning, when Ramu came back from the well which

was used to irrigate his father's fields, he found a crowd of curious children surrounding a jeep and three strangers with guns. Each of the strangers had a gun, and they were accompanied by two bearers and a vast amount of provisions.

They had heard that there was a tiger in the area, and they wanted to shoot it.

One of the hunters, who looked even more strange than the others, had come all the way from America to shoot a tiger, and he vowed that he would not leave the country without a tiger's skin in his baggage. One of his companions had said that he could buy a tiger's skin in Delhi, but the hunter said he preferred to get his own trophies.

These men had money to spend, and as most of the villagers needed money badly they were only too willing to go into the forest to construct a machan for the hunters. The platform, big enough to take the three men, was put up in the branches of a tall tun, or mahogany tree.

It was the only night the hunters used the machan. At the end of March, though the days are warm, the nights are still cold. The hunters had neglected to bring blankets, and by midnight their teeth were chattering. Ramu, having tied up a buffalo calf for them at the foot of the tree, made as if to go home but instead circled the area, hanging up bits and pieces of old clothing on small trees and bushes. He thought he owed that much to the tiger. He knew the wily old king of the jungle would keep well away from the bait if he saw the bits of clothing—for where there were men's clothes, there would be men.

The vigil lasted well into the night but the tiger did not come near the tun tree. Perhaps he wasn't hungry; perhaps he got Ramu's message. In any case, the men in the tree soon gave themselves away.

The cold was really too much for them. A flask of rum was

produced, and passed round, and it was not long before there was more purpose to finishing the rum than to finishing off a tiger. Silent at first, the men soon began talking in whispers; and to jungle creatures a human whisper is as telling as a trumpet call.

Soon the men were quite merry, talking in loud voices. And when the first morning light crept over the forest, and Ramu and his friends came back to fetch the great hunters, they found them fast asleep in the machan.

The hunters looked surly and embarrassed as they trudged back to the village.

'No game left in these parts,' said the American.

'Wrong time of the year for tiger,' said the second man.

'Don't know what the country's coming to,' said the third.

And complaining about the weather, the poor quality of cartridges, the quantity of rum they had drunk, and the perversity of tigers, they drove away in disgust.

It was not until the onset of summer that an event occurred which altered the hunting habits of the old tiger and brought him into conflict with the villagers.

There had been no rain for almost two months, and the tall jungle grass had become a sea of billowy dry yellow. Some refugee settlers, living in an area where the forest had been cleared, had been careless while cooking and had started a jungle fire. Slowly it spread into the interior, from where the acrid smell and the fumes smoked the tiger out towards the edge of the jungle. As night came on, the flames grew more vivid, and the smell stronger. The tiger turned and made for the jheel, where he knew he would be safe provided he swam across to the little island in the centre.

Next morning he was on the island, which was untouched by the fire. But his surroundings had changed. The slopes of the hills were black with burnt grass, and most of the tall bamboo had disappeared. The deer and the wild pig, finding that their natural cover had gone, fled further east.

When the fire had died down and the smoke had cleared, the tiger prowled through the forest again but found no game. Once he came across the body of a burnt rabbit, but he could not eat it. He drank at the jheel and settled down in a shady spot to sleep the day away. Perhaps, by evening, some of the animals would return. If not, he, too, would have to look for new hunting grounds—or a new game.

The tiger spent five more days looking for a suitable game to kill. By that time he was so hungry that he even resorted to rooting among the dead leaves and burnt out stumps of trees, searching for worms and beetles. This was a sad comedown for the king of the jungle. But even now he hesitated to leave the area, for he had a deep suspicion and fear of the forest further east—forests that were fast being swallowed up by human habitation. He could have gone north, into high mountains, but they did not provide him with the long grass he needed. A panther could manage quite well up there, but not a tiger who loved the natural privacy of the heavy jungle. In the hills, he would have to hide all the time.

At daybreak, the tiger came to the jheel. The water was now shallow and muddy, and a green scum had spread over the top. But it was still drinkable and the tiger quenched his thirst.

He lay down across his favourite rock, hoping for a deer but none came. He was about to get up and go away when he heard an animal approach.

The tiger at once leaped off his perch and flattened himself on the ground, his tawny striped skin merging with the dry grass. A heavy animal was moving through the bushes, and the tiger waited patiently.

A buffalo emerged and came to the water.

THE LAST TIGER

The buffalo was alone.

He was a big male, and his long curved horns lay right back across his shoulders. He moved leisurely towards the water, completely unaware of the tiger's presence.

The tiger hesitated before making his charge. It was a long time—many years—since he had killed a buffalo, and he knew the villagers would not like it. But the pangs of hunger overcame his scruples. There was no morning breeze, everything was still, and the smell of the tiger did not reach the buffalo. A monkey chattered on a nearby tree, but his warning went unheeded.

Crawling stealthily on his stomach, the tiger skirted the edge of the jheel and approached the buffalo from the rear. The water birds, who were used to the presence of both animals, did not raise an alarm.

Getting closer, the tiger glanced around to see if there were men, or other buffaloes, in the vicinity. Then, satisfied that he was alone, he crept forward. The buffalo was drinking, standing in shallow water at the edge of the tank, when the tiger charged from the side and bit deep into the animal's thigh.

The buffalo turned to fight, but the tendons of his right hind leg had been snapped, and he could only stagger forward a few paces. But he was a buffalo—the bravest of the domestic cattle. He was not afraid. He snorted, and lowered his horns at the tiger; but the great cat was too fast, and circling the buffalo, bit into the other hind leg.

The buffalo crashed to the ground, both hind legs crippled, and then the tiger dashed in, using both tooth and claw, biting deep into the buffalo's throat until the blood gushed out from the jugular vein.

The buffalo gave one long, last bellow before dying.

The tiger, having rested, now began to gorge himself, but, even though he had been starving for days, he could not finish the huge carcass. At least one good meal still remained when, satisfied and feeling his strength returning, he quenched his thirst at the jheel. Then he dragged the remains of the buffalo into the bushes to hide it from the vultures, and went off to find a place to sleep.

He would return to the kill when he was hungry.

The villagers were upset when they discovered that a buffalo was missing; and the next day, when Ramu and Shyam came running home to say that they had found the carcass near the jheel, half-eaten by a tiger, the men were disturbed and angry. They felt that the tiger had tricked and deceived them. And they knew that once he got a taste for domestic cattle, he would make a habit of slaughtering them.

Kundan Singh, Shyam's father and the owner of the dead buffalo, said he would go after the tiger himself.

'It is all very well to talk about what you will do to the tiger,' said his wife, 'but you should never have let the buffalo go off on its own.'

'It had been out on his own before,' said Kundan. 'This is the first time the tiger has attacked one of our beasts. A devil must have entered the maharaja.'

'He must have been very hungry,' said Shyam.

'Well, we are hungry too,' said Kundan Singh.

'Our best buffalo—the only male in our herd.'

'The tiger will kill again,' said Ramu's father.

'If we let him,' said Kundan.

'Should we send for the shikaris?'

'No. They were not clever. The tiger will escape them easily. Besides, there is no time. The tiger will return for another meal tonight. We must finish him off ourselves!'

'But how?'

Kundan Singh smiled secretively, played with the ends of his moustache for a few moments, and then, with great pride, produced from under his cot a double-barrelled gun of ancient vintage.

'My father bought it from an Englishman,' he said.

'How long ago was that?'

'At the time I was born.'

'And have you ever used it?' asked Ramu's father, who was not sure that the gun would work.

'Well, some years back I let it off at some bandits. You remember the time when those dacoits raided our village? They chose the wrong village, and were severely beaten for their pains. As they left, I fired my gun off at them. They didn't stop running until they crossed the Ganga!'

'Yes, but did you hit anyone?'

'I would have, if someone's goat hadn't got in the way at the last moment. But we had roast mutton that night! Don't worry, brother, I know how the thing fires.'

Accompanied by Ramu's father and some others, Kundan set out for the jheel, where, without shifting the buffalo's—carcass—for they knew that the tiger would not come near them if he suspected a trap—they made another machan in the branches of a tall tree some thirty feet from the kill.

Later that evening Kundan Singh and Ramu's father settled down for the night on their crude platform in the tree.

Several hours passed, and nothing but a jackal was seen by the watchers. And then, just as the moon came up over the distant hills, Kundan and his companion were startled by a low 'A-oonh,' followed by a suppressed, rumbling growl.

Kundan grasped his old gun, whilst his friend drew closer to him for comfort. There was complete silence for a minute or two—time that was an agony of suspense for the watchers—and then the sound of stealthy footfalls on dead leaves under the trees.

A moment later the tiger walked out into the moonlight and

stood over his kill.

At first Kundan could do nothing. He was completely overawed by the size of this magnificent tiger. Ramu's father had to nudge him, and then Kundan quickly put the gun to his shoulder, aimed at the tiger's head, and pressed the trigger.

The gun went off with a flash and two loud bangs, as Kundan fired both barrels. Then there was a tremendous roar. One of the bullets had grazed the tiger's head.

The enraged animal rushed at the tree and tried to leap up into the branches. Fortunately, the machan had been built at a safe height, and the tiger was unable to reach it. It roared again and then bounded off into the forest.

'What a tiger!' exclaimed Kundan, half in fear and half in admiration. 'I feel as though my liver has turned to water.'

'You missed him completely,' said Ramu's father. 'Your gun makes a big noise; an arrow would have done more damage.'

'I did not miss him,' said Kundan, feeling offended. 'You heard him roar, didn't you? Would he have been so angry if he had not been hit? If I have wounded him badly, he will die.'

'And if you have wounded him slightly, he may turn into a man-eater, and then where will we be?'

'I don't think he will come back,' said Kundan. 'He will leave these forests.'

They waited until the sun was up before coming down from the tree. They found a few drops of blood on the dry grass but no trail led into the forest, and Ramu's father was convinced that the wound was only a slight one.

The bullet, missing the fatal spot behind the ear, had only grazed the back of the skull and cut a deep groove at its base. It took a few days to heal, and during this time the tiger lay low and did not go near the jheel except when it was very dark and he was very thirsty.

THE LAST TIGER

The villagers thought the tiger had gone away, and Ramu and Shyam—accompanied by some other youths, and always carrying axes and lathis—began bringing buffaloes to the tank again during the day; but they were careful not to let any of them stray far from the herd, and they returned home while it was still daylight.

It was some days since the jungle had been ravaged by the fire, and in the tropics the damage is repaired quickly. In spite of it being the dry season, new life was creeping into the forest.

While the buffaloes wallowed in the muddy water, and the boys wrestled on their grassy islet, a big tawny eagle soared high above them, looking for a meal—a sure sign that some of the animals were beginning to return to the forest. It was not long before his keen eyes detected a movement in the glade below.

What the eagle, with his powerful eyesight, saw was a baby hare, a small fluffy thing, its long pink-tinted ears laid flat along its sides. Had it not been creeping along between two large stones, it would have escaped notice. The eagle waited to see if the mother was about, and as he waited he realized that he was not the only one who coveted this juicy morsel. From the bushes there had appeared a sinuous yellow creature, pressed low to the ground and moving rapidly towards the hare. It was a yellow jungle cat, hardly noticeable in the scorched grass. With great stealth the jungle cat began to stalk the baby hare.

He pounced. The hare's squeal was cut short by the cat's cruel claws; but it had been heard by the mother hare, who now bounded into the glade and without the slightest hesitation went for the surprised cat.

There was nothing haphazard about the mother hare's attack. She flashed around behind the cat and jumped clean over him. As she landed, she kicked back, sending a stinging jet of dust shooting into the cat's face. She did this again and again.

The bewildered cat, crouching and snarling, picked up the

kill and tried to run away with it. But the hare would not permit this. She continued her leaping and buffeting, till eventually the cat, out of sheer frustration, dropped the kill and attacked the mother.

The cat sprang at the hare a score of times, lashing out with

THE LAST TIGER

his claws; but the mother hare was both clever and agile enough to keep just out of reach of those terrible claws, and drew the cat further and further away from her baby—for she did not as yet know that it was dead.

The tawny eagle saw his chance. Swift and true, he swooped. For a brief moment, as his wings overspread the furry little hare and his talons sank deep into it, he caught a glimpse of the cat racing towards him and the mother hare fleeing into the bushes. And then with a shrill 'kee-ee-ee' of triumph, he rose and whirled away with his dinner.

The boys had heard his shrill cry and looked up just in time to see the eagle flying over the jheel with the small little hare held firmly in his talons.

'Poor hare,' said Shyam. 'Its life was short.'

'That's the law of the jungle,' said Ramu. 'The eagle has a family too, and must feed it.'

'I wonder if we are any better than animals,' said Shyam.

'Perhaps we are a little better, in some ways,' said Ramu. 'Grandfather always says, "To be able to laugh and to be merciful are the only things that make man better than the beast."'

The next day, while the boys were taking the herd home, one of the buffaloes lagged behind. Ramu did not realize that the animal was missing until he heard an agonized bellow behind him. He glanced over his shoulder just in time to see the big striped tiger dragging the buffalo into a clump of young bamboo. At the same time, the herd became aware of the danger, and the buffaloes snorted with fear as they hurried along the forest path. To urge them forward, and to warn his friends, Ramu cupped his hands to his mouth and gave vent to a yodelling call.

The buffaloes bellowed, the boys shouted, and the birds flew shrieking from the trees. It was almost a stampede by the time the herd emerged from the forest. The villagers heard the thunder of hoofs, and saw the herd coming home amidst clouds of dust and confusion, and knew that something was wrong.

'The tiger!' shouted Ramu. 'He is here! He has killed one of the buffaloes.'

'He is afraid of us no longer,' said Shyam.

'Did you see where he went?' asked Kundan Singh, hurrying up to them.

'I remember the place,' said Ramu. 'He dragged the buffalo in amongst the bamboo.'

'Then there is no time to lose,' said his father. 'Kundan, you take your gun and two men, and wait near the suspension bridge, where the Garur stream joins the Ganga. The jungle is narrow there. We will beat the jungle from our side, and drive the tiger towards you. He will not escape us, unless he swims the river!'

'Good!' said Kundan, running into his house for his gun, with Shyam close at his heels. 'Was it one of our buffaloes again?' he asked.

'It was Ramu's buffalo this time,' said Shyam. 'A good milk buffalo.'

'Then Ramu's father will beat the jungle thoroughly. You boys had better come with me. It will not be safe for you to accompany the beaters.'

Kundan Singh, carrying his gun and accompanied by Ramu, Shyam and two men, headed for the river junction, while Ramu's father collected about twenty men from the village and, guided by one of the boys who had been with Ramu, made for the spot where the tiger had killed the buffalo.

The tiger was still eating when he heard the men coming. He had not expected to be disturbed so soon. With an angry 'Whoof!' he bounded into a bamboo thicket and watched the men through a screen of leaves and tall grass.

The men did not seem to take much notice of the dead

THE LAST TIGER

buffalo, but gathered round their leader and held a consultation. Most of them carried hand drums slung from their shoulders. They also carried sticks, spears and axes.

After a hurried conversation, they entered the denser part of the jungle, beating their drums with the palms of their hands. Some of the men banged empty kerosene tins. These made even more noise than the drums.

The tiger did not like the noise and retreated deeper into the jungle. But he was surprised to find that the men, instead of going away, came after him into the jungle, banging away on their drums and tins, and shouting at the top of their voices. They had separated now, and advanced single or in pairs, but nowhere were they more than fifteen yards apart. The tiger could easily have broken through this slowly advancing semicircle of men—one swift blow from his paw would have felled the strongest of them—but his main aim was to get away from the noise. He hated and feared noise made by men.

He was not a man-eater and he would not attack a man unless he was very angry or frightened or very desperate; and he was none of these things as yet. He had eaten well, and he would have liked to rest in peace—but there would be no rest for any animal until the men ceased their tremendous clatter and din.

For an hour Ramu's father and others beat the jungle, calling, drumming and trampling the undergrowth. The tiger had no rest. Whenever he was able to put some distance between himself and the men, he would sink down in some shady spot to rest; but, within five or ten minutes, the trampling and drumming would sound nearer, and the tiger, with an angry snarl, would get up and pad north, pad silently north along the narrowing strip of jungle, towards the junction of the Garur stream and the Ganga. Ten years back, he would have had the jungle on his right in which to hide; but the trees had been felled long ago to make way for humans and houses, and now he could only move to the left, towards the river.

It was about noon when the tiger finally appeared in the open. He longed for the darkness and security of the night, for the sun was his enemy. Kundan and the boys had a clear view of him as he stalked slowly along, now in the open with the sun glinting on his glossy hide, now in the shade or passing through the shorter reeds. He was still out of range of Kundan's gun, but there was no fear of his getting out of the beat, as the 'stops' were all men picked from the village. He disappeared among some bushes but soon reappeared to retrace his steps, the beaters having done their work well. He was now only 150 yards from the rocks where Kundan Singh waited, and he looked very big.

The beat had closed in, and the exit along the bank downstream was completely blocked, so the tiger turned and disappeared into a belt of reeds, and Kundan Singh expected that the head would soon peer out of the cover a few yards away. The beaters were now making a great noise, shouting and beating their drums, but nothing moved; and Ramu, watching from a distance, wondered, *Has he slipped through the beaters?* And he half-hoped so.

Tins clashed, drums beat, and some of the men poked into the reeds with their spears or long bamboos. Perhaps one of these thrusts found a mark, because at last the tiger was roused, and with an angry desperate snarl he charged out of the reeds, splashing his way through an inlet of mud and water.

Kundan Singh fired, and his bullet struck the tiger on the thigh.

The mighty animal stumbled; but he was up in a minute, and rushing through a gap in the narrowing line of beaters, he made straight for the only way across the river—the suspension bridge that passed over the Ganga here, providing a route into

THE LAST TIGER

the high hills beyond.

'We'll get him now,' said Kundan, priming his gun again. 'He's right in the open!'

The suspension bridge swayed and trembled as the wounded tiger lurched across it. Kundan fired, and this time the bullet grazed the tiger's shoulder. The animal bounded forward, lost his footing on the unfamiliar, slippery planks of the swaying bridge, and went over the side, falling headlong into the strong, swirling waters of the river.

He rose to the surface once, but the current took him under and away, and only a thin streak of blood remained on the river's surface.

Kundan and others hurried downstream to see if the dead tiger had been washed up on the river's banks; but though they searched the riverside several miles, they did not find the king of the forest.

He had not provided anyone with a trophy. His skin would not be spread on a couch, nor would his head be hung up on a wall. No claw of his would be hung as a charm round the neck of a child. No villager would use his fat as a cure for rheumatism.

At first the villagers were glad because they felt their buffaloes were safe. Then, the men began to feel that something had gone out of their lives, out of the life of the forest; they began to feel that the forest was no longer a forest. It had been shrinking year by year, but, as long as the tiger had been there and the villagers had heard it roar at night, they had known that they were still secure from the intruders and newcomers who came to fell the trees and eat up the land and let the flood waters into the village. But now that the tiger had gone, it was as though a protector had gone, leaving the forest open and vulnerable, easily destroyable. And once the forest was destroyed they, too, would be in danger...

There was another thing that had gone with the tiger, another thing that had been lost, a thing that was being lost everywhere—something called 'nobility'.

Ramu remembered something that his grandfather had once said, 'The tiger is the very soul of India, and when the last tiger goes, so will the soul of the country.'

The boys lay flat on their stomachs on their little mud island and watched the monsoon clouds gathering overhead.

'The king of our forest is dead,' said Shyam. 'There are no more tigers.'

'There must be tigers,' said Ramu. 'How can there be an India without tigers?'

The river had carried the tiger many miles away from his home, from the forest he had always known, and brought him ashore on a strip of warm yellow sand, where he lay in the sun, quite still, but breathing.

Vultures gathered and waited at a distance, some of them perching on the branches of nearby trees.

But the tiger was more drowned than hurt, and as the river water oozed out of his mouth, and the warm sun made new life throb through his body, he stirred and stretched, and his glazed eyes came into focus. Raising his head, he saw trees and tall grass.

Slowly he heaved himself off the ground and moved at a crouch to where the grass waved in the afternoon breeze. Would he be harried again, and shot at? There was no smell of man. The tiger moved forward with greater confidence.

There was, however, another smell in the air—a smell that reached back to the time when he was young, fresh and full of vigour—a smell that he had almost forgotten but could never quite forget—the smell of a tigress!

He raised his head high, and new life surged through his tired limbs. He gave a full-throated roar and moved purposefully

THE LAST TIGER

through the tall grass. And the roar came back to him, calling him, calling him forward—a roar that meant there would be more tigers in the land!

THE LAST TRUCK RIDE

[*Twice a day Pritam Singh takes his battered old truck on the narrow, mountainous roads to the limestone quarry. He is in the habit of driving fast. The brakes of his truck are in good condition. What happens when a stray mule suddenly appears on the road?*]

A horn blared, shattering the silence of the mountains, and a truck came round the bend in the road. A herd of goats scattered left and right.

The goatherds cursed as a cloud of dust enveloped them, and then the truck had left them behind and was rattling along the stony, unpaved hill road.

At the wheel of the truck, stroking his grey moustache, sat Pritam Singh, a turbaned Sikh. It was his own truck. He did not allow anyone else to drive it. Every day he made two trips to the limestone quarries, carrying truckloads of limestone back to the depot at the bottom of the hill. He was paid by the trip and he was always anxious to get in two trips every day.

Sitting beside him was Nathu, his cleaner-boy. Nathu was a sturdy boy, with a round cheerful face. It was difficult to guess his age. He might have been twelve or he might have been fifteen—he did not know himself, since no one in his village had troubled to record his birthday—but the hard life he led probably made him look older than his years. He belonged to the hills, but his village was far away, on the next range.

Last year the potato crop had failed. As a result there was no money for salt, sugar, soap and flour, and Nathu's parents and

THE LAST TRUCK RIDE

small brothers and sisters couldn't live entirely on the onions and artichokes which were about the only crops that had survived the drought. There had been no rain that summer. So Nathu waved goodbye to his people and came down to the town in the valley to look for work. Someone directed him to the limestone depot. He was too young to work at the quarries, breaking stones and loading them on the trucks; but Pritam Singh, one of the older drivers, was looking for someone to clean and look after his truck. Nathu looked like a bright, strong boy, and he was brought on board at ten rupees a day.

That had been six months ago, and now Nathu was an experienced hand at looking after trucks, riding in them and even sleeping in them. He got on well with Pritam Singh, the grizzled, fifty-year-old Sikh, who had well-to-do sons in Punjab, but whose sturdy independence kept him on the road in his battered old truck.

Pritam Singh pressed hard on his horn. Now there was no one on the road—no animals, no humans—but Pritam was fond of his horn and liked blowing it. It was music to his ears.

'One more year on this road,' said Pritam. 'Then I'll sell my truck and retire.'

'Who will buy this truck?' said Nathu. 'It will retire before you do.'

'Don't be cheeky, boy. She's only twenty years old. There are still a few years left in her!' And as though to prove it, he blew his horn again. Its strident sound echoed and re-echoed down the mountain gorge. A pair of wildfowl, disturbed by the noise, flew out from the bushes and glided across the road in front of the truck.

Pritam Singh's thoughts went to his dinner. 'Haven't had a good meal for days,' he grumbled.

'Haven't had a good meal for weeks,' said Nathu, although he looked quite well fed.

'Tomorrow I'll give you dinner,' said Pritam. 'Tandoori chicken and pulao.'

'I'll believe it when I see it,' said Nathu.

Pritam Singh sounded his horn again before slowing down. The road had become narrow and precipitous, and trotting ahead of them was a train of mules. As the horn blared, one mule ran forward, one ran backwards. One went uphill, one went downhill.

THE LAST TRUCK RIDE

Soon there were mules all over the place.

'You can never tell with mules,' said Pritam, after he had left them behind.

The hills were bare and dry. Much of the forest had long since disappeared. Just a few scraggy old oaks still grew on the steep hillside. This particular range was rich in limestone, and the hills were scarred by quarrying.

'Are your hills as bare as these?' asked Pritam.

'No, they have not started blasting there as yet,' said Nathu. 'We still have a few trees. And there is a walnut tree in front of our house, which gives us two baskets of walnuts every year'.

'And do you have water?'

'There is a stream at the bottom of the hill. But for the fields, we have to depend on the rainfall. And there was no rain last year.'

'It will rain soon,' said Pritam. 'I can smell the rain. It is coming from the north.'

'It will settle the dust.'

The dust was everywhere. The truck was full of it. The leaves of the shrubs and the few trees were thick with it. Nathu could feel the dust near his eyelids and on his lips. As they approached the quarries, the dust increased, but it was a different kind of dust now—whiter, stinging the eyes, irritating the nostrils—limestone dust, hanging in the air.

The blasting was in progress.

Pritam Singh brought the truck to a halt. 'Let's wait a bit,' he said.

They sat in silence, staring through the windscreen at the scarred cliffs about a hundred yards down the road. There was no sign of life around them.

Suddenly, the hillside blossomed outwards, followed by a sharp crack of explosives. Earth and rock hurtled down the hillside.

Nathu watched in awe as shrubs and small trees were flung into the air. It always frightened him—not so much the sight of the rocks bursting asunder, but the trees being flung aside and destroyed. He thought of his own trees at home—the walnut, the pines—and wondered if one day they would suffer the same fate and whether the mountains would all become a desert like this particular range. No trees, no grass, no water—only the choking dust of the limestone quarries.

Pritam Singh pressed hard on his horn again to let the people at the site know he was coming. Soon they were parked outside a small shed, where the contractor and the overseer were sipping cups of tea. A short distance away some labourers were hammering at chunks of rock, breaking them up into manageable blocks. A pile of stones stood ready for loading, while the rock that had just been blasted lay scattered about the hillside.

'Come and have a cup of tea,' called out the contractor.

'Get on with the loading,' said Pritam. 'I can't hang about all afternoon. There's another trip to make and it gets dark early these days.'

But he sat down on a bench and ordered two cups of tea from the stall owner. The overseer strolled over to the group of labourers and told them to start loading. Nathu let down the grid at the back of the truck.

Nathu stood back while the men loaded the truck with limestone rocks. He was glad that he was chubby: thin people seemed to feel the cold much more—like the contractor, a skinny fellow who was shivering in his expensive overcoat.

To keep himself warm, Nathu began helping the labourers with the loading.

'Don't expect to be paid for that,' said the contractor, for whom every extra paise spent was a paisa off his profits.

THE LAST TRUCK RIDE

'Don't worry,' said Nathu, 'I don't work for contractors. I work for Pritam Singh.'

'That's right,' called out Pritam. 'And mind what you say to Nathu—he's nobody's servant!'

It took them almost an hour to fill the truck with stones. The contractor wasn't happy until there was no space left for a single stone. Then four of the six labourers climbed on the pile of stones. They would ride back to the depot on the truck. The contractor, his overseer and the others would follow by jeep. 'Let's go!' said Pritam, getting behind the steering wheel. 'I want to be back here and then home by eight o'clock. I'm going to a marriage party tonight!'

Nathu jumped in beside him, banging his door shut. It never opened at a touch. Pritam always joked that his truck was held together with sellotape.

He was in good spirits. He started his engine, blew his horn and burst into a song as the truck started out on the return journey.

The labourers were singing too, as the truck swung round the sharp bends of the winding mountain road. Nathu was feeling quite dizzy. The door beside him rattled on its hinges.

'Not so fast,' he said.

'Oh,' said Pritam, 'And since when did you become nervous about fast driving?'

'Since today,' said Nathu.

'And what's wrong with today?'

'I don't know. It's just that kind of day, I suppose.'

'You are getting old,' said Pritam. 'That's your trouble.'

'Just wait till you get to be my age,' said Nathu.

'No more cheek,' said Pritam, and stepped on the accelerator and drove faster. As they swung round a bend, Nathu looked out of his window. All he saw was the sky above and the valley below. They were very near the edge. But it was always like that on this narrow road. After a few more hairpin bends, the road started descending steeply to the valley.

'I'll just test the brakes,' said Pritam and jammed down on there so suddenly that one of the labourers almost fell off at the back.

They called out in protest.

'Hang on!' shouted Pritam.

'You're nearly home!'

'Don't try any shortcuts,' said Nathu.

Just then a stray mule appeared in the middle of the road. Pritam swung the steering wheel over to his right; but the road turned left, and the truck went straight over the edge.

As it tipped over, hanging for a few seconds on the edge of the cliff, the labourers leapt from the back of the truck.

The truck pitched forward, bouncing over the rocks, turning over on its side and rolling over twice before coming to rest against the trunk of a scraggy old oak tree. Had it missed the tree, the truck would have plunged a few hundred feet down to the bottom of the gorge.

Two labourers sat on the hillside, stunned and badly shaken.

The other two had picked themselves up and were running back to the quarry for help.

Nathu had landed in a bed of nettles. He was smarting all over, but he wasn't really hurt.

His first impulse was to get up and run back with the labourers. Then he realized that Pritam was still in the truck. If he wasn't dead, he would certainly be badly injured.

Nathu skidded down the steep slope, calling out, 'Pritam, Pritam, are you all right?'

There was no answer.

Then he saw Pritam's arm and half his body jutting out of

THE LAST TRUCK RIDE

the open door of the truck. It was a strange position to be in, half in and half out. When Nathu came nearer, he saw Pritam was jammed in the driver's seat, held there by the steering wheel which was pressed hard against his chest. Nathu thought he was dead. But as he was about to turn away and clamber back up the hill, he saw Pritam open one blackened, swollen eye. It looked straight up at Nathu.

'Are you alive?' whispered Nathu, terrified.

'What do you think?' muttered Pritam. He closed his eye again.

When the contractor and his men arrived, it took them almost an hour to get him to a hospital in the town. He had a broken collarbone, a dislocated shoulder and several fractured ribs. But the doctors said he was repairable—which was more than what could be said for his truck.

'The truck's finished,' said Pritam, when Nathu came to see him a few days later. 'Now I'll have to go home and live with my sons. But you can get work on another truck.'

'No,' said Nathu. 'I'm going home too.'

'And what will you do there?'

'I'll work on the land. It's better to grow things on the land than to blast things out of it.'

They were silent for some time.

'Do you know something?' said Pritam finally. 'But for that tree, the truck would have ended up at the bottom of the hill and I wouldn't be here, all bandaged up and talking to you. It was the tree that saved me. Remember that, boy.'

'I'll remember,' said Nathu.

THE BOY WHO BROKE THE BANK

Nathu, the sweeper-boy, grumbled to himself as he swept the steps of a small local bank, owned for the most part by Seth Govind Ram, a man of wealth whose haphazard business dealings had often brought him to the verge of ruin. Nathu used the small broom hurriedly and carelessly; the dust, after rising in a cloud above his head, settled down again on the steps. As Nathu was banging his pan against a dustbin, Sitaram, the washerman's son, passed by.

Sitaram was on his delivery round. He had a bundle of pressed clothes balanced on his head.

'Don't raise such a dust!' he called out to Nathu. 'Are you annoyed because they are still refusing to pay you another five rupees a month?'

'I don't want to talk about it,' complained the sweeper-boy. 'I haven't even received my regular pay. And this is the end of the month. Soon two months' pay will be due. Who would think this was a bank? holding up a poor man's salary! As soon as I get my money, I'm off! Not another week will I work in this place.'

And Nathu banged his pan against the dustbin two or three times more, just to emphasize his point and give himself confidence.

'Well, I wish you luck,' said Sitaram. 'I'll be on the lookout for a new job for you.' And he plodded barefoot along the road, the big bundle of clothes hiding most of his head and shoulders.

At the fourth house he visited, delivering the washing, Sitaram

THE BOY WHO BROKE THE BANK

overheard the woman of the house saying how difficult it was to get someone to sweep the courtyard. Tying up his bundle, Sitaram said: 'I know a sweeper-boy who's looking for work. He might be able to work for you from next month. He's with Seth Govind Ram's bank right now, but they are not giving him his pay, and he wants to leave.'

'Oh, is that so?' said Mrs Prakash. 'And why aren't they paying him?'

'They must be short of money,' said Sitaram with a shrug.

Mrs Prakash laughed, 'Well, tell him to come and see me when he's free.'

Sitaram, glad that he had been of some service both to a friend and to a customer, hoisted his bag on his shoulders and went on his way.

Mrs Prakash had to do some shopping. She gave instructions to her maidservant with regard to the baby and told the cook what she wanted for lunch. Her husband worked for a large company, and they could keep servants and live in style. Having given her orders, she set out for the bazaar to make her customary tour of the clothes' shops.

A large, shady tamarind tree grew near the clock tower, and it was here that Mrs Prakash found her friend, Mrs Bhushan, sheltering from the heat. Mrs Bhushan was fanning herself with a large peacock's feather. She complained that this summer was the hottest in the history of the town. She then showed Mrs Prakash a sample of the cloth she was going to buy, and for five minutes they discussed its shade, texture, and design.

When they had exhausted the subject, Mrs Prakash said: 'Do you know, my dear, Seth Govind Ram's bank can't even pay its employees. Only this morning I heard a complaint from their sweeper-boy, who hasn't received his pay for two months!'

'It's disgraceful!' exclaimed Mrs Bhushan. 'If they can't pay their sweeper, they must be in a bad way. The others would not be getting paid either.'

She left Mrs Prakash under the tamarind tree and went in search of her husband, who was found sitting under the fan in Jugal Kishore's electrical goods shop, playing cards with the owner.

'So, there you are!' cried Mrs Bhushan. 'I've been looking for you for nearly an hour. Where did you disappear to?'

'Nowhere,' replied Mr Bhushan. 'Had you remained stationary in one shop, you might have found me. But you go from one to another, like a bee in a flower garden.'

'Now, don't start grumbling. The heat is bad enough. I don't know what's happening to this town. Even the bank is going bankrupt.'

'What did you say?' said Mr Jugal Kishore, sitting up suddenly. 'Which bank?'

'Why, Seth Govind Ram's bank, of course. I hear they've stopped paying their employees—no salary for over three months! Don't tell me you have an account with them, Mr Kishore?'

'No, but my neighbour does!' he said, and he called out to the keeper of the barbershop next door: 'Faiz Hussain, have you heard the latest? Seth Govind Ram's bank is about to collapse! You'd better take your money out while there's still time.'

Faiz Hussain, who was cutting the hair of an elderly gentleman, was so startled that his hand shook and he nicked his customer's ear. The customer yelped with pain and distress: pain, because of the cut, and distress, because of the awful news he had just heard. With one side of his neck still unshorn, he leapt out of his chair and sped across the road to a general merchant's store, where there was a telephone. He dialled Seth Govind Ram's number. The Seth was not at home. Where was he, then? The Seth was holidaying in Kashmir. Oh, was that

THE BOY WHO BROKE THE BANK

so? The elderly gentleman did not believe it. He hurried back to the barbershop and told Faiz Hussain: 'The bird has flown! Seth Govind Ram has left town. Definitely, it means a collapse. I'll have the rest of my haircut another time.' And he dashed out of the shop and made a beeline for his office and chequebook.

∞

The news spread through the bazaar with the rapidity of a forest fire. From the general merchant's it travelled to the tea shop, circulated amongst the customers; and then spread with them in various directions—to the paan-seller, the tailor, the fruit vendor, the jeweller, the beggar sitting on the pavement.

Old Ganpat, the beggar, had a crooked leg and had been squatting on the pavement for years, calling for alms. In the evening someone would come with a barrow and take him away. He had never been known to walk. But now, on learning that the bank was about to collapse, Ganpat astonished everyone by leaping to his feet and actually running at a good speed in the direction of the bank. It soon became known that he had well over a thousand rupees in savings.

Men stood in groups in street corners, discussing the situation. There hadn't been so much excitement since India last won a Test match. The small town in the foothills seldom had a crisis, never had floods or earthquakes or droughts. And so the imminent crash of the local bank set everyone talking and speculating and rushing about in a frenzy.

Some boasted of their far-sightedness, congratulating themselves on having taken out their money, or on never putting any in. Others speculated on the reasons for the crash, putting it all down to Seth Govind Ram's pleasure-loving ways. The Seth had fled the state, said one. He had fled the country, said another. He had a South American passport, said a third. Others insisted that he was hiding somewhere in the town. And there was a rumour that he had hanged himself from the tamarind tree, where he had been found that morning by the sweeper-boy.

Someone who had a relative working as a clerk in the bank decided to phone him and get the facts.

'I don't know anything about it,' said the clerk, 'except that half the town is here, trying to take their money out. Everyone seems to have gone mad!'

'There's a rumour that none of you have been paid.'

'Well, all the clerks have had their salaries. We wouldn't be working otherwise. It may be that some of the part-time workers are getting paid late, but that isn't due to a shortage of money—only a few hundred rupees—it's just that the clerk who looks after their payments is on sick leave. You don't expect me to do his work, do you?' And he put the telephone down.

By afternoon the bank had gone through all its ready money, and the harassed manager was helpless. Emergency funds could only be obtained from one of the government banks, and now it was nearly closing time. He wasn't sure he could persuade the crowd outside to wait until the following morning. And Seth Govind Ram could be of no help from his luxury houseboat in Kashmir, five hundred miles away.

The clerks shut down their counters. But the people gathered outside on the steps of the bank, shouting: 'We want our money!' 'Give it to us today, break in!' 'Fetch Seth Govind Ram, we know he's hiding in the vaults!'

Mischief-makers, who did not have a paisa in the bank, joined the crowd. The manager stood at the door and tried to calm his angry customers. He declared that the bank had plenty of money, that they could withdraw all they wanted the following morning.

'We want it now!' chanted the people. 'Now, now, now!'

THE BOY WHO BROKE THE BANK

A few stones were thrown, and the manager retreated indoors, closing the iron-grilled gate.

A brick hurtled through the air and smashed into the plate-glass window which advertised the bank's assets.

Then the police arrived. They climbed the steps of the bank and, using their long sticks, pushed the crowd back until people began falling over each other. Gradually everyone dispersed, shouting that they would be back in the morning.

∞

Nathu arrived next morning to sweep the steps of the bank.

He saw the refuse and the broken glass and the stones cluttering up the steps. Raising his hands in horror, he cried: 'Goondas! Hooligans! May they suffer from a thousand ills! It was bad enough being paid irregularly—now I must suffer an increase of work!' He smote the steps with his broom, scattering the refuse.

'Good morning, Nathu,' said Sitaram, the washerman's son, getting down from his bicycle. 'Are you ready to take up a new job from the first of next month? You'll have to, I suppose, now that the bank is closing.'

'What did you say?' said Nathu.

'Haven't you heard? The bank's gone bankrupt. You'd better hang around until the others arrive, and then start demanding your money too. You'll be lucky if you get it!' He waved cheerfully, and pedalled away on his bicycle.

Nathu went back to sweeping the steps, muttering to himself. When he had finished, he sat down on the bottom step to await the arrival of the manager. He was determined to get his pay.

'Who would have thought the bank would collapse,' he said to himself, and looked thoughtfully across the street. 'I wonder how it could have happened....'

ROMI AND THE WILDFIRE

I

As Romi was about to mount his bicycle, he saw smoke rising from behind the distant line of trees.

'It looks like a forest fire,' said Prem, his friend and classmate.

'It's well to the east,' said Romi. 'Nowhere near the road.'

'There's a strong wind,' said Prem, looking at the dry leaves swirling across the road.

It was the middle of May, and it hadn't rained in the Terai for several weeks. The grass was brown, the leaves of the trees covered with dust. Even though it was getting on to six o'clock in the evening, the boys' shirts were damp with sweat.

'It will be getting dark soon,' said Prem. 'You'd better spend the night at my house.'

'No, I said I'd be home tonight. My father isn't keeping well. The doctor has given me some tablets for him.'

'You'd better hurry, then. That fire seems to be spreading.'

'Oh, it's far off. It will take me only forty minutes to ride through the forest. 'Bye, Prem—see you tomorrow!'

Romi mounted his bicycle and pedalled off down the main road of the village, scattering stray hens, stray dogs and stray villagers.

'Hey, look where you're going!' shouted an angry villager, leaping out of the way of the oncoming bicycle. 'Do you think you own the road?'

'Of course I own it,' called Romi cheerfully, and cycled on.

His own village lay about seven miles distant, on the other side of the forest; but there was only a primary school in his village, and Romi was now in high school. His father, who was a fairly wealthy sugarcane farmer, had only recently bought him the bicycle. Romi didn't care too much for school and felt there weren't enough holidays; but he enjoyed the long rides, and he got on well with his classmates.

He might have stayed the night with Prem had it not been for the tablets which the Vaid—the village doctor—had given him for his father.

Romi's father was having back trouble, and the medicine had been specially prepared from local herbs.

Having been given such a fine bicycle, Romi felt that the least he could do in return was to get those tablets to his father as early as possible.

He put his head down and rode swiftly out of the village. Ahead of him, the smoke rose from the burning forest and the sky glowed red.

II

He had soon left the village far behind. There was a slight climb, and Romi had to push harder on the pedals to get over the rise. Once over the top, the road went winding down to the edge of the subtropical forest.

This was the part Romi enjoyed most. He relaxed, stopped pedalling, and allowed the bicycle to glide gently down the slope. Soon the wind was rushing past him, blowing his hair about his face and making his shirt billow out behind. He burst into song.

A dog from the village ran beside him, barking furiously. Romi shouted at the dog, encouraging him in the race.

ROMI AND THE WILDFIRE

Then the road straightened out, and Romi began pedalling again.

The dog, seeing the forest ahead, turned back to the village. It was afraid of the forest.

The smoke was thicker now, and Romi caught the smell of burning timber. But ahead of him, the road was clear. He rode on.

It was a rough, dusty road, cut straight through the forest. Tall trees grew on either side, cutting off the last of the daylight. But the spreading glow of the fire on the right lit up the road, and giant tree-shadows danced before the boy on the bicycle.

Usually the road was deserted. This evening it was alive with wild creatures fleeing from the forest fire.

The first animal that Romi saw was a hare, leaping across the road in front of him. It was followed by several more hares. Then a band of monkeys streamed across, chattering excitedly.

They'll be safe on the other side, thought Romi. The fire won't cross the road.

But it was coming closer. And realizing this, Romi pedalled harder. In half an hour he should be out of the forest.

Suddenly, from the side of the road, several pheasants rose in the air, and with a *whoosh*, flew low across the path, just in front of the oncoming bicycle. Taken by surprise, Romi fell off. When he picked himself up and began brushing his clothes, he saw that his knee was bleeding. It wasn't a deep cut, but he allowed it to bleed a little, took out his handkerchief and bandaged his knee. Then he mounted the bicycle again.

He rode a bit slower now, because birds and animals kept coming out of the bushes.

Not only pheasants but smaller birds, too, were streaming across the road—parrots, jungle crows, owls, magpies—and the air was filled with their cries.

Everyone's on the move, thought Romi. *It must be a really big fire.*

He could see the flames now, reaching out from behind the trees on his right, and he could hear the crackling as the dry leaves caught fire. The air was hot on his face. Leaves, still alight or turning to cinders, floated past.

A herd of deer crossed the road, and Romi had to stop until they had passed. Then he mounted again and rode on; but now, for the first time, he was feeling afraid.

III

From ahead came a faint clanging sound. It wasn't an animal sound, Romi was sure of that. A fire engine? There were no fire engines within fifty miles.

The clanging came nearer, and Romi discovered that the noise came from a small boy who was running along the forest path, two milk cans clattering at his side.

'Teju!' called Romi, recognizing the boy from a neighbouring village. 'What are you doing out here?'

'Trying to get home, of course,' said Teju, panting along beside the bicycle.

'Jump on,' said Romi, stopping for him.

Teju was only eight or nine—a couple of years younger than Romi. He had come to deliver milk to some road workers, but the workers had left at the first signs of the fire, and Teju was hurrying home with his cans still full of milk.

He got up on the crossbar of the bicycle, and Romi moved on again. He was quite used to carrying friends on the crossbar.

'Keep beating your milk cans,' said Romi. 'Like that, the animals will know we are coming. My bell doesn't make enough noise. I'm going to get a horn for my cycle!'

'I never knew there were so many animals in the jungle,' said Teju. 'I saw a python in the middle of the road. It stretched right across!'

'What did you do?'

'Just kept running and jumped right over it!'

Teju continued to chatter but Romi's thoughts were on the fire, which was much closer now. Flames shot up from the dry grass and ran up the trunks of trees and along the branches. Smoke billowed out above the forest.

Romi's eyes were smarting and his hair and eyebrows felt scorched. He was feeling tired but he couldn't stop now, he had to get beyond the range of the fire. Another ten or fifteen minutes of steady riding would get them to the small wooden bridge that spanned the little river separating the forest from the sugarcane fields.

Once across the river, they would be safe. The fire could not touch them on the other side, because the forest ended at the river's edge. But could they get to the river in time?

IV

Clang, clang, clang, went Teju's milk cans. But the sound of the fire grew louder too.

A tall silk-cotton tree, its branches leaning across the road, had caught fire. They were almost beneath it when there was a crash and a burning branch fell to the ground, a few yards in front of them.

The boys had to get off the bicycle and leave the road, forcing their way through a tangle of thorny bushes on the left, dragging and pushing at the bicycle and only returning to the road some distance ahead of the burning tree.

'We won't get out in time,' said Teju, back on the crossbar but feeling disheartened.

'Yes, we will,' said Romi, pedalling with all his might. 'The fire hasn't crossed the road as yet.'

Even as he spoke, he saw a small flame leap up from the grass on the left. It wouldn't be long before more sparks and burning leaves were blown across the road to kindle the grass on the other side.

'Oh, look!' exclaimed Romi, bringing the bicycle to a sudden stop.

'What's wrong now?' asked Teju, rubbing his sore eyes. And then, through the smoke, he saw what was stopping them.

An elephant was standing in the middle of the road.

Teju slipped off the crossbar, his cans rolling on the ground, bursting open and spilling their contents.

The elephant was about forty feet away. It moved about restlessly, its big ears flapping as it turned its head from side to side, wondering which way to go.

From far to the left, where the forest was still untouched, a herd of elephants moved towards the river. The leader of the herd raised his trunk and trumpeted a call. Hearing it, the elephant on the road raised its own trunk and trumpeted a reply. Then it shambled off into the forest, in the direction of the herd, leaving the way clear.

'Come, Teju, jump on!' urged Romi. 'We can't stay here much longer!'

V

Teju forgot about his milk cans and pulled himself up on the crossbar. Romi ran forward with the bicycle, to gain speed, and mounted swiftly. He kept as far as possible to the left of the road, trying to ignore the flames, the crackling, the smoke and the scorching heat.

It seemed that all the animals who could get away, had done

ROMI AND THE WILDFIRE

so. The exodus across the road had stopped.

'We won't stop again,' said Romi, gritting his teeth. 'Not even for an elephant!'

'We're nearly there!' said Teju. He was perking up again.

A jackal, overcome by the heat and smoke, lay in the middle of the path, either dead or unconscious. Romi did not stop. He swerved round the animal. Then he put all his strength into one final effort.

He covered the last hundred yards at top speed, and then they were out of the forest, freewheeling down the sloping road to the river.

'Look!' shouted Teju. 'The bridge is on fire!'

Burning embers had floated down on to the small wooden bridge, and the dry, ancient timber had quickly caught fire. It was now burning fiercely.

Romi did not hesitate. He left the road, riding the bicycle over sand and pebbles. Then with a rush they went down the riverbank and into the water.

The next thing they knew, they were splashing around, trying to find each other in the darkness.

'Help!' cried Teju. 'I'm drowning!'

IV

'Don't be silly,' said Romi. 'The water isn't deep—it's only up to the knees. Come here and grab hold of me.'

Teju splashed across and grabbed Romi by the belt.

'The water's so cold,' he said, his teeth chattering.

'Do you want to go back and warm yourself?' asked Romi. 'Some people are never satisfied. Come on, help me get the bicycle up. It's down here, just where we are standing.'

Together they managed to heave the bicycle out of the water and stand it upright.

'Now sit on it,' said Romi. 'I'll push you across.'

'We'll be swept away,' said Teju.

'No, we won't. There's not much water in the river at this time of the year. But the current is quite strong in the middle, so sit still. All right?'

'All right,' said Teju nervously.

Romi began guiding the bicycle across the river, one hand on the seat and one hand on the handlebar. The river was shallow and sluggish in midsummer; even so, it was quite swift in the middle. But having got safely out of the burning forest, Romi

ROMI AND THE WILDFIRE

was in no mood to let a little river defeat him.

He kicked off his shoes, knowing they would be lost; and then gripping the smooth stones of the riverbed with his toes, he concentrated on keeping his balance and getting the bicycle and Teju through the middle of the stream. The water here came up to his waist, and the current would have been too strong for Teju. But when they reached the shallows, Teju got down and helped Romi push the bicycle.

They reached the opposite bank, and sank down on the grass.

'We can rest now,' said Romi. 'But not all night—I've got some medicine to give to my father.' He felt in his pockets and found that the tablets, in their envelope, had turned into a soggy mess. 'Oh well, he had to take them with water anyway,' he said.

They watched the fire as it continued to spread through the forest. It had crossed the road down which they had come. The sky was a bright red, and the river reflected the colour of the sky.

Several elephants had found their way down to the river. They were cooling off by spraying water on each other with their trunks. Further downstream there were deer and other animals.

Romi and Teju looked at each other in the glow from the fire. They hadn't known each other very well before. But now they felt they had been friends for years.

'What are you thinking about?' asked Teju.

'I'm thinking,' said Romi, 'that even if the fire is out in a day or two, it will be a long time before the bridge is repaired. So it will be a nice long holiday from school!'

'But you can walk across the river,' said Teju. 'You just did it.'

'Impossible,' said Romi. 'It's much too swift.'

PANTHER'S MOON

I

In the entire village, he was the first to get up. Even the dog, a big hill mastiff called Sheroo, was asleep in a corner of the dark room, curled up near the cold embers of the previous night's fire. Bisnu's tousled head emerged from his blanket. He rubbed the sleep from his eyes and sat up on his haunches. Then, gathering his wits, he crawled in the direction of the loud ticking that came from the battered little clock which occupied the second most honoured place in a niche in the wall. The most honoured place belonged to a picture of Ganesha, the god of learning, who had an elephant's head and a fat boy's body. Bringing his face close to the clock, Bisnu could just make out the hands. It was five o'clock. He had half an hour in which to get ready and leave.

He got up, in vest and underpants, and moved quietly towards the door. The soft tread of his bare feet woke Sheroo and the big black dog rose silently and padded behind the boy. The door opened and closed and then the boy and the dog were outside in the early dawn. The month was June and the nights were warm, even in the Himalayan valleys; but there was fresh dew on the grass. Bisnu felt the dew beneath his feet. He took a deep breath and began walking down to the stream.

The sound of the stream filled the small valley. At that early hour of the morning, it was the only sound; but Bisnu was hardly conscious of it. It was a sound he lived with and took for granted. It was only when he had crossed the hill, on his way to the town—and the sound of the stream grew distant—that he really began to notice it. And it was only when the stream was too far away to be heard that he really missed its sound.

He slipped out of his underclothes, gazed for a few moments at the goose pimples rising on his flesh, and then dashed into the shallow stream. As he went further in, the cold mountain water reached his loins and navel and he gasped with shock and pleasure. He drifted slowly with the current, swam across to a small inlet which formed a fairly deep pool and plunged into the water. Sheroo hated cold water at this early hour. Had the sun been up, he would not have hesitated to join Bisnu. Now he contented himself with sitting on a smooth rock and gazing placidly at the slim brown boy splashing about in the clear water, in the widening light of dawn.

Bisnu did not stay long in the water. There wasn't time. When he returned to the house, he found his mother up, making tea and chapattis. His sister, Puja, was still asleep. She was a little older than Bisnu, a pretty girl with large black eyes, good teeth and strong arms and legs. During the day, she helped her mother in the house and in the fields. She did not go to the school with Bisnu. But when he came home in the evenings, he would try teaching her some of the things he had learnt. Their father was dead. Bisnu, at twelve, considered himself the head of the family.

He ate two chapattis, after spreading butter-oil on them. He drank a glass of hot sweet tea. His mother gave two thick chapattis to Sheroo and the dog wolfed them down in a few minutes. Then she wrapped two chapattis and a gourd curry in some big green leaves and handed these to Bisnu. This was his lunch packet. His mother and Puja would take their meal afterwards.

When Bisnu was dressed, he stood with folded hands before the picture of Ganesha. Ganesha is the god who blesses all beginnings. The author who begins to write a new book, the banker who opens a new ledger, the traveller who starts on a journey, all invoke the kindly help of Ganesha. And as Bisnu made a journey every day, he never left without the goodwill of the elephant-headed god.

How, one might ask, did Ganesha get his elephant's head? When born, he was a beautiful child. Parvati, his mother, was so proud of him that she went about showing him to everyone.

Unfortunately she made the mistake of showing the child to that envious planet, Saturn, who promptly burnt off poor Ganesha's head. Parvati in despair went to Brahma, the Creator, for a new head for her son. He had no head to give her but advised her to search for some man or animal caught in a sinful or wrong act. Parvati wandered about until she came upon an elephant sleeping with its head the wrong way, that is, to the south. She promptly removed the elephant's head and planted it on Ganesha's shoulders, where it took root.

Bisnu knew this story. He had heard it from his mother. Wearing a white shirt and black shorts and a pair of worn white keds, he was ready for his long walk to school, five miles up the mountain.

His sister woke up just as he was about to leave. She pushed the hair away from her face and gave Bisnu one of her rare smiles.

'I hope you have not forgotten,' she said.

'Forgotten?' said Bisnu, pretending innocence. 'Is there anything I am supposed to remember?'

'Don't tease me. You promised to buy me a pair of bangles, remember? I hope you won't spend the money on sweets, as you did last time.'

'Oh, yes, your bangles,' said Bisnu. 'Girls have nothing better to do than waste money on trinkets. Now, don't lose your temper! I'll get them for you. Red and gold are the colours you want?'

PANTHER'S MOON

'Yes, Brother,' said Puja gently, pleased that Bisnu had remembered the colours.

'And for your dinner tonight we'll make you something special. Won't we, Mother?'

'Yes. But hurry up and dress. There is some ploughing to be done today. The rains will soon be here, if the Gods are kind.'

'The monsoon will be late this year,' said Bisnu. 'Mr Nautiyal, our teacher, told us so. He said it had nothing to do with the Gods.'

'Be off, you are getting late,' said Puja, before Bisnu could begin an argument with his mother. She was diligently winding the old clock. It was quite light in the room. The sun would be up any minute.

Bisnu shouldered his school bag, kissed his mother, pinched his sister's cheeks and left the house. He started climbing the steep path up the mountainside. Sheroo bounded ahead; for he, too, always went with Bisnu to school.

Five miles to school. Every day, except Sunday, Bisnu walked five miles to school; and in the evening, he walked home again. There was no school in his own small village of Manjari, for the village consisted of only five families. The nearest school was at Kemptee, a small township on the bus route through the district of Garhwal. A number of boys walked to school, from distances of two or three miles; their villages were not quite as remote as Manjari. But Bisnu's village lay right at the bottom of the mountain, a drop of over two thousand feet from Kemptee. There was no proper road between the village and the town.

In Kemptee there was a school, a small mission hospital, a post office and several shops. In Manjari village there were none of these amenities. If you were sick, you stayed at home until you got well; if you were very sick, you walked or were carried to the hospital, up the five-mile path. If you wanted to buy something, you went without it; but if you wanted it very badly, you could walk the five miles to Kemptee.

Manjari was known as the Five-Mile Village.

Twice a week, if there were any letters, a postman came to the village. Bisnu usually passed the postman on his way to and from school.

There were other boys in Manjari village, but Bisnu was the only one who went to school. His mother would not have fussed if he had stayed at home and worked in the fields. That was what the other boys did; all except lazy Chittru, who preferred fishing in the stream or helping himself to the fruit off other people's trees. But Bisnu went to school. He went because he wanted to. No one could force him to go; and no one could stop him from going. He had set his heart on receiving a good schooling. He wanted to read and write as well as anyone in the big world, the world that seemed to begin only where the mountains ended. He felt cut off from the world in his small valley. He would rather live at the top of a mountain than at the bottom of one. That was why he liked climbing to Kemptee, it took him to the top of the mountain; and from its ridge he could look down on his own valley to the north and to the wide endless plains stretching towards the south.

The plainsman looks to the hills for the needs of his spirit but the hillman looks to the plains for a living. Leaving the village and the fields below him, Bisnu climbed steadily up the bare hillside, now dry and brown. By the time the sun was up, he had entered the welcome shade of an oak and rhododendron forest. Sheroo went bounding ahead, chasing squirrels and barking at langurs.

A colony of langurs lived in the oak forest. They fed on oak leaves, acorns and other green things and usually remained in the trees, coming down to the ground only to play or bask in the sun. They were beautiful, supple-limbed animals, with black faces and silver-grey coats and long, sensitive tails. They leapt from tree to tree with great agility. The young ones wrestled on the grass like boys.

A dignified community, the langurs did not have the cheekiness or dishonest habits of the red monkeys of the plains; they did not approach dogs or humans. But they had grown used to Bisnu's comings and goings and did not fear him. Some of the older ones would watch him quietly, a little puzzled. They did not go near the town, because the Kemptee boys threw stones at them. And anyway, the oak forest gave them all the food they required. Emerging from the trees, Bisnu crossed a small brook. Here he stopped to drink the fresh clean water of a spring. The brook tumbled down the mountain and joined the river a little below Bisnu's village. Coming from another direction was a second path and at the junction of the two paths Sarru was waiting for him.

Sarru came from a small village about three miles from Bisnu's and closer to the town. He had two large milk cans slung over his shoulders. Every morning he carried this milk to town, selling one can to the school and the other to Mrs Taylor, the lady doctor at the small mission hospital. He was a little older than Bisnu but not as well built.

They hailed each other and Sarru fell into step beside Bisnu. They often met at this spot, keeping each other company for the remaining two miles to Kemptee.

'There was a panther in our village last night,' said Sarru.

This information interested but did not excite Bisnu. Panthers were common enough in the hills and did not usually present a problem except during the winter months, when their natural prey was scarce. Then, occasionally, a panther would take to haunting the outskirts of a village, seizing a careless dog or a stray goat.

'Did you lose any animals?' asked Bisnu.

'No. It tried to get into the cowshed but the dogs set up an alarm. We drove it off.'

'It must be the same one which came around last winter. We lost a calf and two dogs in our village.'

'Wasn't that the one the shikaris wounded? I hope it hasn't become a cattle lifter.'

'It could be the same. It has a bullet in its leg. These hunters are the people who cause all the trouble. They think it's easy to shoot a panther. It would be better if they missed altogether but they usually wound it.'

'And then the panther's too slow to catch the barking deer and starts on our own animals.'

'We're lucky it didn't become a man-eater. Do you remember the man-eater six years ago? I was very small then. My father told me all about it. Ten people were killed in our valley alone. What happened to it?'

'I don't know. Some say it poisoned itself when it ate the headman of another village.'

Bisnu laughed. 'No one liked that old villain. He must have been a man-eater himself in some previous existence!' They linked arms and scrambled up the stony path. Sheroo began barking and ran ahead. Someone was coming down the path. It was Mela Ram, the postman.

II

'Any letters for us?' asked Bisnu and Sarru together. They never received any letters but that did not stop them from asking. It was one way of finding out who had received letters.

'You're welcome to all of them,' said Mela Ram, 'if you'll carry my bag for me.'

'Not today,' said Sarru. 'We're busy today. Is there a letter from Corporal Ghanshyam for his family?'

'Yes, there is a postcard for his people. He is posted on the Ladakh border now and finds it very cold there.'

Postcards, unlike sealed letters, were considered public property and were read by everyone. The senders knew that too, and so Corporal Ghanshyam Singh was careful to mention that he expected a promotion very soon. He wanted everyone in his village to know it.

Mela Ram, complaining of sore feet, continued on his way and the boys carried on up the path. It was eight o'clock when they reached Kemptee. Dr Taylor's outpatients were just beginning to trickle in at the hospital gate. The doctor was trying to prop up a rose creeper which had blown down during the night. She liked attending to her plants in the mornings, before starting on her patients. She found this helped her in her work. There was a lot in common between ailing plants and ailing people.

Dr Taylor was fifty, white-haired but fresh in the face and full of vitality. She had been in India for twenty years and ten of these had been spent working in the hill regions.

She saw Bisnu coming down the road. She knew about the boy and his long walk to school and admired him for his keenness and sense of purpose. She wished there were more like him.

Bisnu greeted her shyly. Sheroo barked and put his paws up on the gate.

'Yes, there's a bone for you,' said Dr Taylor. She often put aside bones for the big black dog, for she knew that Bisnu's people could not afford to give the dog a regular diet of meat—though he did well enough on milk and chapattis.

She threw the bone over the gate and Sheroo caught it before it fell. The school bell began ringing and Bisnu broke into a run.

Sheroo loped along behind the boy.

When Bisnu entered the school gate, Sheroo sat down on

the grass of the compound. He would remain there until the lunch break. He knew of various ways of amusing himself during school hours and had friends among the bazaar dogs. But just then he didn't want company. He had his bone to get on with.

Mr Nautiyal, Bisnu's teacher, was in a bad mood. He was a keen rose grower and only that morning, on getting up and looking out of his bedroom window, he had been horrified to see a herd of goats in his garden. He had chased them down the road with a stick but the damage had already been done. His prize roses had all been consumed.

Mr Nautiyal had been so upset that he had gone without his breakfast. He had also cut himself whilst shaving. Thus, his mood had gone from bad to worse. Several times during the day, he brought down his ruler on the knuckles of any boy who irritated him. Bisnu was one of his best pupils. But even Bisnu irritated him by asking too many questions about a new sum which Mr Nautiyal didn't feel like explaining.

That was the kind of day it was for Mr Nautiyal. Most school teachers know similar days.

'Poor Mr Nautiyal,' thought Bisnu. 'I wonder why he's so upset. It must be because of his pay. He doesn't get much money. But he's a good teacher. I hope he doesn't take another job.'

But after Mr Nautiyal had eaten his lunch, his mood improved (as it always did after a meal) and the rest of the day passed serenely. Armed with a bundle of homework, Bisnu came out from the school compound at four o'clock and was immediately joined by Sheroo. He proceeded down the road in the company of several of his class-fellows. But he did not linger long in the bazaar. There were five miles to walk and he did not like to get home too late. Usually, he reached his house just as it was beginning to get dark.

Sarru had gone home long ago and Bisnu had to make the

return journey on his own. It was a good opportunity to memorize the words of an English poem he had been asked to learn. Bisnu had reached the little brook when he remembered the bangles he had promised to buy for his sister.

'Oh, I've forgotten them again,' he said aloud. 'Now I'll catch it—and she's probably made something special for my dinner!'

Sheroo, to whom these words were addressed, paid no attention but bounded off into the oak forest. Bisnu looked around for the monkeys but they were nowhere to be seen.

'Strange,' he thought, 'I wonder why they have disappeared.'

He was startled by a sudden sharp cry, followed by a fierce yelp. He knew at once that Sheroo was in trouble. The noise came from the bushes down the khud, into which the dog had rushed but a few seconds previously.

Bisnu jumped off the path and ran down the slope towards the bushes. There was no dog and not a sound. He whistled and called but there was no response. Then he saw something lying on the dry grass. He picked it up. It was a portion of a dog's collar, stained with blood. It was Sheroo's collar and Sheroo's blood.

Bisnu did not search further. He knew, without a doubt, that Sheroo had been seized by a panther. No other animal could have attacked so silently and swiftly and carried off a big dog without a struggle. Sheroo was dead—must have been dead within seconds of being caught and flung into the air. Bisnu knew the danger that lay in wait for him if he followed the blood trail through the trees. The panther would attack anyone who interfered with its meal.

With tears starting in his eyes, Bisnu carried on down the path to the village. His fingers still clutched the little bit of bloodstained collar that was all that was left to him of his dog.

III

Bisnu was not a very sentimental boy but he sorrowed for his dog who had been his companion on many a hike into the hills and forests. He did not sleep that night but turned restlessly from side to side, moaning softly. After some time he felt Puja's hand on his head. She began stroking his brow. He took her hand in his own and the clasp of her rough, warm familiar hand gave him a feeling of comfort and security.

Next morning, when he went down to the stream to bathe, he missed the presence of his dog. He did not stay long in the water. It wasn't as much fun when there was no Sheroo to watch him.

When Bisnu's mother gave him his food, she told him to be careful and hurry home that evening. A panther, even if it is only a cowardly lifter of sheep or dogs, is not to be trifled with. And this particular panther had shown some daring by seizing the dog even before it was dark.

Still, there was no question of staying away from school. If Bisnu remained at home every time a panther put in an appearance, he might just as well stop going to school altogether.

He set off even earlier than usual and reached the meeting of the paths long before Sarru. He did not wait for his friend because he did not feel like talking about the loss of his dog. It was not the day for the postman and so Bisnu reached Kemptee without meeting anyone on the way. He tried creeping past the hospital gate unnoticed, but Dr Taylor saw him and the first thing she said was: 'Where's Sheroo? I've got something for him.'

When Dr Taylor saw the boy's face, she knew at once that something was wrong.

'What is it, Bisnu?' she asked. She looked quickly up and down the road. 'Is it Sheroo?'

He nodded gravely.

'A panther took him,' he said.

'In the village?'

'No, while we were walking home through the forest. I did not see anything—but I heard.'

Dr Taylor knew that there was nothing she could say that would console him and she tried to conceal the bone which she had brought out for the dog, but Bisnu noticed her hiding it behind her back and the tears welled up in his eyes. He turned away and began running down the road.

His school-fellows noticed Sheroo's absence and questioned Bisnu. He had to tell them everything. They were full of sympathy but they were also quite thrilled at what had happened and kept pestering Bisnu for all the details. There was a lot of noise in the classroom, and Mr Nautiyal had to call for order. When he learnt what had happened, he patted Bisnu on the head and told him that he need not attend school for the rest of the day. But Bisnu did not want to go home. After school, he got into a fight with one of the boys, and that helped him forget.

IV

The panther that plunged the village into an atmosphere of gloom and terror may not have been the same panther that took Sheroo. There was no way of knowing and it would have made no difference, because the panther that came by night and struck at the people of Manjari was that most feared of wild creatures, a man-eater.

Nine-year-old Sanjay, son of Kalam Singh, was the first child to be attacked by the panther.

Kalam Singh's house was the last in the village and nearest the stream. Like the other houses, it was quite small, just a room above and a stable below, with steps leading up from outside the house. He lived there with his wife, two sons (Sanjay was the youngest) and little daughter Basanti, who had just turned three.

Sanjay had brought his father's cows home after grazing them on the hillside in the company of other children. He had also brought home an edible wild plant, which his mother cooked into a tasty dish for their evening meal. They had their food at dusk, sitting on the floor of their single room, and soon after settled down for the night. Sanjay curled up in his favourite spot, with his head near the door, where he got a little fresh air. As the nights were warm, the door was usually left a little ajar. Sanjay's mother piled ash on the embers of the fire and the family was soon asleep.

No one heard the stealthy padding of a panther approaching the door, pushing it wider open. But suddenly there were sounds of a frantic struggle, and Sanjay's stifled cries were mixed with the grunts of the panther. Kalam Singh leapt to his feet with a shout. The panther had dragged Sanjay out of the door and was pulling him down the steps, when Kalam Singh started battering at the animal with a large stone. The rest of the family screamed in terror, rousing the entire village. A number of men came to Kalam Singh's assistance and the panther was driven off. But Sanjay lay unconscious.

Someone brought a lantern and the boy's mother screamed when she saw her small son with his head lying in a pool of blood. It looked as if the side of his head had been eaten off by the panther. But he was still alive, and as Kalam Singh plastered ash on the boy's head to stop the bleeding, he found that though the scalp had been torn off on one side of the head, the bare bone was smooth and unbroken.

'He won't live through the night,' said a neighbour. 'We'll have to carry him down to the river in the morning.'

The dead were always cremated on the banks of a small river

which flowed past Manjari village.

Suddenly the panther, still prowling about the village, called out in rage and frustration, and the villagers rushed to their homes in panic and barricaded themselves in for the night.

Sanjay's mother sat by the boy for the rest of the night, weeping and watching. Towards dawn he started to moan and show signs of coming round. At this sign of returning consciousness, Kalam Singh rose determinedly and looked around for his stick.

He told his elder son to remain behind with the mother and daughter, as he was going to take Sanjay to Dr Taylor at the hospital.

'See, he is moaning and in pain,' said Kalam Singh. 'That means he has a chance to live if he can be treated at once.'

With a stout stick in his hand, and Sanjay on his back, Kalam Singh set off on the two miles of hard mountain track to the hospital at Kemptee. His son, a bloodstained cloth around his head, was moaning but still unconscious. When at last Kalam Singh climbed up through the last fields below the hospital, he asked for the doctor and stammered out an account of what had happened.

It was a terrible injury, as Dr Taylor discovered. The bone over almost one-third of the head was bare and the scalp was torn all round. As the father told his story, the doctor cleaned and dressed the wound, and then gave Sanjay a shot of penicillin to prevent sepsis. Later, Kalam Singh carried the boy home again.

V

After this, the panther went away for some time. But the people of Manjari could not be sure of its whereabouts. They kept to their houses after dark and shut their doors. Bisnu had to stop going to school, because there was no one to accompany him and it was dangerous to go alone. This worried him because his final exam was only a few weeks away and he would be missing important classwork. When he wasn't in the fields, helping with the sowing of rice and maize, he would be sitting in the shade of a chestnut tree, going through his well-thumbed second-hand schoolbooks. He had no other reading, except for a copy of the Ramayana and a Hindi translation of *Alice in Wonderland*. These were well-preserved, read only in fits and starts and usually kept locked in his mother's old tin trunk.

Sanjay had nightmares for several nights and woke up screaming. But with the resilience of youth, he quickly recovered. At the end of the week he was able to walk to the hospital, though his father always accompanied him. Even a desperate panther will hesitate to attack a party of two. Sanjay, with his thin little face and huge bandaged head, looked a pathetic figure, but he was getting better and the wound looked healthy.

Bisnu often went to see him, and the two boys spent long hours together near the stream. Sometimes Chittru would join them, and they would try catching fish with a homemade net. They were often successful in taking home one or two mountain trout. Sometimes, Bisnu and Chittru wrestled in the shallow water or on the grassy banks of the stream. Chittru was a chubby boy with a broad chest, strong legs and thighs, and when he used his weight, he got Bisnu under him. But Bisnu was hard and wiry and had very strong wrists and fingers. When he had Chittru in a vice, the bigger boy would cry out and give up the struggle. Sanjay could not join in these games.

He had never been a very strong boy and he needed plenty of rest if his wounds were to heal well.

The panther had not been seen for over a week and the people of Manjari were beginning to hope that it might have moved on over the mountain or further down the valley.

'I think I can start going to school again,' said Bisnu. 'The panther has gone away.'

'Don't be too sure,' said Puja. 'The moon is full these days and perhaps it is only being cautious.'

'Wait a few days,' said their mother. 'It is better to wait. Perhaps you could go the day after tomorrow when Sanjay goes to the hospital with his father. Then you will not be alone.'

And so, two days later, Bisnu went up to Kemptee with Sanjay and Kalam Singh. Sanjay's wound had almost healed over. Little islets of flesh had grown over the bone. Dr Taylor told him that he needed to come see her only once a fortnight, instead of every third day.

Bisnu went to his school and was given a warm welcome by his friends and by Mr Nautiyal.

'You'll have to work hard,' said his teacher. 'You have to catch up with the others. If you like, I can give you some extra time after classes.'

'Thank you, sir, but it will make me late,' said Bisnu. 'I must get home before it is dark, otherwise my mother will worry. I think the panther has gone but nothing is certain.'

'Well, you mustn't take risks. Do your best, Bisnu. Work hard and you'll soon catch up with your lessons.'

Sanjay and Kalam Singh were waiting for him outside the school. Together they took the path down to Manjari, passing the postman on the way. Mela Ram said he had heard that the panther was in another district and that there was nothing to fear. He was on his rounds again.

Nothing happened on the way. The langurs were back in their favourite part of the forest. Bisnu got home just as the kerosene lamp was being lit. Puja met him at the door with a winsome smile.

'Did you get the bangles?' she asked.

But Bisnu had forgotten again.

VI

There had been a thunderstorm and some rain—a short, sharp shower which gave the villagers hope that the monsoon would arrive on time. It brought out the thunder lilies—pink, crocus-like flowers which sprang up on the hillsides immediately after a summer shower.

Bisnu, on his way home from school, was caught in the rain. He knew the shower would not last, so he took shelter in a small cave and, to pass the time, began doing sums, scratching figures in the damp earth with the end of a stick.

When the rain stopped, he came out from the cave and continued down the path. He wasn't in a hurry. The rain had made everything smell fresh and good. The scent from fallen pine needles rose from the wet earth. The leaves of the oak trees had been washed clean and a light breeze turned them about, showing their silver undersides. The birds, refreshed and high-spirited, set up a terrific noise. The worst offenders were the yellow-bottomed bulbuls who squabbled and fought in the blackberry bushes. A barbet, high up in the branches of a deodar, set up its querulous, plaintive call. And a flock of bright green parrots came swooping down the hill to settle on a wild plum tree and feast on the unripe fruit. The langurs, too, had been revived by the rain. They leapt friskily from tree to tree, greeting Bisnu with little grunts.

He was almost out of the oak forest when he heard a faint bleating. Presently, a little goat came stumbling up the path towards him. The kid was far from home and must have strayed from the rest of the herd. But it was not yet conscious of being lost. It came to Bisnu with a hop, skip and a jump and started nuzzling against his legs like a cat.

'I wonder who you belong to,' mused Bisnu, stroking the

little creature. 'You'd better come home with me until someone claims you.'

He didn't have to take the kid in his arms. It was used to humans and followed close at his heels. Now that darkness was coming on, Bisnu walked a little faster.

He had not gone very far when he heard the sawing grunt of a panther.

The sound came from the hill to the right and Bisnu judged the distance to be anything from a hundred to two hundred yards. He hesitated on the path, wondering what to do. Then he picked the kid up in his arms and hurried on in the direction of home and safety.

The panther called again, much closer now. If it was an ordinary panther, it would go away on finding that the kid was with Bisnu. If it was the man-eater, it would not hesitate to attack the boy, for no man-eater fears a human. There was no time to lose and there did not seem much point in running. Bisnu looked up and down the hillside. The forest was far behind him and there were only a few trees in his vicinity. He chose a spruce.

The branches of the Himalayan spruce are very brittle and snap easily beneath a heavy weight. They were strong enough to support Bisnu's light frame. It was unlikely they would take the weight of a full-grown panther. At least that was what Bisnu hoped.

Holding the kid with one arm, Bisnu gripped a low branch and swung himself up into the tree. He was a good climber. Slowly but confidently he climbed halfway up the tree, until he was about twelve feet above the ground. He couldn't go any higher without risking a fall.

He had barely settled himself in the crook of a branch when the panther came into the open, running into the clearing at a brisk trot. This was no stealthy approach, no wary stalking of its prey. It was the man-eater, all right. Bisnu felt a cold shiver run down his spine. He felt a little sick.

The panther stood in the clearing with a slight thrusting forward of the head. This gave it the appearance of gazing intently and rather short-sightedly at some invisible object in the clearing. But there is nothing short-sighted about a panther's vision. Its sight and hearing are acute.

Bisnu remained motionless in the tree and sent up a prayer to all the Gods he could think of. But the kid began bleating. The panther looked up and gave its deep-throated, rasping grunt—a fearsome sound, calculated to strike terror in any tree-borne animal. Many a monkey, petrified by a panther's roar, has fallen from its perch to make a meal for Mr Spots. The man-eater was trying the same technique on Bisnu. But though the boy was trembling with fright, he clung firmly to the base of the spruce tree.

The panther did not make any attempt to leap into the tree. Perhaps, it knew instinctively that this was not the type of tree that it could climb. Instead, it described a semicircle round the tree, keeping its face turned towards Bisnu. Then it disappeared into the bushes.

The man-eater was cunning. It hoped to put the boy off his guard, perhaps entice him down from the tree. For, a few seconds later, with a half-pitched growl, it rushed back into the clearing and then stopped, staring up at the boy in some surprise. The panther was getting frustrated. It snarled, and putting its forefeet up against the tree trunk, began scratching at the bark in the manner of an ordinary domestic cat. The tree shook at each thud of the beast's paw.

Bisnu began shouting for help.

The moon had not yet come up. Down in Manjari village, Bisnu's mother and sister stood in their lighted doorway, gazing anxiously up the pathway. Every now and then, Puja would turn to take a look at the small clock.

Sanjay's father appeared in a field below. He had a kerosene lantern in his hand.

'Sister, isn't your boy home as yet?' he asked.

'No, he hasn't arrived. We are very worried. He should have been home an hour ago. Do you think the panther will be about tonight? There's going to be a moon.'

'True, but it won't be dark for another hour. I will fetch the other menfolk and we will go up the mountain for your boy.

There may have been a landslide during the rain. Perhaps the path has been washed away.'

'Thank you, brother. But arm yourselves, just in case the panther is about.'

'I will take my spear,' said Kalam Singh. 'I have sworn to spear that devil when I find him. There is some evil spirit dwelling in the beast and it must be destroyed!'

'I am coming with you,' said Puja.

'No, you cannot go,' said her mother. 'It's bad enough that Bisnu is in danger. You stay at home with me. This work is for men.'

'I shall be safe with them,' insisted Puja. 'I am going, Mother!'

And she jumped down the embankment into the field and followed Sanjay's father through the village.

Ten minutes later, two men armed with axes had joined Kalam Singh in the courtyard of his house and the small party moved silently and swiftly up the mountain path. Puja walked in the middle of the group, holding the lantern. As soon as the village lights were hidden by a shoulder of the hill, the men began to shout—both to frighten the panther, if it was about, and to give themselves courage.

Bisnu's mother closed the front door and turned to the image of Ganesha for comfort and help.

Bisnu's calls were carried on the wind and Puja and the men heard him while they were still half a mile away. Their own shouts increased in volume and, hearing their voices, Bisnu felt strength return to his shaking limbs. Emboldened by the approach of his own people, he began shouting insults at the snarling panther, then throwing twigs and small branches at the enraged animal. The kid added its bleats to the boy's shouts, the birds took up the chorus. The langurs squealed and grunted, the searchers shouted themselves hoarse and the panther howled with rage.

PANTHER'S MOON

The forest had never before been so noisy.

As the search party drew near, they could hear the panther's savage snarls, and hurried, fearing that perhaps Bisnu had been seized. Puja began to run.

'Don't rush ahead, girl,' said Kalam Singh. 'Stay between us.'

The panther, now aware of the approaching humans, stood still in the middle of the clearing, head thrust forward in a familiar stance. There seemed too many men for one panther. When the animal saw the light of the lantern dancing between the trees, it turned, snarled defiance and hate, and without another look at the boy in the tree, disappeared into the bushes. It was not yet ready for a showdown.

VII

Nobody turned up to claim the little goat, so Bisnu kept it. A goat was a poor substitute for a dog, but, like Mary's lamb, it followed Bisnu wherever he went, and the boy couldn't help being touched by its devotion. He took it down to the stream, where it would skip about in the shallows and nibble the sweet grass that grew on the banks.

As for the panther, frustrated in its attempt on Bisnu's life, it did not wait long before attacking another human.

It was Chittru who came running down the path one afternoon, bubbling excitedly about the panther and the postman.

Chittru, deeming it safe to gather ripe bilberries in the daytime, had walked about half a mile up the path from the village, when he had stumbled across Mela Ram's mailbag lying on the ground. Of the postman himself there was no sign. But a trail of blood led through the bushes.

Once again, a party of men headed by Kalam Singh and accompanied by Bisnu and Chittru, went out to look for the postman. But though they found Mela Ram's bloodstained clothes, they could not find his body. The panther had made no mistake this time.

It was to be several weeks before Manjari had a new postman.

A few days after Mela Ram's disappearance, an old woman was sleeping with her head near the open door of her house. She had been advised to sleep inside with the door closed but the nights were hot and anyway the old woman was a little deaf, and in the middle of the night, an hour before moonrise, the panther seized her by the throat. Her strangled cry woke her grown-up son, and all the men in the village woke up at his shouts and came running.

The panther dragged the old woman out of the house and down the steps, but left her when the men approached with their axes and spears, and made off into the bushes. The old woman was still alive and the men made a rough stretcher of bamboo and vines and started carrying her up the path. But they had not gone far when she began to cough, and because of her terrible throat wounds, her lungs collapsed and she died.

It was the 'dark of the month'—the week of the new moon when nights are darkest.

Bisnu, closing the front door and lighting the kerosene lantern, said, 'I wonder where that panther is tonight!'

The panther was busy in another village: Sarru's village.

A woman and her daughter had been out in the evening bedding the cattle down in the stable. The girl had gone into the house and the woman was following. As she bent down to go in at the low door, the panther sprang from the bushes. Fortunately, one of its paws hit the doorpost and broke the force of the attack, or the woman would have been killed. When she cried out, the men came round shouting and the panther slunk off. The woman had deep scratches on her back and was badly shocked.

PANTHER'S MOON

The next day, a small party of villagers presented themselves in front of the magistrate's office at Kemptee and demanded that something be done about the panther. But the magistrate was away on tour and there was no one else in Kemptee who had a gun. Mr Nautiyal met the villagers and promised to write to a well-known shikari but said that it would be at least a fortnight before the shikari would be able to come.

Bisnu was fretting because he could not go to school. Most boys would be only too happy to miss school, but when you are living in a remote village in the mountains and having an education is the only way of seeing the world, you look forward to going to school, even if it is five miles from home. Bisnu's exams were only two weeks off and he didn't want to remain in the same class while the others were promoted. Besides, he knew he could pass even though he had missed a number of lessons. But he had to sit for the exams. He couldn't miss them.

'Cheer up, brother,' said Puja, as they sat drinking glasses of hot tea after their evening meal. 'The panther may go away once the rains break.'

'Even the rains are late this year,' said Bisnu. 'It's so hot and dry. Can't we open the door?'

'And be dragged down the steps by the panther?' said his mother. 'It isn't safe to have the window open, let alone the door.'

And she went to the small window—through which a cat would have found difficulty in passing—and bolted it firmly.

With a sigh of resignation, Bisnu threw off all his clothes except his underwear and stretched himself out on the earthen floor.

'We will be rid of the beast soon,' said his mother. 'I know it in my heart. Our prayers will be heard, and you shall go to school and pass your exams.'

To cheer up her children, she told them a humorous story

which had been handed down to her by her grandmother. It was all about a tiger, a panther and a bear, the three of whom were made to feel very foolish by a thief hiding in the hollow trunk of a banyan tree. Bisnu was sleepy and did not listen very attentively. He dropped off to sleep before the story was finished.

When he woke, it was dark and his mother and sister were asleep on the cot. He wondered what it was that had woken him. He could hear his sister's easy breathing and the steady ticking of the clock. Far away an owl hooted—an unlucky sign, his mother would have said; but she was asleep and Bisnu was not superstitious.

And then he heard something scratching at the door, and the hair on his head felt tight and prickly. It was like a cat scratching, only louder. The door creaked a little whenever it felt the impact of the paw—a heavy paw, as Bisnu could tell from the dull sound it made.

'It's the panther,' he muttered under his breath, sitting up on the hard floor.

The door, he felt, was strong enough to resist the panther's weight. And if he set up an alarm, he could rouse the village. But the middle of the night was no time for the bravest of men to tackle a panther.

In a corner of the room stood a long bamboo stick with a sharp knife tied to one end, which Bisnu sometimes used for spearing fish. Crawling on all fours across the room, he grasped the homemade spear, and then scrambling on to a cupboard, he drew level with the skylight window. He could get his head and shoulders through the window.

'What are you doing up there?' said Puja, who had woken up at the sound of Bisnu shuffling about the room.

'Be quiet,' said Bisnu. 'You'll wake Mother.'

Their mother was awake by now. 'Come down from there,

Bisnu. I can hear a noise outside.'

'Don't worry,' said Bisnu, who found himself looking down on the wriggling animal which was trying to get its paw in under the door. With his mother and Puja awake, there was no time to lose.

He had got the spear through the window, and though he could not manoeuvre it so as to strike the panther's head, he brought the sharp end down with considerable force on the animal's rump.

With a roar of pain and rage the man-eater leapt down from the steps and disappeared into the darkness. It did not pause to see what had struck it. Certain that no human could have come upon it in that fashion, it ran fearfully to its lair, howling until the pain subsided.

VIII

A panther is an enigma. There are occasions when it proves itself to be the most cunning animal under the sun and yet the very next day it will walk into an obvious trap that no self-respecting jackal would ever go near. One day a panther will prove itself to be a complete coward and run like a hare from a couple of dogs and the very next it will dash in amongst half a dozen men sitting round a campfire and inflict terrible injuries on them.

It is not often that a panther is taken by surprise, as its power of sight and hearing are very acute. It is a master at the art of camouflage and its spotted coat is admirably suited for the purpose. It does not need a heavy jungle to hide in. A couple of bushes and the light and shade from surrounding trees are enough to make it almost invisible.

Because the Manjari panther had been fooled by Bisnu, it did not mean that it was a stupid panther. It simply meant that it had been a little careless. And Bisnu and Puja, growing in confidence since their midnight encounter with the animal, became a little careless themselves.

Puja was hoeing the last field above the house and Bisnu, at the other end of the same field, was chopping up several branches of green oak, prior to leaving the wood to dry in the loft. It was late afternoon and the descending sun glinted in patches on the small river. It was a time of day when only the most desperate and daring of man-eaters would be likely to show itself.

Pausing for a moment to wipe the sweat from his brow, Bisnu glanced up at the hillside and his eye caught sight of a rock on the brow of the hill which seemed unfamiliar to him. Just as he was about to look elsewhere, the round rock began to grow and then alter its shape, and Bisnu watching in fascination was at last able to make out the head and forequarters of the panther. It looked enormous from the angle at which he saw it and for a moment he thought it was a tiger. But Bisnu knew instinctively that it was the man-eater.

Slowly, the wary beast pulled itself to its feet and began to walk round the side of the great rock. For a second, it disappeared and Bisnu wondered if it had gone away. Then it reappeared and the boy was all excitement again. Very slowly and silently the panther walked across the face of the rock until it was in direct line with the corner of the field where Puja was working.

With a thrill of horror Bisnu realized that the panther was stalking his sister. He shook himself free from the spell which had woven itself round him and shouting hoarsely ran forward.

'Run, Puja, run!' he called. 'It's on the hill above you!'

Puja turned to see what Bisnu was shouting about. She saw him gesticulate to the hill behind her and looked up just in time to see the panther crouching for his spring.

With great presence of mind, she leapt down the banking of the field and tumbled into an irrigation ditch.

PANTHER'S MOON

The springing panther missed its prey, lost its foothold on the slippery shale banking and somersaulted into the ditch a few feet away from Puja. Before the animal could recover from its surprise, Bisnu was dashing down the slope, swinging his axe and shouting, 'Maro, maro!'

Two men came running across the field. They, too, were armed with axes. Together with Bisnu they made a half-circle around the snarling animal, which turned at bay and plunged at them in order to get away. Puja wriggled along the ditch on her stomach. The men aimed their axes at the panther's head and Bisnu had the satisfaction of getting in a well-aimed blow between the eyes. The animal then charged straight at one of the men, knocked him over and tried to get at his throat. Just then Sanjay's father arrived with his long spear. He plunged the end of the spear into the panther's neck.

The panther left its victim and ran into the bushes, dragging the spear through the grass and leaving a trail of blood on the ground.

The men followed cautiously—all except the man who had been wounded and who lay on the ground, while Puja and the other womenfolk rushed up to help him.

The panther had made for the bed of the stream and Bisnu, Sanjay's father and their companion were able to follow it quite easily. The water was red where the panther had crossed the stream and the rocks were stained with blood. After they had gone downstream for about a furlong, they found the panther lying still on its side at the edge of the water. It was mortally wounded but it continued to wave its tail like an angry cat. Then, even the tail lay still.

'It is dead,' said Bisnu. 'It will not trouble us again in this body.'

'Let us be certain,' said Sanjay's father and he bent down and pulled the panther's tail.

There was no response.

'It is dead,' said Kalam Singh. 'No panther would suffer such an insult were it alive!'

They cut down a long piece of thick bamboo and tied the panther to it by its feet. Then, with their enemy hanging upside down from the bamboo pole, they started back for the village.

'There will be a feast at my house tonight,' said Kalam Singh. 'Everyone in the village must come. And tomorrow we will visit all the villages in the valley and show them the dead panther, so that they may move about again without fear.'

'We can sell the skin in Kemptee,' said their companion. 'It will fetch a good price.'

'But the claws we will give to Bisnu,' said Kalam Singh, putting his arm around the boy's shoulders. 'He has done a man's work today. He deserves the claws.'

A panther's or tiger's claws are considered to be lucky charms.

'I will take only three claws,' said Bisnu. 'One each for my mother and sister, and one for myself. You may give the others to Sanjay and Chittru and the smaller children.'

As the sun set, a big fire was lit in the middle of the village of Manjari and the people gathered round it, singing and laughing. Kalam Singh killed his fattest goat and there was meat for everyone.

IX

Bisnu was on his way home. He had just handed in his first paper, arithmetic, which he had found quite easy. Tomorrow it would be algebra, and when he got home he would have to practise square roots and cube roots and fractional coefficients.

Mr Nautiyal and the entire class had been happy that he had been able to sit for the exams. He was also a hero to them for his part in killing the panther. The story had spread through the villages with the rapidity of a forest fire, a fire which was now raging in Kemptee town.

When he walked past the hospital, he was whistling cheerfully.

Dr Taylor waved to him from the verandah steps.

'How is Sanjay now?' she asked.

'He is well,' said Bisnu.

'And your mother and sister?'

'They are well,' said Bisnu.

'Are you going to get yourself a new dog?'

'I am thinking about it,' said Bisnu. 'At present I have a baby goat—I am teaching it to swim!'

He started down the path to the valley. Dark clouds had gathered and there was a rumble of thunder. A storm was imminent.

'Wait for me!' shouted Sarru, running down the path behind Bisnu, his milk pails clanging against each other. He fell into step beside Bisnu.

'Well, I hope we don't have any more man-eaters for some time,' he said. 'I've lost a lot of money by not being able to take milk up to Kemptee.'

'We should be safe as long as a shikari doesn't wound another panther. There was an old bullet wound in the man-eater's thigh. That's why it couldn't hunt in the forest. The deer were too fast for it.'

'Is there a new postman yet?'

'He starts tomorrow. A cousin of Mela Ram's.'

When they reached the parting of their ways, it had begun to rain a little.

'I must hurry,' said Sarru. It's going to get heavier any minute.'

'I feel like getting wet,' said Bisnu. 'This time it's the monsoon, I'm sure.'

Bisnu entered the forest on his own and at the same time the rain came down in heavy opaque sheets. The trees shook in the wind and the langurs chattered with excitement.

It was still pouring when Bisnu emerged from the forest, drenched to the skin. But the rain stopped suddenly, just as the village of Manjari came into view. The sun appeared through a rift in the clouds. The leaves and the grass gave out a sweet, fresh smell.

Bisnu could see his mother and sister in the field transplanting the rice seedlings. The menfolk were driving the yoked oxen through the thin mud of the fields while the children hung on to the oxen's tails, standing on the plain wooden harrows, and with weird cries and shouts sending the animals almost at a gallop along the narrow terraces.

Bisnu felt the urge to be with them, working in the fields. He ran down the path, his feet falling softly on the wet earth. Puja saw him coming and waved at him. She met him at the edge of the field.

'How did you find your paper today?' she asked.

'Oh, it was easy.' Bisnu slipped his hand into hers and together they walked across the field. Puja felt something smooth and hard against her fingers, and before she could see what Bisnu was doing, he had slipped a pair of bangles on her wrist.

'I remembered,' he said, with a sense of achievement.

Puja looked at the bangles and blurted out: 'But they are blue, Bhai, and I wanted red and gold bangles!' And then, when she saw him looking crestfallen, she hurried on: 'But they are very pretty and you did remember…. Actually, they are just as nice as red and gold bangles! Come into the house when you are ready. I have made something special for you.'

'I am coming,' said Bisnu, turning towards the house. 'You don't know how hungry a man gets, walking five miles to reach home!'

DUST ON THE MOUNTAIN

I

Winter came and went, without so much as a drizzle. The hillside was brown all summer and the fields were bare. The old plough that was dragged over the hard ground by Bisnu's lean oxen made hardly any impression. Still, Bisnu kept his seeds ready for sowing. A good monsoon, and there would be plenty of maize and rice to see the family through the next winter.

Summer went its scorching way, and a few clouds gathered on the southwestern horizon.

'The monsoon is coming,' announced Bisnu.

His sister Puja was at the small stream, washing clothes. 'If it doesn't come soon, the stream will dry up,' she said. 'See, it's only a trickle this year. Remember when there were so many different flowers growing here on the banks of the stream? This year there isn't one.'

'The winter was dry. It did not even snow,' said Bisnu.

'I cannot remember another winter when there was no snow,' said his mother. 'The year your father died, there was so much snow the villagers could not light his funeral pyre for hours. And now there are fires everywhere.' She pointed to the next mountain, half-hidden by the smoke from a forest fire. At night they sat outside their small house, watching the fire spread. A red line stretched right across the mountain. Thousands of

Himalayan trees were perishing in the flames. Oaks, deodars, maples, pines; trees that had taken hundreds of years to grow. And now a fire started carelessly by some campers had been carried up the mountain with the help of the dry grass and strong breeze.

There was no one to put it out. It would take days to die down by itself.

'If the monsoon arrives tomorrow, the fire will go out,' said Bisnu, ever the optimist. He was only twelve, but he was the man in the house; he had to see that there was enough food for the family and for the oxen, for the big black dog and the hens.

There were clouds the next day but they brought only a drizzle. 'It's just the beginning,' said Bisnu, as he placed a bucket of muddy water on the steps.

'It usually starts with a heavy downpour,' said his mother. But there were to be no downpours that year. Clouds gathered on the horizon but they were white and puffy and soon disappeared.

True monsoon clouds would have been dark and heavy with moisture. There were other signs—or lack of them—that warned of a long, dry summer. The birds were silent, or simply absent. The Himalayan barbet, who usually heralded the approach of the monsoon with strident calls from the top of a spruce tree, hadn't been seen or heard. And the cicadas, who played a deafening overture in the oaks at the first hint of rain, seemed to be missing altogether.

Puja's apricot tree usually gave them a basket full of fruit every summer. This year it produced barely a handful of apricots, lacking juice and flavour. The tree looked ready to die, its leaves curled up in despair. Fortunately, there was a store of walnuts, and a bin full of wheat grain and another of rice stored from the previous year, so they would not be entirely without food; but it looked as though there would be no fresh fruit or vegetables. And there would be nothing to store away for the following winter.

Money would be needed to buy supplies in Tehri, some thirty miles distant. And there was no money to be earned in the village.

'I will go to Mussoorie and find work,' announced Bisnu.

'But Mussoorie is a two-day journey by bus,' said his mother. 'There is no one there who can help you. And you may not get any work.'

'In Mussoorie there is plenty of work during the summer. Rich people come up from the plains for their holidays. It is full of hotels and shops and places where they can spend their money.'

'But they won't spend any money on you.'

'There is money to be made there. And if not, I will come home. I can walk back over the Nag Tibba mountain. It will take only two-and-a-half days and I will save the bus fare!'

'Don't go, Bhai,' pleaded Puja.

'There will be no one to prepare your food, you will only get sick.'

But Bisnu had made up his mind so he put a few belongings in a cloth shoulder bag, while his mother prised several rupee coins out of a cache in the wall of their living room. Puja prepared a special breakfast of parathas and an egg scrambled with onions, the hen having laid just one for the occasion. Bisnu put some of the parathas in his bag. Then, waving goodbye to his mother and sister, he set off down the road from the village. After walking for a mile, he reached the highway where there was a hamlet with a bus stop. A number of villagers were waiting patiently for a bus. It was an hour late but they were used to that. As long as it arrived safely and got them to their destination, they would be content. They were patient people. And although Bisnu wasn't quite so patient, he too had learnt how to wait—for late buses and late monsoons.

II

Along the valley and over the mountains went the little bus with its load of frail humans. A little misjudgement on the part of the driver, and they would all be dashed to pieces on the rocks far below.

How tiny we are, thought Bisnu, looking up at the towering peaks and the immensity of the sky. *Each of us no more than a raindrop... And I wish we had a few raindrops!*

There were still fires burning to the north but the road went south, where there were no forests anyway, just bare brown hillsides. Down near the river there were small paddy fields but unfortunately rivers ran downhill and not uphill, and there was no inexpensive way in which the water could be brought up the steep slopes to the fields that depended on rainfall.

Bisnu stared out of the bus window at the river running far below. On either bank huge boulders lay exposed, for the level of the water had fallen considerably during the past few months. 'Why are there no trees here?' he asked aloud, and received the attention of a fellow passenger, an old man in the next seat who had been keeping up a relentless dry coughing. Even though it was a warm day, he wore a woollen cap and had an old muffler wrapped about his neck.

'There were trees here once,' he said. 'But the contractors took the deodars for furniture and houses. And the pines were tapped to death for resin. And the oaks were stripped of their leaves to feed the cattle—you can still see a few tree skeletons if you look hard—and the bushes that remained were finished off by the goats!'

'When did all this happen?' asked Bisnu.

'A few years ago. And it's still happening in other areas, although it's forbidden now to cut trees. The only forests that remain are in remote places where there are no roads.' A fit of coughing came over him, but he had found a good listener and was eager to continue. 'The road helps you and me to get about but it also makes it easier for others to do mischief. Rich men from the cities come here and buy up what they want—land, trees, people!'

'What takes you to Mussoorie, Uncle?' asked Bisnu politely. He always addressed elderly people as uncle or aunt.

'I have a cough that won't go away. Perhaps they can do something for it at the hospital in Mussoorie. Doctors don't like coming to villages, you know—there's no money to be made in villages. So we must go to the doctors in the towns. I had a brother who could not be cured in Mussoorie. They told him to go to Delhi. He sold his buffaloes and went to Delhi, but there they told him it was too late to do anything. He died on the way back. I won't go to Delhi. I don't wish to die amongst strangers.'

'You'll get well, Uncle,' said Bisnu.

'Bless you for saying so. And you? What takes you to the big town?'

'Looking for work—we need money at home.'

'It is always the same. There are many like you who must go out in search of work. But don't be led astray. Don't let your friends persuade you to go to Bombay to become a film star! It is better to be hungry in your village than to be hungry on the streets of Bombay. I had a nephew who went to Bombay. The smugglers put him to work selling afeem (opium) and now he is in jail. Keep away from the big cities, boy. Earn your money and go home.'

'I'll do that, Uncle. My mother and sister will expect me to return before the summer season is over.'

The old man nodded vigorously and began coughing again. Presently he dozed off. The interior of the bus smelt of tobacco smoke and petrol fumes and as a result Bisnu had a headache. He kept his face near the open window to get as much fresh air as possible, but the dust kept getting into his mouth and eyes.

Several dusty hours later the bus got into Mussoorie, honking its horn furiously at everything in sight. The passengers, looking dazed, got down and went their different ways. The old man trudged off to the hospital.

Bisnu had to start looking for a job straightaway. He needed a lodging for the night and he could not afford even the cheapest of hotels. So he went from one shop to another, and to all the

little restaurants and eating places, asking for work—anything in exchange for a bed, a meal, and a minimum wage. A boy at one of the sweet shops told him there was a job at the Picture Palace, one of the town's three cinemas. The hill station's main road was crowded with people, for the season was just starting. Most of them were tourists who had come up from Delhi and other large towns.

The street lights had come on, and the shops were lighting up, when Bisnu presented himself at the Picture Palace.

III

The man who ran the cinema's tea stall had just sacked the previous helper for his general clumsiness. Whenever he engaged a new boy (which was fairly often) he started him off with the warning: 'I will be keeping a record of all the cups and plates you break, and their cost will be deducted from your salary at the end of the month.'

As Bisnu's salary had been fixed at fifty rupees a month, he would have to be very careful if he were going to receive any of it.

'In my first month,' said Chittru, one of the three tea stall boys, 'I broke six cups and five saucers, and my pay came to three rupees! Better be careful!'

Bisnu's job was to help prepare the tea and samosas, serve these refreshments to the public during intervals in the film, and later wash up the dishes. In addition to his salary, he was allowed to drink as much tea as he wanted or could hold in his stomach. But the sugar supply was kept to a minimum.

Bisnu went to work immediately and it was not long before he was as wellversed in his duties as the other two tea boys, Chittru and Bali. Chittru was an easy-going, lazy boy who always tried to place the brunt of his work on someone else's shoulders.

But he was generous and lent Bisnu five rupees during the first week. Bali, besides being a tea boy, had the enviable job of being the poster boy. As the cinema was closed during the mornings, Bali would be busy either pushing the big poster board around Mussoorie, or sticking posters on convenient walls.

'Posters are very useful,' he claimed. 'They prevent old walls from falling down.'

Chittru had relatives in Mussoorie and slept at their house. But both Bisnu and Bali were on their own and had to sleep at the cinema. After the last show the hall was locked up, so they could not settle down in the expensive seats as they would have liked! They had to sleep on a dirty mattress in the foyer, near the ticket office, where they were often at the mercy of icy Himalayan winds.

Bali made things more comfortable by setting his poster board at an angle to the wall, which gave them a little alcove where they could sleep protected from the wind. As they had only one blanket each, they placed their blankets together and rolled themselves into a tight warm ball.

During shows, when Bisnu took the tea around, there was nearly always someone who would be rude and offensive. Once when he spilt some tea on a college student's shoes, he received a hard kick on the shin. He complained to the tea stall owner, but his employer said, 'The customer is always right. You should have got out of the way in time!'

As he began to get used to this life, Bisnu found himself taking an interest in some of the regular customers.

There was, for instance, the large gentleman with the soup-strainer moustache, who drank his tea from the saucer. As he drank, his lips worked like a suction pump, and the tea, after a brief agitation in the saucer, would disappear in a matter of seconds. Bisnu often wondered if there was something lurking in the forest of that gentleman's upper lip, something that would suddenly spring out and fall upon him! The boys took great pleasure in exchanging anecdotes about the peculiarities of some of the customers.

Bisnu had never seen such bright, painted women before. The girls in his village, including his sister Puja, were good-looking and often sturdy; but they did not use perfumes or make-up like these more prosperous women from the towns of the plains. Wearing expensive clothes and jewellery, they never gave Bisnu more than a brief, bored glance. Other women were more inclined to notice him, favouring him with kind words and a small tip when he took away the cups and plates. He found he could make a few rupees a month in tips; and when he received his first month's pay, he was able to send some of it home.

Chittru accompanied him to the post office and helped him to fill in the money order form. Bisnu had been to the village school, but be wasn't used to forms and official paperwork. As Chittru had been in the town for a while, he knew all about them, even though he could just about read and write.

Walking back to the cinema, Chittru said, 'We can make more money at the limestone quarries.'

'All right, let's try them,' said Bisnu.

'Not now,' said Chittru, who enjoyed the busy season in the hill station. 'After the season—after the monsoon.'

But there was still no monsoon to speak of, just an occasional drizzle which did little to clear the air of the dust that blew up from the plains. Bisnu wondered how his mother and sister were faring at home. A wave of homesickness swept over him. The hill station, with all its glitter, was just a pretty gift box with nothing inside.

One day in the cinema, Bisnu saw the old man who had been with him on the bus. He greeted him like a long lost friend. At first, the old man did not recognize the boy, but when Bisnu asked him if he had recovered from his illness, the old man remembered, and said, 'So you are still in Mussoorie, boy. That is good. I thought you might have gone down to Delhi to make more money.' He added that he was a little better and that he was undergoing a course of treatment at the hospital. Bisnu brought him a cup of tea and refused to take any money for it; it could be included in his own quota of free tea. When the show was over, the old man went his way and Bisnu did not see him again.

In September, the town began to get empty. The taps were running dry or giving out just a trickle of muddy water. A thick mist lay over the mountain for days on end, but there was no rain. When the mists cleared, an autumn wind came whispering through the deodars.

At the end of the month, the manager of the Picture Palace gave everyone a week's notice, a week's pay, and announced that the cinema would be closing for the winter.

IV

Bali said, 'I'm going to Delhi to find work. I'll come back next summer. What about you, Bisnu, why don't you come with me? It's easier to find work in Delhi.'

'I'm staying with Chittru,' said Bisnu. 'We may work at the quarries.'

'I like the big towns,' said Bali. 'I like shops and people and lots of noise. I will never go back to my village. There is no money there, no fun.'

Bali made a bundle of his things and set out for the bus stand. Bisnu bought himself a pair of cheap shoes, for his old ones had fallen to pieces. With what was left of his money, he sent another money order home. Then he and Chittru set out

DUST ON THE MOUNTAIN

for the limestone quarries, an eight-mile walk from Mussoorie.

They knew they were nearing the quarries when they saw clouds of limestone dust hanging in the air. The dust hid the next mountain from view. When they did see the mountain, they found that the top of it was missing—blasted away by dynamite to enable the quarries to get at the rich strata of limestone rock below the surface.

The skeletons of a few trees remained on the lower slopes. Almost everything else had gone—grass, flowers, shrubs, birds, butterflies, grasshoppers, ladybirds. A rock lizard popped its head out of a crevice to look at the intruders. Then, like some prehistoric survivor, it scuttled back into its underground shelter.

'I used to come here when I was small,' announced Chittru cheerfully.

'Were the quarries here then?'

'Oh, no. My friends and I—we used to come for the strawberries. They grew all over this mountain. Wild strawberries, but very tasty.'

'Where are they now?' asked Bisnu, looking around at the devastated hillside.

'All gone,' said Chittru. 'Maybe there are some on the next mountain.'

Even as they approached the quarries, a blast shook the hillside. Chittru pulled Bisnu under an overhanging rock to avoid the shower of stones that pelted down on the road. As the dust enveloped them, Bisnu had a fit of coughing. When the air cleared a little, they saw the limestone dump ahead of them.

Chittru, who was older and bigger than Bisnu, was immediately taken on as a labourer; but the quarry foreman took one look at Bisnu and said, 'You're too small. You won't be able to break stones or lift those heavy rocks and load them into the trucks. Be off, boy. Find something else to do.'

He was offered a job in the labourers' canteen, but he'd had enough of making tea and washing dishes. He was about to turn around and walk back to Mussoorie when he felt a heavy hand descend on his shoulder. He looked up to find a grey-bearded, turbaned Sikh looking down at him in some amusement.

'I need a cleaner for my truck,' he said. 'The work is easy, but the hours are long!'

Bisnu responded immediately to the man's gruff but jovial manner.

'What will you pay?' he asked.

'Fifteen rupees a day, and you'll get food and a bed at the depot.'

'As long as I don't have to cook the food,' said Bisnu.

The truck driver laughed. 'You might prefer to do so, once you've tasted the depot food. Are you coming on my truck? Make up your mind.'

'I'm your man,' said Bisnu; and waving goodbye to Chittru, he followed the Sikh to his truck.

V

A horn blared, shattering the silence of the mountains, and the truck came round a bend in the road. A herd of goats scattered left and right.

The goatherds cursed as a cloud of dust enveloped them, and then the truck had left them behind and was rattling along the bumpy, unmetalled road to the quarries.

At the wheel of the truck, stroking his grey moustache with one hand, sat Pritam Singh. It was his own truck. He had never allowed anyone else to drive it. Every day he made two trips to the quarries, carrying truckloads of limestone back to the depot at the bottom of the hill. He was paid by the trip and he was always anxious to get in two trips every day. Sitting beside him was Bisnu, his new cleaner. In less than a month, Bisnu had become an experienced hand at looking after trucks, riding in them, and even sleeping in them. He got on well with Pritam, the grizzled, fifty-year-old Sikh, who boasted two well off sons—one a farmer in Punjab, the other a wine merchant in far-off London. He could have gone to live with either of them, but his sturdy independence kept him on the road, in his battered, old truck.

Pritam pressed hard on his horn. Now there was no one on the road—neither beast nor man—but Pritam was fond of the sound of his horn and liked blowing it. He boasted that it was the loudest horn in northern India. Although it struck terror into the hearts of all who heard it—for it was louder than the trumpeting of an elephant—it was music to Pritam's ears.

Pritam treated Bisnu as an equal and a friendly banter had grown between them during their many trips together.

'One more year on this bone-breaking road,' said Pritam, 'and then I'll sell my truck and retire.'

'But who will buy such a shaky old truck?' asked Bisnu. 'It will retire before you do!'

'Now don't be insulting, boy. She's only twenty years old—there are still a few years left in her!' And as though to prove it he blew the horn again. Its strident sound echoed and re-echoed down the mountain gorge. A pair of wildfowl burst from the bushes and fled to more silent regions.

Pritam's thoughts went to his dinner. 'Haven't had a good meal for days.'

'Haven't had a good meal for weeks,' said Bisnu, although in fact he looked much healthier than when he had worked at the cinema's tea stall.

'Tonight I'll give you a dinner in a good hotel. Tandoori chicken and rice pulao.'

He sounded his horn again as though to put a seal on his promise. Then he slowed down, because the road had become narrow and precipitous, and trotting ahead of them was a train of mules.

As the horn blared, one mule ran forward, another ran backward. One went uphill, another went downhill. Soon there were mules all over the place. Pritam cursed the mules and the mule drivers cursed Pritam; but he had soon left them far behind.

Along this range, all the hills were bare and dry. Most of the forest had long since disappeared.

'Are your hills as bare as these?' asked Pritam. 'No, we still have some trees,' said Bisnu. 'Nobody has started blasting the hills as yet. In front of our house, there is a walnut tree which gives us two baskets of walnuts every year. And there is an apricot tree. But it was a bad year for fruit. There was no rain. And the stream is too far away.'

'It will rain soon,' said Pritam. 'I can smell rain. It is coming from the north. The winter will be early.'

'It will settle the dust.'

Dust was everywhere. The truck was full of it. The leaves of the shrubs and the few trees were thick with it. Bisnu could feel the dust under his eyelids and in his mouth. And as they approached the quarries, the dust increased. But it was a different kind of dust now—whiter, stinging the eyes, irritating the nostrils.

They had been blasting all morning.

'Let's wait here,' said Pritam, bringing the truck to a halt. They sat in silence, staring through the windscreen at the scarred cliffs a little distance down the road. There was a sharp crack of explosives and the hillside blossomed outwards. Earth and rocks hurtled down the mountain.

Bisnu watched in awe as shrubs and small trees were flung into the air. It always frightened him—not so much the sight

DUST ON THE MOUNTAIN

of the rocks bursting asunder, as the trees being flung aside and destroyed. He thought of the trees at home—the walnut, the chestnuts, the pines—and wondered if one day they would suffer the same fate, and whether the mountains would all become a desert like this particular range. No trees, no grass, no water—only the choking dust of mines and quarries.

VI

Pritam pressed hard on his horn again to let the people at the site know that he was approaching. He parked outside a small shed where the contractor and the foreman were sipping cups of tea. A short distance away, some labourers, Chittru among them, were hammering at chunks of rock, breaking them up into manageable pieces. A pile of stones stood ready for loading; while the rock that had just been blasted lay scattered about the hillside.

'Come and have a cup of tea,' called out the contractor.

'I can't hang about all day,' said Pritam. 'There's another trip to make—and the days are getting shorter. I don't want to be driving by night.'

But he sat down on a bench and ordered two cups of tea from the stall. The foreman strolled over to the group of labourers and told them to start loading. Bisnu let down the grid at the back of the truck. Then, to keep himself warm, he began helping Chittru and the men with the loading.

'Don't expect to be paid for helping,' said Sharma, the contractor, for whom every rupee spent was a rupee off his profits.

'Don't worry,' said Bisnu. 'I don't work for contractors, I work for friends.'

'That's right,' called out Pritam. 'Mind what you say to

Bisnu—he's no one's servant!'

Sharma wasn't happy until there was no space left for a single stone. Then Bisnu had his cup of tea and three of the men climbed on the pile of stones in the open truck.

'All right, let's go!' said Pritam. 'I want to finish early today. Bisnu and I are having a big dinner!'

Bisnu jumped in beside Pritam, banging the door shut. It never closed properly unless it was slammed really hard. But it opened at a touch.

'This truck is held together with sticking plaster,' joked Pritam.

He was in good spirits. He started the engine, and blew his horn just as he passed the foreman and the contractor.

'They are deaf in one ear from the blasting,' said Pritam. 'I'll make them deaf in the other ear!'

The labourers were singing as the truck swung round the sharp bends of the winding road. The door beside Bisnu rattled on its hinges. He was feeling quite dizzy.

'Not too fast,' he said.

'Oh,' said Pritam. 'About my driving?'

'It's just today,' said Bisnu uneasily.

'You're getting old,' said Pritam. 'And since when did you become nervous?'

'It's a feeling, that's all.'

'That's your trouble.'

'I suppose so,' said Bisnu.

Pritam was feeling young, exhilarated. He drove faster. As they swung round a bend, Bisnu looked out of his window.

All he saw was the sky above and the valley below. They were very near the edge; but it was usually like that on this narrow mountain road.

After a few more hairpin bends, the road descended steeply

to the valley. Just then a stray mule ran into the middle of the road. Pritam swung the steering wheel over to the right to avoid the mule, but here the road turned sharply to the left. The truck went over the edge.

As it tipped over, hanging for a few seconds on the edge of the cliff, the labourers leapt from the back of the truck. It pitched forward, and as it struck a rock outcrop, the loose door burst open. Bisnu was thrown out.

The truck hurtled forward, bouncing over the rocks, turning over on its side and rolling over twice before coming to rest against the trunk of a scraggly old oak tree. But for the tree, the truck would have plunged several hundred feet down to the bottom of the gorge.

Two of the labourers sat on the hillside, stunned and badly shaken. The third man had picked himself up and was running back to the quarry for help.

Bisnu had landed in a bed of nettles. He was smarting all over, but he wasn't really hurt; the nettles had broken his fall. His first impulse was to get up and run back to the road. Then he realized that Pritam was still in the truck.

Bisnu skidded down the steep slope, calling out, 'Pritam Uncle, are you all right?'

There was no answer.

VII

When Bisnu saw Pritam's arm and half his body jutting out of the open door of the truck, he feared the worst. It was a strange position, half in and half out. Bisnu was about to turn away and climb back up the hill, when he noticed that Pritam had opened a bloodied and swollen eye. It looked straight up at Bisnu.

'Are you alive?' whispered Bisnu, terrified.

'What do you think?' muttered Pritam. He closed his eye again. When the contractor and his men arrived, it took them almost an hour to get Pritam Singh out of the wreckage of the truck, and another hour to get him to the hospital in the next big town. He had broken bones, fractured ribs, and a dislocated shoulder. But the doctors said he was repairable—which was more than could be said for the truck.

'So the truck's finished,' said Pritam, between groans, when Bisnu came to see him after a couple of days. 'Now I'll have to go home and live with my son. And what about you, boy? I can get you a job on a friend's truck.'

'No,' said Bisnu, 'I'll be going home soon.'

'And what will you do at home?'

'I'll work on my land. It's better to grow things on the land, than to blast things out of it.'

They were silent for some time.

'There is something to be said for growing things,' said Pritam. 'But for that tree, the truck would have finished up at the foot of the mountain, and I wouldn't be here, all bandaged up and talking to you. It was the tree that saved me. Remember that, boy.'

'I'll remember, and I won't forget the dinner you promised me, either.'

It snowed during Bisnu's last night at the quarries. He slept on the floor with Chittru, in a large shed meant for the labourers. The wind blew the snowflakes in at the entrance; it whistled down the deserted mountain pass. In the morning, Bisnu opened his eyes to a world of dazzling whiteness. The snow was piled high against the walls of the shed, and they had some difficulty getting out. Bisnu joined Chittru at the tea stall, drank a glass of hot, sweet tea, and ate two stale buns. He said goodbye to Chittru and set out on the long march home. The road would be closed to traffic because of the heavy snow, and he would have to walk all the way.

He trudged over the hills all day, stopping only at small villages to take refreshment. By nightfall he was still ten miles from home.

But he had fallen in with other travellers, and with them he took shelter at a small inn. They built a fire and crowded around it, and each man spoke of his home and fields and all were of the opinion that the snow and rain had come just in time to save the winter crops. Someone sang, and another told a ghost story. Feeling at home already, Bisnu fell asleep listening to their tales. In the morning they parted and went their different ways. It was almost noon when Bisnu reached his village. The fields were covered with snow and the mountain stream was in spate. As he climbed the terraced fields to his house, he heard the sound of barking, and his mother's big black mastiff came bounding towards him over the snow. The dog jumped on him and licked his arms and then went bounding back to the house to tell the others.

Puja saw him from the courtyard and ran indoors shouting, 'Bisnu has come, my brother has come!'

His mother ran out of the house, calling, 'Bisnu, Bisnu!'

Bisnu came walking through the fields, and he did not hurry, he did not run; he wanted to savour the moment of his return, with his mother and sister smiling, waiting for him in front of the house.

There was no need to hurry now. He would be with them for a long time, and the manager of the Picture Palace would have to find someone else for the summer season... It was his home, and these were his fields! Even the snow was his. When the snow melted he would clear the fields, and nourish them, and make them rich.

He felt very big and very strong as he came striding over the land he loved.